RICK PARTLOW
DROP TROOPER BOOK NINE
KILLBOX

www.aethonbooks.com

KILL BOX
©2022 RICK PARTLOW

This book is a work of fiction. Names, characters, places, and incidents are the product of the author's imagination or are used fictitiously. Any resemblance to actual events, locales, or persons, living or dead is coincidental.

CONTACT FRONT
KINETIC STRIKE
DANGER CLOSE
DIRECT FIRE
HOME FRONT
FIRE BASE
SHOCK ACTION
RELEASE POINT
KILL BOX
DROP ZONE

[1]

"The range is no longer clear! Shooters! Take up a prone, unsupported position and lock and load one fifty-round magazine into your M345A rifle!"

Top's voice boomed like she was using public-address speakers, though, for her, none were necessary. Somehow, the translation program managed to pass her tone and the authority behind it through to the Vergai language, because the transplanted humans did exactly as they were told, with various degrees of clumsiness. Not that I blamed them. Most of them hadn't handled a weapon of any sort prior to a few weeks ago. Finally, the series of metallic click-clacks from the magazines seating in the receiver ended and I scanned the line of shooting positions carefully, like it was my job to make sure none of them did anything stupid and shot each other.

Because it *was* my job, even if I'd never supervised an infantry range before.

"Why couldn't the Force Recon platoon leader do this shit?" I murmured aside to Vicky.

"Because Matis trusts *you*," she reminded me, the corner of her mouth turning up in a sadistic grin.

Which was true, if inconvenient. Matis was, at least, showing more promise than most of the others. The farmer snugged the buttstock of his rifle into his shoulder just as he'd been taught and cuddled the cheek rest like it was his wife's shoulder, putting his eyes in just the right position for the electronic reticle to float over the target. It would have been better if we could have fabricated helmets for all of them with built-in Heads-Up Displays so they could see where the rifle was shooting no matter what position their heads were in, but there just hadn't been enough raw material to work with for the fabricators. Even the so-called M345A's were mostly metal and ceramic because the people of Yfingam—whether human, Tahni, or Resscharr—didn't have enough plastic to feed the machine.

"Are we ready on the right?" Top called, craning her neck around in the jury-rigged, home-built range master platform at the center of the firing line. I shot her a thumbs-up. "The right is ready! Are we ready on the left?" About two hundred meters down the line of tan dirt scraped bare with rakes, Captain Solano gave an identical signal. "The left is ready! Shooters! Place your selector on semi-auto and commence fire!"

If the loading had been a shambolic series of echoing clicks, the gunfire was an ocean wave, trickling in at first and then breaking against the shore as each of the Vergai waited for someone else to shoot first. Matis did, of course. I'd come to appreciate the spine on the man since we'd met him in the farms outside the Resscharr fortress. Despite being an indentured servant farmer for most of his life, he hadn't surrendered to fate. The crack-snap of his weapon firing started the cascade, and in a couple of seconds, I was glad I'd taken Top's advice and worn hearing protection.

This wasn't what I was used to. Even when I wasn't stuffed inside a Vigilante battlesuit, insulated from the sounds of combat by centimeters of BiPhase Carbide alloy, the individual weapons I'd become accustomed to were Gauss rifles and lasers, and while they weren't silent by any means, neither did they have the concussive report of the rifles we'd fabricated for the Vergai. God knows, I *wished* we'd been able to make them Gauss rifles, but the problem, again, was raw materials. Fabricators could make whatever you had patterns for, but they needed the shit to make them, and we just didn't have a ready supply of tungsten...not without taking a few years to get an asteroid mining operation up. Not to mention the superconductors for the capacitors, and the ultra-lightweight alloys that could only be manufactured in orbit with a dedicated fusion reactor.

We'd done the best we could, certainly better than the black powder shit the Karai had been carrying around before.

Before.

Colonel Ten-Lenon-Zan-Karan-Thint had changed all that, of course. He'd come prepared, unlike us.

"Look over to the north," Vicky told me, as quiet as she could be talking over sporadic gunfire. "Hundred meters out, at the crest of the hill."

I did, trying not to be obvious. The crest of a hill was a shitty place to set up an OP from a tactical standpoint, but the Karai weren't trying to be subtle, nor were they arranging an ambush. They were sending a message. There were eight of them, because that was a Tahni thing, and if the Karai called themselves something different, having been pulled off of Tahn-Skyyiah centuries before the planet united, they still shared elements of the ancient culture. And apparently, the Mohawk haircut and the queue wrapped around their necks were older than the Tahni Imperium, though their clothes were much different, without the multicolored striping prevalent in modern Tahni designs.

But the guns were new...to the Karai, if not to us. They were

KE rifles, electromagnetic weapons that fired tantalum needles at hypersonic velocities, decades ahead of what we were supplying to the human residents of Yfingam.

"Fuckers," I muttered. Vicky shrugged. Her hair was getting long...really long. Longer than would have been allowed in the military, and I felt like it was an act of rebellion against getting shanghaied into this mission.

"There are disadvantages," she pointed out. "We're leaving the Vergai with the equipment and the training to produce ammunition and spare parts. Those things...." She nodded toward the hilltop and the tall, broad-chested figures silhouetted against the morning sun. "They can't repair them, they can't make more ammo, and they'll barely be able to recharge them."

"*They* can't," I corrected her. "But Zan-Thint and his people can. And they're not leaving them unsupported the way we are the Vergai. They'll be right there to train and equip them."

"Cease fire, cease fire!" Top bellowed. I shouldn't have been calling her "Top" anymore...she wasn't a first sergeant; she was Sergeant-Major Ellen Campbell, Commonwealth Marine Corps, detached for assignment to Fleet Intelligence for the duration of this mission. But she'd been "Top" to me for so many years, I couldn't break the habit. "Are there any alibis?"

That probably took a bit more effort for the translators, but I assumed they'd briefed the Vergai that an alibi was a weapons malfunction that prevented someone from firing off their entire fifty rounds.

"No alibis! Shooters, clear all weapons!"

And this was where I actually had to pay close attention. All it would take was one Vergai farmer not realizing they'd left a live round in the chamber for us to have our first training fatality, which would cost us their trust and instill a fear of the new weapons we really didn't need.

"There," Vicky said, pointing at a younger man with a

sparse beard and sweat rolling down his face...and not just from the summer heat.

"Got it."

I snatched the weapon out of the nervous kid's hands, then held it receiver-up so he could see it, and yanked back the charging handle. A brass cartridge with a steel-core bullet popped out and I caught it in mid-air and held it up for him.

"You dropped your magazine," I explained to him, my 'link translating it into the local lingo, spouting the gibber-gabber from its external speaker since I wasn't wearing armor with a public-address system, "but you didn't clear the chamber. If you didn't fire all your ammo, there'll always be a round in the chamber. And you skipped the last step in clearing the weapon—you didn't inspect the chamber visually. Do that again, I'll kick your ass all over this range in front of all your friends. You know why? Because we treat *all* guns as if they're loaded. You understand me?"

"Y-yes, my lord," the kid stuttered, face going red.

"Don't fucking call me that," I warned him, shoving the rifle back at him, a surge of anger coursing through me even though I couldn't figure out exactly why. "*Captain* or *sir*. I command Marines in battle, I don't rule them."

"Yes, sir!" the kid said, making sure to keep the rifle barrel pointed downrange.

"Is the firing line clear on the right?" Top demanded, and even from a hundred meters away, I could feel her eyes boring into me. I flashed her the go-ahead. "The right is clear. Is the firing line clear on the left? The left is clear. Shooters and range officers, you may move downrange to score, repair, and replace your targets!"

"This should be fun," Vicky said, sauntering down to check the humanoid-shaped wood silhouettes. I'd been in favor of giving them Mohawks and queues, but Colonel Hachette had vetoed the idea, since technically, we had a truce with Zan-Thint and the Tahni.

Even from this distance, I could tell that most of the silhouettes were undamaged or, at best, had bites nibbled away at their edges. Most, but not all. A few of the shooters looked promising, as if they lacked fear of the new weapons, if not a complete knowledge of how to use them. And, of course, Matis' target was chewed up at center-mass. The bearded farmer walked up to me, grinning ear to ear, his new rifle slung over his right shoulder as we'd taught them. If I'd been forced to guess, I would have put his age in the early forties, but I knew the lines in his face were from hardship and exposure to sun and wind rather than years—even years without the benefit of anti-aging treatments. I also knew he wasn't yet even thirty, was younger than me, despite having three children already. The ones who'd lived.

"Captain Alvarez," he enthused, "these weapons are incredible! You have our eternal gratitude for finally giving us the means to defend ourselves against the Karai and the Resscharr!"

I forced a smile, not wanting to discourage him.

"It's the least we can do," I said, meaning it more than he knew. "I just wish we had the resources to provide something even better." *Like a decent Gauss rifle. Or powered armor.*

"It is surely better than what we had before," he said, waving the thought away. "Now that they see we have these weapons, the Karai will think twice about attempting to enslave us as their masters, the Resscharr, did. Even if they could overwhelm us in the end, we would kill dozens of them with these rifles. Not even the Karai are foolish enough to risk this."

He hurried downrange, eager to see his targets, and likely to brag about them to his friends. It was a good thing we couldn't provide the Vergai with 'links, or he would have been taking selfies with his shot-up silhouette and posting them to social media. I shook my head, sighing in preparation to join him, but Top was somehow standing right beside me. How a woman of her age could be that silent was a mystery I didn't care to delve into.

"You saw the hostiles." It wasn't a question and I didn't have to guess what she meant.

"We saw them. They *wanted* to be seen." I nodded toward the Vergai chattering to each other about their shooting, and knew if we hadn't drilled into them that rifles weren't to be handled downrange, they would have been finger-fucking the damn things in their excitement. "Not that the Vergai took the hint. Matis thinks we've saved him by giving him the guns."

Top snorted, not quite a laugh, and it didn't reach her eyes. She was a small woman, the top of her head not reaching my nose, but I would never make the mistake of underestimating her. I'd seen her kill too many enemy soldiers for that.

"Zan-Thint *might* keep his word," she ventured, not sounding convinced. "I mean, he'll still have most of this planet."

"You've heard the story about the frog and the scorpion, right?" I asked, casting a doubtful sidelong glance her way.

"I know," Top admitted. "But the colonel doesn't have a lot of choice in the matter. We don't have the firepower to take them on right now."

"And that's stopping *us* from taking on *them*," I agreed. "But it sounds like a damned good reason for him to decide to hit us now, before we're ready. And if we leave—if he *lets* us leave, even if he tries to keep his word, then they...." I gestured toward the Vergai and then up at the Karai. "...are going to wind up killing each other."

"Yeah, they are. But I'm just a Marine, Cam." She shook her head. "Not a miracle worker."

[2]

"We need," Kyler Dunstan opined, "to get the fuck out of here."

I expected Colonel Hachette to glower at the pilot for his lack of decorum, but maybe Dunstan had worn the Intelligence officer down, because Hachette just nodded.

"I don't disagree, in principle." He leaned back in his chair, a solid, local build, hand-worked out of wood, and stared out the window of the small building we'd been given as an office, just outside the city walls. Through it, Vergai farmers were hauling in crops from their fields under the midday sun like some kind of ViR simulation of the Middle Ages. "But I can't help thinking it's only our presence here that's keeping a lid on things." He turned and eyed Matis, who seemed uncomfortable not just in the unfamiliar office but sitting in the chair. His people had stools, but chairs with backs were strange to them. "What do your people say, Matis? Do they think us remaining here in Yfingam is protecting them or simply provoking the Karai?"

"It's difficult for me to say, Colonel Hachette." I'd almost gotten used to having to wait for the translation after hearing the utterly incomprehensible words of his language, but it still gave everything a surreal air. "I do not know these Karai you call the

Tahni. But if I had to guess the intention of the Karai I *have* known, I would say they fear nothing except harm coming to their offspring, and they respect nothing but power. You of the Commonwealth would not threaten their children, and as powerful as you are, you do not have the numbers of the Tahni." He made a gesture of hands and head that might have been a shrug. "I don't think your presence or your absence will mean a great deal to them."

"Have your people given any more consideration to emigrating to the second planet?" Top asked him, then corrected herself. "To Laisvas Miestas?" It translated, roughly, to "the Islands," or possibly "the Islanders." The second planet out was mostly ocean, with the land confined to island chains, and it was populated mostly by humans, with the only Tahni barely possessing the technology to cross the ocean. "I know they'd be happy for the extra hands. Though it would likely mean you'd have to learn fishing as a way of feeding yourselves."

Matis exchanged a look with his wife, Carella. She was short, plain, and mousy-looking, but it was camouflage. She had just as much spine as Matis and a huge stubborn streak, and had been just as valuable organizing the Vergai. The stubborn streak shone through her expression and Matis didn't argue with her.

"This is our home," he said, giving voice to the words his wife didn't need to say. "It's true that the Resscharr brought us here to be their slaves, but we've made a life here, had children of our own. To take them from this place and force them to live on Laisvas Miestas would be to do the same to them as the Resscharr did to us."

I didn't agree with his logic, but I wasn't going to bother debating him, not when the real anchor behind that argument was Carella. And she didn't talk to us because, Matis had explained, she found the translation program creepy and disturbing.

Hachette sighed, rubbing a hand over his face.

"You understand that we're going to have to leave soon. We need to find the gateway back to our home, and it has to be soon, before we burn through our resources." Hachette winced, realizing he'd need to explain that. "We can only generate power while our fuel holds out. And the fuel is being burned constantly, whether we're traveling or fighting or just sitting in orbit. We have enough to last a long time, but not forever. And we can't get any more of it here."

"Not to mention," Dunstan chimed in again, leaning against the wall in a corner, arms folded, "that if that Tahni son of a bitch decides he wants to fight, we'll get our asses kicked." He looked around at the ceiling as if he were searching for someone. "That is, unless Dwight has found us one of those handy Predecessor power plants that has a black hole as its creamy nougat."

"Unfortunately, Captain Dunstan, I have not." Dwight didn't appear in his usual holographic form as a Commonwealth Space Fleet officer because Hachette hadn't bothered to bring down the hologram projector for his dirtside office. The disembodied voice was less off-putting, but not by much. "The only remaining energy cells of a suitable output to power your ship are beneath the Resscharr palace, and getting at them would require heavy equipment and the cooperation of the Karai and the Tahni...which I am sure you agree, we would not get."

"Can I ask you something, Dwight?" Vicky said, sitting beside me on the opposite side of Hachette's desk, elbows resting on its polished wood. Vicky was looking upward as well, used to seeing the Predecessor AI projected overhead. "Now that there are three of you, what with the copy you smuggled aboard the Tahni ships and the AI we found here in the Resscharr palace complex, Presteri, which one is...." She shrugged, spreading her hands. "...well, *you?*" I raised an eyebrow, the unspoken implication being that this was a weird time to ask that question, and she scowled at me. "I just want to know who we're talking to," she insisted.

"I take no offense at the question, Captain Sandoval," Dwight assured her, though I don't know that any of us had been concerned that he would. "Presteri is not any version of me. He was installed centuries, possibly even millennia after my construction. However, it is true that there is a version of my personality on the Tahni destroyer." Dwight lacked even the holographic shoulders to shrug, but I could have sworn I heard one in his voice. "Think of it this way. If someone were to clone you, force-age this copy to match your own development and imprint your memories into it, then separate the two of you for months, would this clone still be identical to you in every way? Would not those months of living separate lives have created differences in experience? And what is a sentient being other than the sum of their experiences?"

"No room for a soul, huh?" I wondered, trying not to obsess over the idea of two versions of Vicky running around.

"Souls are unquantifiable by nature. If they exist in any meaningful, physical way, it would be as an emergent property of consciousness...."

Colonel Hachette cleared his throat loud enough that Matis nearly jumped out of his skin.

"While this is all fascinating, I believe we're getting pretty far afield." Hachette closed his eyes as if trying to reclaim his train of thought. "Matis, we could use some reinforcements on this mission. And I think it might do your people some good to get experience serving with real combat troops. What do you think about putting together a platoon to go with us? If we did find the gateway," he hastened to add, "we'd be sure to give your people an opportunity to return here before we used it."

I didn't say anything and kept my face carefully neutral, but that was bullshit. Hachette had no idea whether the gateway would be—if it existed at all—and couldn't possibly make a promise that we'd be able to return to Yfingam before going through it. But I suppose being a full-bird colonel promotable required something of the politician, and politicians and making empty promises went together like peanut butter and bananas.

"I'll come myself," Matis volunteered, and his wife's eyes went wide. He noticed and put an arm around her, squeezing tight. "How can I lead in the defense of our people if I have no experience fighting?"

She jabbered something in their annoyingly fast-paced language and the translator repeated it in English, even though it wasn't meant for our ears.

"Without you, who will hold us together in the face of the Karai?"

"You will, Carella," he said, his hand on top of hers. "You, your brother, and your father. You have all kept me strong when I was ready to give up hope."

"Sir," I blurted, knowing Hachette wouldn't like me speaking out in front of the locals, "are you sure this is a good idea? We have no idea what we're going to run into out there. Maybe we should wait until they've had more training dirtside."

I'd expected the glare from the colonel and the eye-roll from Top, but I didn't expect the frown from Matis.

"If we are not ready to simply be on your ship," he said, "then are we to be treated as children, never trusted to do anything but shoot at lifeless wooden targets?"

"No, Matis," Hachette said, jumping in before I had the chance. "We *do* trust you, and I will be happy to have you lead the contingent aboard the *Orion*." And his stare dared me to say anything different.

I was about to do it anyway, but Vicky kicked me in the ankle and I grunted softly then kept my mouth shut. She was probably right. Going any further would just alienate Matis and his wife, or scare the shit out of them, neither of which would help us.

Hachette stood from behind his desk and the rest of us—except Dunstan, who hadn't sat down—did as well, those of us in the military because he was our superior officer and Matis and Carella presumably because they saw everyone else doing it. Hachette offered a hand in the Earth fashion and Matis shook it.

"Thank you for coming, both of you." Hachette nodded toward me. "Captain Alvarez will be making arrangements for equipping and organizing your platoon."

Ouch. There it was, my punishment for questioning him. That was technically Top's job, or possibly Solano's, but now it was mine.

"I will go and seek the best of us for this task," Matis assured him, edging toward the door as Hachette escorted him out. "It is a great honor for us."

And then he was out the door and Hachette pushed it shut, not slamming it but clearly wanting to.

"What was that all about, Alvarez?" he snapped. "I know you were out of the military for a couple years, but by God, I hope you still know not to second-guess your commanding officer in public!"

"Yes, sir," I said, stiffening to attention. "Sorry, sir."

"Oh, stow that shit, Marine!" Hachette waved away my attempts at military decorum. "*What* is your problem?"

"The same one I have, sir," Vicky said, her hand on my shoulder. "You're taking their best people on what could be a one-way mission. What are the Vergai going to do if we don't come back? Not only will they not have our protection, we'll also have stripped away their leadership."

Hachette regarded us both with his chin down, just slits of his eyes visible below his brows.

"Neither of you is stupid enough to believe that if the Karai attack, having Matis and a platoon of his best is going to slow them down for more than a few minutes."

"No, sir." The admission was easy. I was a captain, I didn't have to have all the answers. That was the colonel's job.

"But I understand the concern," Hachette allowed. "The key to all this is Zan-Thint. And Captain Alvarez, if you're that concerned about what he's going to do once we're gone...well, I suggest you go and have a talk with him about it."

Oh, shit. Why can't I keep my mouth shut?

———

Of all the things I'd seen during the war, I'd never actually had the opportunity to visit a Tahni military headquarters. So I didn't know if Zan-Thint was a traditionalist or the equivalent of an *avant-garde* when it came to furnishings and architecture. Though I *could* tell who had more political pull in Yfingam from the size of the building, at least three times what Hachette had been given, and by the fact that it was closer to the city walls than ours was.

The guards outside stared at me with unreadable expressions, their beady black eyes nearly hidden under the over-hanging brows. The muzzles of their KE rifles didn't move, but their fingers tightened around the grips, and I knew what they would have done had they been given the leave.

"I'm Captain Alvarez," I told them, my 'link translating it to Tahni. "I'm here to see Colonel Zan-Thint."

No response, not so much as a twitch. Eyeing the gap between the two, I considered whether I could squeeze through it and if they'd stop me if I tried. Fortunately, the door opened inward before I had to make the decision and Zan-Thint himself stood before me. He wasn't much different from any other

Tahni male except for the tell-tale signs of age, and I might have forgiven myself for not recognizing him if it hadn't been for his uniform. I *did* know the rank insignia of the Tahni equivalent of a colonel.

"Captain Alvarez," he said, his English still jarring and stilted, but better than any other Tahni I'd heard attempt it. "So nice of you to stop by. Would you mind if we talked as we walk? I promised to inspect the Karai troops this afternoon and I'd hate to disappoint them."

"Of course," I said, nodding. Because what the hell else was I going to say? Plus, I was one hundred percent certain this was all some message he was trying to send to me, and when an adversary is sharing information for free, you let him.

The two Tahni guards followed us, trailing at three meters, a respectful enough distance, far enough back that they wouldn't hear our conversation if we kept our voices low. Not that I expected them to speak English. The area surrounding the city walls was a buzz of activity this time of day, just before dusk. Tasks that had taken all day had to be wrapped up, herd animals had to be brought inside the fences, harvested food stored inside grain silos. The smell of sweat and fresh-cut wheat was strong in the air, though the inherent musk of the Tahni drowned some of it out.

"Tell me, Cameron Alvarez," Zan-Thint urged, "what can I do for you?"

"We're going to be leaving soon to search for the gate back to the Cluster," I told him.

"I had assumed so." He nearly stepped on the end of my sentence and I fought an urge to repeat the words of my instructors at OCS that ASSUME meant making an ASS out of U and ME. "After all, you didn't ask to be here," he added, with what might have sounded like reason coming from someone I trusted. "This is not your home."

It's not yours either, asshole. I didn't say that, but I thought it hard.

"But it is the home of the Vergai," I said instead. "They've been exploited by the Resscharr for generations, and Colonel Hachette and I are worried there will be a sentiment among the Karai to maintain that status quo once we're out of the way."

"And you expect me to do what, exactly?" He stopped walking so abruptly that I nearly stumbled to stay with him. Karai workers moved around us, guiding ox-carts laden with wood or stone into the gates of the city. An occasional Resscharr walked by, though not into the city. They'd been forced out into the former quarters where they'd kept the Karai females and children. "Tell them to be good little children and not bully the weaker humans?"

The hackles rose on the back of my neck, a cold weight settling in the pit of my stomach, something that had always been a prelude to violent action. I was very conscious of the handgun holstered at my right hip, its mass seeming to increase, weighing down that side of my body. It was a credit to the years of military training and my service as an officer under the Skipper, Captain Covington, that I was able to control my anger. There'd been a time once, not all that long ago, when I wouldn't have been talking, and the fact that I would have died in the process wouldn't have stopped me from drawing that gun and splashing Zan-Thint's brains all over the ground. But I had matured. That was what I told myself.

"Your command of our idiom is as impressive as your knowledge of our society," I complimented him, though I'm sure my tone would have sounded anything but congenial to someone who could read human expressions and body language. "But no, I don't expect you to lecture them. I expect you to take responsibility for their actions. You've given them high-tech armaments and made it clear that you intend to act as their protector, so that makes you the one who gets the credit or the blame for anything you allow them to do."

"I have armed and trained my people, as you have armed and trained yours." If he had been a human, I would have expected a shrug. Tahni didn't shrug. "Am I to blame if your numbers and resources are fewer than my own? Am I to believe that you wouldn't give the humans here an upper hand if you had the capability?"

Now *that* was a damned fine point, and one I had no argument against...at least none he would listen to. But I had to try.

"If we had the ability to arm the Vergai as you have the Karai, we would, you're right. What we would also do is encourage them to use the security those weapons gave them to ensure an enforceable peace with the Karai, with mutual respect for both sides."

I was no expert on Tahni, but I did know what it looked like when they were amused. They didn't laugh, but there was a set to their shoulders, a tilt of their head, that was their equivalent.

"Forgive me if I lack faith in your assurance of peace, human. All we have ever known from you is war."

"Your people fired the first shots in both wars," I reminded him. "And maybe that doesn't mean anything in your culture, but it does in mine. The one who shoots first has given up any claim to wanting peace."

"You're correct. It doesn't mean anything to us. To the Tahni, he who puts the other in a position where he *has* to shoot first is the one to blame." He turned and looked out at the Resscharr, reduced to a fraction of their population during the revolt, then back at the city, now in the hands of the Karai. "You've come to me seeking assurances. But we have the power, and with that power comes the lack of any need to give assurances. You may believe that I have no designs on wiping out the Vergai here, that their existence is neither a threat nor an insult to me.

That much I will tell you, and if it is enough, you may return to your people and say you've done your duty."

"And if it's not enough?" The question was academic, but I wanted to hear his answer, for my own curiosity if nothing else.

"If it's not...." He turned back toward me, his hands out to his sides, palms facing the ground. I knew this gesture too. It was one of defiance. "Then I would use your idiom once more, Captain Alvarez. What are you going to do about it?"

[3]

Nothing. That was what we were going to do about it.

Not that I didn't try hard enough to nearly get Colonel Hachette have me relieved for insubordination before Top grabbed him by the arm and pulled him aside. Whatever she told him saved my ass for the moment, but I wasn't in the mood for gratitude. I had twenty-eight puking, terrified Vergai to deal with.

"Will this never end?" Matis groaned. He would have been doubled over, but doubled over wasn't a thing in free-fall. Space sickness surely was, and not even our best medicines could keep the inner ears of our new recruits from rebelling.

If there was any comfort, it was that the ship's exhaust fans sucked up the nauseating chunks of whatever the Vergai had last eaten and disposed of it, usually before it smacked into anything, but the crew compartment the locals had been given on board the *Orion* still retained a stench unlike anything I'd smelled since I lived in the Trans Angeles Underground as a teenager. I'd put the bulkhead viewscreens on an external view of the planet, hoping it would give them something to focus on to soothe the mental anguish of free-fall, but all that had accomplished was to remind them they were in orbit, in perhaps the most unnatural situation any of them could imagine.

"Yes, it will end," I assured Matis, putting a hand on his shoulder to steady him, anchored down myself by ship boots. They had them too, but hadn't mastered the use of them. "In just a few minutes, we're going to be boosting out of orbit, and then you'll feel more normal." For a while, but I didn't tell him that. "But I need all of you to strap into your acceleration couches right now, or we won't be able to get underway, and the feeling you all have right now won't stop."

I motioned to Sgt. Motte, one of the Force Recon NCOs who had been shanghaied into this detail along with his squad, the poor bastards. At least I'd done something to piss Hachette off. They'd just drawn the short straw.

"Help get them strapped in," I told Motte, guiding Matis toward one of the row of acceleration couches arrayed in the center of the common area between troop compartments.

It was a different arrangement than I'd ever seen on a troop ship, but the *Orion* wasn't just a troop transport, wasn't merely a warship. She was unique, constructed specially for this mission, and there were a lot of features she didn't share with any other Commonwealth military vessel, including a railgun as her main armament.

"I am so sorry for this, Captain," Matis said once I'd buckled him in and he seemed to be recovering a bit from the shock of exposure to microgravity.

It hadn't happened on the shuttle up, mostly because the bird had been under thrust the whole time, and once it had docked, the collection of trainees had been so flabbergasted by the experience of the interior of a starship that they hadn't even thought about the lack of normal gravity. That had all changed once they'd left the docking bay and began trying to traverse the passageways to their quarters. We'd left a trail of green and yellow globules behind us, orbiting in a spiral toward the nearest vents like DNA double-helixes.

"I feel as if we are letting you down," Matis went on, wiping at his mouth with the back of his hand. "We act like children who must be bundled in their beds." He was staring at the Force Recon Marines strapping down his people. "I fear we will be nothing more than a burden to you."

It could have been worse. He could have been panicking, as a few of his men had. And they *were* all men, which had annoyed the hell out of Vicky and amused Top. They were a typical semi-feudal farming community for one thing, and for another, the only military force they'd had to emulate before we came was the Karai, and the Tahni didn't have female warriors. The Vergai had allowed women to take part in the shooting instructions, mostly because Cam had reminded them that numbers were the only advantage they had over the Karai, but when the time had come to pick the platoon for this mission, somehow they'd wound up all male.

Oh well. They're used to everything being raw muscle. They'll learn the difference modern weapons can make. And time and experience were better teachers than any scolding lecture Cam could give them.

"Don't worry about it, Matis," I assured him. "Everyone gets sick their first time up here. It's nothing to be ashamed of."

"Boost in three minutes," the automated systems warned over the PA system. "All personnel must be strapped in and prepared for acceleration."

I didn't hear the translation, but I knew it was repeating in the earbuds we'd given to each of the Vergai. They'd learn English eventually, maybe, if we were around that long, but it wouldn't be quick enough for this operation. I began to push away from Matis with some vague words of encouragement, but his hand on my forearm stopped me.

"Would you mind staying here with us?" He had a little-lost-boy expression and he must have realized it because his face screwed up with forced sternness. "It would help reassure the men."

Sure. The men.

"Of course," I said, slipping into the empty seat beside him and pulling the straps into place. If I'd been honest, I would rather have been on the bridge with Vicky, but I understood his trepidation. This was about as alien an experience as he could have.

I'd barely had time to get settled in when the acceleration alarm sounded and we broke orbit. The boost was gentle since we weren't in a combat situation, just a standard gravity, and Matis' sigh of relief was audible over the rumble of the fusion drive. But the vibration from the engine twisted in my gut, bringing with it the knowledge that every second we boosted was more fuel burned away, precious and irreplaceable. We had a portable fusion reactor, of course, meant for extended ground operations, and a small conversion plant that could let it run on seawater, but the fuel it produced wasn't concentrated enough for a drive...well, maybe a passenger ship that never had to boost higher than one gravity, but not a combat ship. Warships required metallic hydrogen, and the facilities to produce it were huge and expensive, and beyond our capability to build.

And once it was gone, well...that was pretty much where we were staying. Hachette knew it, knew my opinion on it, that we should settle into the Islander planet and bring everything down that we could, build ourselves as close to a technological civilization as we could, and try to make the best of it. Neither Vicky nor I had anything in particular holding us to the Cluster, not even the sense of duty driving Hachette. We'd done our duty and had only signed back up to prevent Zan-Thint from destroying the whole Cluster because that was where we lived.

"And it will be like this the rest of the way?" one of Matis' people asked, and I realized he had to be asking me, since my Force Recon helpers had beat feet to get back to their boost positions. I sighed,

"We'll be accelerating at one gravity..." I stopped when I saw the incomprehension in his eyes. I'd have to try again. "It'll be like this for the next several minutes. Then you'll be weightless again for a few minutes until we do what we call a Transition, the thing that lets us travel great distances. Once we do that, you'll be able to walk around again."

For a few days, maybe a week. But by then, I'd have a chance to sit down and talk to them some more, and hopefully, they'd be calmer about the whole thing by then.

"You do this all the time?" That was from someone behind me, a voice I didn't recognize. Not that I could have put a name with any of the faces without their IFF transponders.

"I've been doing it since I was nineteen years old."

I paused, trying to remember how I'd felt that first time, when I'd been taken straight out of the Trans-Angeles Detention Center and put on a shuttle to orbit still wearing my orange coveralls marked *Prisoner*. I'd never even been off the ground before, much less out of the gravity well.

"The first time," I confessed, grinning in self-deprecation, "I not only barfed, I pissed myself." No one had noticed, of course. Those detention coveralls were very efficient and keeping prisoners from expressing themselves through bodily functions was one of their many features.

Once the translation went through, the Vergai laughed softly, each of them probably relieved it hadn't been *that* bad for them. Except, of course, for the ones who *had* pissed themselves, and those would be laughing so no one else thought they'd done anything so humiliating.

"It got better for me, and it will for you too. The thing to remember is, you're not *really* falling. It's just part of not being on a planet." Someone started to ask a technical question and I waved it off. "I'll explain that later." Or someone would. Someone *else* if I had my way. "You're going to be feeling a lot of new sensations. If we have to fly into battle, your stomach will feel as though it wants to claw its way out of your throat, and it's going to scare you because it's something new. But the key is, you have to refuse to let the fear rule you. We've all done this before and we know what we're doing." I nearly choked on the next words. "You just have to trust us."

"You still back there slumming with the Vergai, Alvarez?" Hachette called, his voice an annoying buzz in my ear.

"Just where you ordered me to be, sir."

He chuckled, apparently enjoying this a lot more than I was.

"We'll be Transitioning in five minutes. Once we do, get your ass to the Ops center. We're going to go over the star charts Dwight has in his records and try to figure out what might be waiting for us."

I glanced aside at Matis, knowing he couldn't hear Hachette's voice and wouldn't be able to make out my end of the conversation if I subvocalized for my throat mic. Just in case, I touched a control on my 'link and turned off the translation routine.

"Should I bring Matis or any of his people, sir?"

"Negative. This is a high-level planning session. Since you're so concerned about his professional development, you can personally brief him and his people on it later."

"Yes, sir."

Matis was staring at me, eyes narrowed. He could tell, I think, that something was up, that I was talking to someone. The man wasn't stupid, for all that he'd spent his formative years as a dirt farmer.

"We're about to Transition," I said, pretending that was what I'd been talking about. I pitched my voice to carry to the others. "We'll be cutting off the drive just before we do, so you're going to be weightless for just a minute. Then, when we jump, you're going to feel something strange. I can't describe it, really, but it's going to scare you a little. It only lasts for a second."

It was difficult trying to tell them about things that were as normal to me as getting dressed in the morning, difficult to remember the thoughts and feelings of that kid who'd never been off Earth. Sure, I remembered soiling myself, but that was an event. What had I thought in that moment? What had I felt the first time I'd experienced a Transition from our spacetime to something so totally outside the human experience that we couldn't see it even if we looked directly at it?

What use was I to these people? What could I do except get them killed?

"One minute to Transition." Damn that automated voice. This was the military; couldn't they afford the inefficiency of a real person warning us? "Prepare for free-fall."

Some of the Vergai took that announcement as a warning to cover their mouths, which wasn't a bad idea. The fusion drive cut off, leaving us traveling forward with the momentum of our previous burn. Not that it would matter. T-space ate momentum the way whales ate krill, and when we emerged from the jump, we'd be as close to motionless as was possible for anything in realspace.

Someone retched and I rolled my eyes.

"God's sake," I snapped, "keep it together. It's only for a minute."

It seemed longer, I'd grant them that. And it would probably feel as if it took forever for the Vergai, who only knew something strange and unpleasant was coming.

"Transitioning now."

Was this jump worse than usual? Or had I built it up so much to the Vergai that it had penetrated my subconscious and made me as paranoid and sensitive as they were?

Either way, the jump dug its talons into my soul and ripped me free of one reality, dragging me kicking and screaming into another. Figuratively, in my case. Literally for at least three of the Vergai.

"It's okay!" I yelled at them, yanking the quick-release on my restraints and sprinting across the compartment, laying my palm against the chest of one of them, a burly, thick-bodied man close to middle age, wires of grey shot through his beard. "We're all right! Everyone can take off their safety straps and walk around. It's over."

The man's breathing slowed down and he quieted, looking around as if he'd just realized the gravity had returned.

"These are your rooms," I told them, motioning at the open hatches on either side of the passageway. "Matis knows who goes in which, and your clothes and personal belongings have already been secured in the wall lockers in each room. Get settled in, take a shower if you need it. Dinner will be in two hours." Remembering that they probably told time by the position of their primary star in the sky, I amended that. "I'll come get you for dinner, or I'll send one of the others."

The casual way I was treating the whole thing had calmed down the others who'd screamed in fright from the jump, and the ones who had already figured out how to take off their seatbelts began helping those who were having trouble with it.

"Congratulations," I told them, smiling as broadly and artificially as any politician or colonel I had ever despised. "You're all spacers. You've done what no Vergai has done before...jumped into Transition Space. You're traveling to another star. When you return home, they'll tell stories about you to their grand-children."

That brought their spirits up and many were laughing and clapping each other on the back when I left them, heading for the lift banks. I was glad for the chance to turn away from them. That fake smile came closer to making me puke than free-fall ever could have.

[4]

"You're a real gloomy Gus lately," Vicky said softly just beside my ear, so the crewmembers stuffed into the lift with us wouldn't hear it. Not that I expected them to pay attention. They were bluesuits, Fleet personnel, and they generally considered us Marines as excess baggage. Of course, we were minor celebrities due to the circumstances of the mission, which might mean they'd have their ears open for gossip.

"I've been playing kindergarten teacher to a bunch of pre-industrial farmers all week long," I reminded her. "And by the way, you promised to *help* with that, I recall."

"Hey, I got my own responsibilities," she protested, raising a hand to end my complaint. "And anyway, *I* wasn't the one who pissed off Colonel Hachette."

"What happened to 'for better or for worse?' I seem to remember hearing something like that in our marriage vows."

"Do you?" She arched an eyebrow at me. "I don't remember taking *any* vows, just filing the marriage with the Personnel Command so that if they ever activated us again, they'd have to station us at the same base. I also recall *someone* saying we didn't need a religious ceremony, that it was just a waste of time. I wonder if that someone is in this elevator right now?"

"I only remember saying that God already knew we were married in our hearts," I protested weakly. One of the bluesuits *did* hear that, because she snickered. "At the time, you thought it was very romantic."

"At the time, I just wanted to get as far away from the Marine Corps as possible." She nudged me. "Just be glad Colonel Hachette is letting you back on the bridge for the Transition instead of making you hold the Vergai's hands and read them bedtime stories."

"Ma'am, sir?" The voice wasn't familiar and I had to search through the faces of the half-dozen Fleet officers and enlisted in the lift car before I found the one who'd spoken. She was young, a Lieutenant-JG, still just a rank down and a few years younger than me, but there was a gap of worlds of experience. She'd probably still been in the Academy when the war ended.

"Yes, Lt. Sienna?" I replied, reading the name off the plate at her chest.

"Do you know why we picked this system to Transition into?" She shrugged, her expression apologetic. "We were briefed about the destination, but I was curious whether this was just the next stop, or if there was something special about it."

What she was curious about, I thought but had the brains not to say, was whether we were wasting our fuel chasing our tails all over the galaxy, or if there was any hope we'd actually find the gateway. Unfortunately, I didn't have an answer to that...at least not one she would like.

"You know about Dwight, I assume?" It was a stupid question, of course. Who on the ship didn't know about the ten-thousand-year-old AI who'd stranded us here? At her nod, I went on. "He has records from before, from when the Predecessors dropped him back in the Cluster. They don't say what'll be here now, but they show the surveys the Predecessors did of this area, and we all figured the best place to check would be in systems with habitables."

"But, sir," she said, tentative, though I didn't know whether her hesitation came from a reluctance to question me or from a desperate hope that we and Hachette knew what we were doing, "wasn't the gateway we came through to get here in a life-less system?"

I winced. I couldn't help it. A glance at Vicky offered no support nor any suggestion she'd take over this answer.

"You're absolutely right," I admitted. "But there are hundreds, even thousands of lifeless systems for every habitable. We're hoping that we can find more remnants of the Resscharr and track down any old records they might have."

"And you think that'll work, sir?"

I wished she would stop calling me "sir." And asking me questions I didn't want to answer.

"I think it's the best chance we have. And so does Colonel Hachette." And as for Captain Nance, the *Orion*'s master...I didn't know. The man was closed-mouthed at the best of times, and this was certainly not the best of times.

"Thank you, sir," she said just as the lift doors opened with a hiss that could have echoed my sigh of relief.

Hachette and Nance were speaking at the center of the bridge when we arrived, their tones low and businesslike, showing none of the tension I was feeling. Vicky and I waited just the other side of the railing encircling the command posi-tions, a practical device meant to help the crew get around in free-fall, and Hachette finally noticed us.

"Now we get to find out if this whole trip is just a huge boondoggle, eh?" he asked, offering me a grin that might have been meant to seem mischievous, but instead reeked of desperation.

"It's just one system, sir," Vicky said, offering the olive branch I wasn't willing to part with. "Just one chance out of many."

"I may have my fair share of the sometimes-unwarranted self-confidence for which colonels are infamous," Hachette said, "but in this job, I've cultivated at least the self-awareness to admit it and to admit I'm not always right." And he didn't seem shy about saying it in front of the whole bridge, which surprised me. "We only have enough fuel for a few more Transitions, if we expect to be able to return to Yfingam." He looked around at the crew, who were staring at him. "You've all had the thought and so have I. I want you to know, I'm not blind to our situation. We have a duty to try to return home, but not to die doing it. If we find nothing, if this is a dry hole, we're not doubling down on a bad hand." He nodded toward the ship's master. "Captain Nance and I have discussed it and calculated our stores and their capacity. We have enough fuel to keep this ship running for another two months, given our usual usage, and barring high-g combat maneuvers. At the end of that period, if we've found no way back, we're going to Transition back to Yfingam and do what we can to survive and thrive there, or perhaps on the Islander planet." There was rumbling from around the bridge, though not by me. I was silent, frozen, watching him. Hachette held up a hand to forestall the chatter. "I know some of us have families back home, and I know you don't want to hear that, but this isn't a decision I've made lightly."

"For what it's worth," Dwight interjected, appearing over Hachette's shoulder on the main screen, like the ghost of Hamlet's father, "I am very confident in the promise of this course. If there's anything to be found, we're on the right track to find it."

"Your lips to God's ears," Hachette told him, not seeming at all perturbed by the sudden manifestation of the alien AI. "Helm, Transition in one minute. Comms, announce secure for microgravity and possible emergency boost."

While the Communications officer sounded the alerts, Vicky and I heeded them ourselves, folding down the spare acceleration couches at the rear of the bridge and strapping in. I tightened the last restraint just seconds before the alarm sounded and the *Orion* Transitioned into realspace. Lacking any preemptive lecture to the Vergai, I barely noticed the parapsychological effects, but I did start at the blare of alarms that went off in the wake of the jump.

I was no Fleet spacer, but I recognized them. Proximity alerts, collision alarms.

"Helm, adjust forty-eight degrees relative north, eighteen west! One-gravity burn for thirty seconds!" Nance's orders were clipped, instinctive, not waiting for confirmation from Hachette. The safety of the ship was *his* purview, and no Intelligence colonel was going to second-guess him.

"Report!" Hachette demanded. "What are we looking at?"

It was a damned good question and even the sudden *bangbangbang* of the maneuvering thrusters and the return of thrust gravity couldn't distract me from the main screens. We'd come out of T-space about two light-seconds from a planet, the one Dwight's data had indicated was habitable and probably settled by the Resscharr.

It was a blackened cinder. It was clear where the oceans had been once, but they were gone, leaving one of those naked photos of Earth meant to show the mountains and valleys under the sea. No trace of green or blue or white tainted the black and brown that were all that was left of the world. It had once had a moon much like ours. That was nearly a universal law, I think, though Dwight hadn't been able to confirm it. Wherever there was life, there was a moon. I was of the opinion that the Predecessors had dragged moons into the orbit of the planets they terraformed, but I couldn't have said whether this one was transplanted or simply came to be here the old-fashioned way.

What I *could* tell was that it had been blasted to bits. Its core still held together, though with the look of a loose collection of rocks, a spherical cairn that could come apart with the least application of force, but the rest...

"There's a ring of debris orbiting the planet, sir," Lt.-Commander Wojtera, the Tactical Officer, informed Hachette. "I'm guessing here, but by the amount of it and its distribution, I'd say it's from the moon."

"Holy hell," Vicky murmured. "What could *do* that to it?"

"Resscharr gravity weapons," Dwight provided the unexpected answer. "Or, more likely, the rupture of a Resscharr power plant and the uncontrolled release of the singularity contained within it. A large one."

"Helm," Nance told Lt. Yanayev, an undercurrent to the tension running through the bridge, "cut thrust, execute turnover, and perform braking for one minute. Take us to station-keeping."

The Newtonian gravity of boost faded and I pushed against the restraints as my body wanted to cut loose of their surly bonds and fly toward the overhead. I barely registered it beyond a slight feeling of gratitude that we weren't about to smack into one of the fragments of the devastated moon at several thousand meters per second.

"I'm picking up other debris, sir," Wojtera put in, tracing lines across his control board, the view on the Tactical screen zooming in tighter toward the dead planet, red halos flashing around a few dozen fragments invisible with the naked eye. "They're a different spectrographic consistency than the rest of the ring."

"They're Skrela seed ships," Dwight announced. "Or rather, what remains of them. And there's something more...."

"Captain, Colonel," Lt. Chase, the Comms officer cut in, excitement trembling in his voice, in the wide whiteness of his eyes, "something down there is transmitting. It's low-power, not enough juice to make it out of this system, but it's not EM frequency. It's gravimetic."

I stared at the holographic projection that was our only tangible perception of Dwight. He'd gotten very good at pantomiming our emotional responses, and just now, he was showing a disturbed expression, something between fear and sorrow, yet still with a glint of intrigue in those simulated eyes.

"I know what it's saying," he informed us. "It's a beacon. It *should* be bright enough and loud enough to reach light-years, dozens of them. That was how they designed it."

"A beacon saying what?" I asked him, though I thought I knew.

"Calling for help. Warning the others. This was a Resscharr colony, a living world. Something killed it, either the Skrela or the Resscharr themselves in their attempt to destroy the invading force." Disgust this time on that simulated face, as if he'd bitten into something rotten. "This was, far too often, how any confrontation with the Skrela turned out. To truly defeat them, nothing less than total destruction would suffice. This...." He pointed toward the image of the world. "...is why the Predecessors left your Cluster and never returned."

Colonel Hachette was watching Dwight as well, and I had the sense he was reading him as cannily as he'd ever read any other intellectual opponent.

"What's down there, Dwight? If we go, what will we find?"

"I can't be sure." Dwight shook his head in the simulation. "It's been so long, and the power must be so low after this long, after this much damage. There's no guarantee you'll find anything except a mindless automated system repeating this message."

"But?" Hachette insisted.

"But there's a possibility," Dwight admitted, "that there could be another of us down there."

"Another of us?" I said, wondering if I was misunderstanding him.

"Another of me," he elaborated. "The AI. There was generally one of us with every expedition."

"Just one?" Vicky asked.

"The Resscharr were wary of gathering too many of us in one place." I couldn't be sure, since Dwight only showed us the emotions he wanted to share, but I thought I detected resentment in his voice. "They feared that we might be tempted to assume too much control."

"A fear not unique to the Predecessors," Hachette allowed. "If there's an AI down there, can you contact it?"

"If you'll allow me to access your communications?" The mild-looking man in the projection tilted his head toward Hachette in a question.

"Could I stop you if I wanted to?"

"Of course! I was forced to follow my programming and send you through the gate, but otherwise, I am merely here to help."

Hachette grunted noncommittally but nodded.

"Very well, give it a try."

Silence for a few seconds and just as I was wondering how long the process was going to take, Dwight spoke up again.

"I...detect his presence, yet I am unable to contact him."

I frowned, and I thought my face must be a mirror of Hachette's.

"You're going to have to walk us through that one," I told

him, beating the colonel to the punch. "If you can't contact him, how do you know he's there?"

"It's complicated to explain. There's a certain pattern to gravimetic communications...I'm sure you haven't gotten a feel for this yet, since your ability to communicate with gravimetic waves is still extremely limited. It's not the same as an electromagnetic signal, just a modulation of the field. It's dependent on what sort of equipment you're using, how fast the computations are being run. You'll just have to take my word that I can *feel* the presence of one like me in the signal. But no, I can't communicate with him because he is unable to receive." Dwight pointed toward the planet on the main screen. "But if you were to land there and get close enough to the source using something with enough computing power for me to piggyback a connection to it, such as one of your battlesuits, I may be able to access its memories."

Hachette looked to Nance, and the captain glanced between Yanayev and Wojtera, his Helm and Tactical officers.

"We're clear of the debris field," Wojtera announced. "I believe I can chart a safe course to orbit through the ring, but if you want my opinion, we should stay out here and send an Intercept through if we're going to land."

Hachette's eyes were on me, and I knew what he was going to ask, but I let him go ahead anyhow because why should I make it easy for him?

"How many Vigilantes can you fit in the utility bay of an Intercept cutter?"

It sounded like the beginning of a bad joke, but I figured Hachette was serious.

"In a pinch, four," I told him. "But unless it's an emergency, I'd rather keep it to two." I nudged Vicky. "You wanna come along or should I ask Solano?"

She snorted a derisive laugh.

"Yeah, right, like he'd actually come along of his own free will. He'd probably order one of his platoon leaders, or better yet, one of his platoon *sergeants* to go with you. Anyway, you're not wading into the shit anymore unless I'm there to watch your ass, Alvarez."

I sighed but I couldn't help grinning.

"I guess that means we volunteer, sir," I told Hachette, pretending we'd had a choice. "We'll take Dunstan's bird, if that's all right with you."

"And me," Dwight added with the enthusiasm of a younger brother hanging out with the older kids.

"And of course, you," I assured him, wondering if his knowledge of human expressions was complete enough to tell a sincere smile from a sneer. "How could I forget *you*? Without you, none of us would be here."

He smiled back as if it were a compliment, and I got my answer.

[5]

"I can't believe," Kyler Dunstan said, shaking his head, "that this place used to be habitable."

I wasn't in the cockpit with him or his crew, but I'd learned how to link my Vigilante's Heads-Up Display to the internal viewers many years ago as an NCO, long before I'd technically been allowed to do it. A quarter of my HUD was the view from the cockpit's visual comm pickup, showing the look of disgust on Dunstan's face, the three-quarters which remained revealing what had provoked the reaction.

Intercept One was hovering two kilometers over what I guess had once been the planet's northernmost continent, back when the world's landmasses had been separated by ocean. Now, it was just another piece of charcoal, baked lifeless by the unfettered fury of the primary star. That was what happened when a planet had its atmosphere ripped away by a gravity bomb or whatever the hell had done it.

"The thought of anyone having weapons that powerful...." I didn't finish the thought, but Dunstan scoffed at the sentiment.

"Dude, we can destroy planets with what we have now. Hell, we've been able to do it for two hundred years, ever since we got nukes. It just took more effort. Honest, man, I don't think these Predecessors were that smart. Yeah, they had shit we don't. But give us another couple hundred years, we might have. And you know what? I think if we were fighting some bad-ass bug monsters who wouldn't stop coming, we'd figure something out and we wouldn't wind up destroying everything we'd built along the way."

"Someone," Vicky countered, her tone dry enough to kindle a fire, "has forgotten the Sino-Russian War. I know they still teach history in the Academy, right? Nuclear exchange about midway through the Twenty-First Century? Three billion people dead in the war, another three in the aftermath? Civilization ground to a halt, riots in all major cities, refugee crises all along eastern Europe and Australia, famine, pestilence? Any of this ring a bell?"

"Yeah, yeah," Dunstan admitted. "And we came back from it and made sure it wouldn't happen again. I still say we'd find a better way."

"If your people are more fortunate than mine," Dwight told him, his tone more reserved and introspective than I was used to from the chatty AI, "you'll never have to find out. Now, if you wouldn't mind, I believe the source of the signal is north by northwest, one hundred kilometers."

"I'm picking up something that way," the copilot, Lt. Quaresma, agreed. "Thermal output, though not much...maybe some kind of generator."

"Jesus, these fuckers were sure built to last." That was the gunner. I couldn't remember her name until I checked the IFF transponder readings from her uniform. Lt. Tuduri.

"Singularities take billions of years to degrade," Dwight said. "A bit more to the west, Captain Dunstan."

"I wonder what sort of place this was." I hadn't meant to say it out loud, but the thought slipped away before I could grab on to it. I shrugged and finished the sentiment. "I mean, was it like a huge city, stretching from one horizon to another? Or some half-assed feudal kingdom like Yfingam? Did they still have all the knowledge of the ones who came here or were they just scrabbling around in the dark, fighting an enemy they didn't understand with weapons left to them?"

"We'll find out in approximately seven minutes," Dwight replied. "Depending on how long it takes you to reach the source of the signal once we land."

———

It took a while.

I couldn't recall the last time I'd sweated with effort while wearing the suit. From ambient heat, sure. From fear, yeah. But from actual work...that had been a while. The suit's muscles and servos were actually lifting the two-hundred-kilo chunks of granite, but my body had to do the follow-through, had to start the effort to send it through the feedback, even with the interface jacks. Those were more for balance, coordination, but I had to send the commands for its limbs to move in order to pass them through the implants in my temples, and when that happened, my limbs moved...and took a ton of battlesuit along with them.

Sweat poured down my forehead and I blinked it out of my eyes.

"How much fucking deeper, Dwight?" I demanded, pausing to stare at the three-meter-tall pile of rocks Vicky and I had removed from where the AI insisted the source of the signal was located.

"Another meter," he assured me, with the same sort of confidence of a parent telling their child "just a little further."

I didn't say anything and Vicky's only comment was a terse

profanity. I took a sip of water from the nipple off to the side of my head. At least it was cold. Hell, the suit heaters were probably working overtime just to keep it from freezing solid. It was night on this side of the planet, though with no atmosphere, the only difference was the bone-chilling cold or the searing heat.

And the stars. When the primary was out, I couldn't see anything but the glare and the blackness. Now, all I could see was stars coating the sky, as if we weren't on a planet at all, but simply floating free in space.

"It's almost beautiful," Vicky said, reading my mind as usual. "If we didn't know how it got this way."

"Yeah," I agreed, reluctantly looking away, bending over to grab another chunk of rock.

It landed amidst the rest of the pile, soundless in the vacuum, though a slight vibration reached up through the soles of my feet, conducted by the uninsulated stone. Nothing else was quite as eerie and surreal as working on an airless world. Vacuum was natural, but it always seemed to go hand-in-hand with free-fall in my head. Free-fall without vacuum, I was used to from being in starships. Vacuum without free-fall was the part that weirded me out. And this world, as close as I could tell, had slightly over Earth-normal gravity, which made it even worse, made breathing and moving harder.

"Is that a tunnel?" Vicky asked, her metal fist ringing off my shoulder plastron.

I turned my attention from the pile of rocks to the area we'd been clearing. She was right. I'd been so busy concentrating on moving rocks, I hadn't noticed, but we'd opened up the end of a tunnel, and not a natural one. The walls were too smooth for that, too perfect. And too bright. Everything else was black, or a brown so dark as to not make a difference. The walls were a light gray, almost shining under the glow of the beams from our helmet lights.

I pushed aside a few last bits of rock and slid down the crest of built-up dirt and sand, landing with a dull thump only I could hear. The beam from my headlamp reached down ten meters before it curved into the unknown.

"Can we fit through this, Dwight?"

"We?" Vicky repeated. "You think I'm going in there?"

"Yes, Captain Alvarez," Dwight answered. "It should widen around the curve."

"If I get stuck down here," I warned him, ducking into the passageway, "I'm going to make sure someone scrambles your neural network for you."

"There's no need for threats, Captain Alvarez." Dwight seemed hurt.

"Oh, there's always room for threats," I muttered back, trying to get a reading on the far end of the tunnel. The suit had laser rangefinders, but the rock wall wasn't very reflective. It also had sonar, but sound wouldn't travel without air, which left me only the old-fashioned way to find out if he was right.

I suppose there were worse things than getting trapped underground in a Vigilante suit. I wouldn't be crushed, I had plenty of water and air, and they'd undoubtedly land more people to come and dig me out. But it would have been damned embarrassing, and when my shoulder plastrons scraped against the walls on either side, I was convinced I was going to be there for the foreseeable future.

"Damn it," I muttered, digging my spiked soles in and pushing with all the might of the suit, taking the chance of getting stuck even worse.

I had a fifty-fifty shot and that was better odds than you get in any casino. I popped through the curve into a larger chamber, twenty meters in diameter and empty except for a single plat-form at the center.

Jackpot.

"That's it," Dwight told me. "Go to the dais."

I wouldn't have thought of the thing as a dais, but then *dais* wasn't a word I'd ever used in my life and I barely knew the definition. The thing reminded me of a speaker's platform except for what seemed like a crystal in the center of it.

"What do I do?" I asked him. "Touch it? Make a fucking wish?"

He didn't answer immediately, and I wondered why an AI would hesitate.

"I still can't connect. I think yes, you will need to make direct contact with the control panel."

"Why did I ask?" I muttered.

Now that I was closer, I could see the pale, purple light glowing through a layer of centuries-old dirt, still stuck in place because there was no wind to stir it. No thermal readings from the thing, though something deeper, somewhere under the floor was glowing a gentle yellow. If I could see that much heat through layers of rock, something down there was red hot.

"Hope you don't expect me to bare-hand the thing."

I reached out hesitantly, half-expecting the thing to blow up when I touched it, but the claw-like appendage on my suit's right hand clicked against it, pushing aside a layer of black dirt, coming up short against something solid and perhaps crystalline. Nothing happened, or nothing that I could see or feel. No spark, no hologram springing to life to tell us the secrets of the universe. I was sure it wasn't working and that the whole trip had been a waste.

"He is here." Dwight sounded like the leader of a cult, announcing the arrival of some eldritch god. "We are connected. Please don't move your hand."

Great. Not that I would get tired of holding the suit in the same position, but I was already feeling awkward and now I had to tempt fate by keeping my suit pressed against what was essentially a live wire.

"How long is this going to take?" I asked him after I'd held the same pose for a few more minutes.

"I am constrained by the capacity of your suit computers and the bandwidth of your connection to the Intercept cutter," Dwight explained. "The data stored inside this facility is quite beyond your technological capability, so I am forced to choose which bits to send over. This is requiring more time than I would like."

"The Intercept has Quantum-core storage," I protested. "How the hell could your system manage to store more than that?"

"The Predecessors stored data in Transition Space."

"Of course they did," Vicky said. I couldn't see her, but I could picture the expression on her face, the roll of her eyes.

"All right. That's enough. You may break the connection."

"You sound sad," I told him, surprised at how pronounced the emotion was in his voice.

"He is a friend. More, a brother. And I am forced to leave what most makes him who he is on this desolate world with no chance of rescue."

"Damn." I felt as if I'd been punched in the gut. "I hadn't thought of it that way."

"You would not. Just as the Predecessors, you think of us as tools, as machines rather than thinking beings."

"We're not used to you yet," I insisted. "We don't allow research into sentient AIs because our government is afraid of what they could become. I think, given enough time, they'll learn to accept you for who you are."

"And who do you say I am, Cameron Alvarez?"

The question had a familiar ring to it, something Biblical, I thought, and I wondered if he wanted me to answer that he was the son of God. I wasn't going to.

"I think you're a thinking being who was given a shitty job. I think you're doing the best you can with what you have, just like the rest of us." I felt like I was back counseling enlisted Marines about their personal problems, and honestly, it probably wasn't much different. "You did your duty and some of us still resent that, but eventually, they'll get over it."

"You are my friend, Cameron?"

Another odd question, especially from an alien computer. Was he serious? Was he sincere? Or was this another affectation, a conscious decision to try to appear more human? He'd done it before, and while it could have been an innocent attempt to fit in with us, my instincts were way too far on the skeptical side to accept that.

"Of course, Dwight," I said, telling him what he wanted to hear. God knows, maybe it was the truth. I'd certainly had stranger friends.

I wasn't sure if he believed me, but the answer seemed to satisfy him.

"Then we must go, my friend. I have discovered much, and Colonel Hachette needs to know."

I wished there were some way I could speak to Vicky privately without the AI listening in, because I sure would have liked to ask her if she thought this was as weird as I did.

[6]

The city gleamed white in the mid-day sun, beautiful, like something out of a dream. Spires twisted in designs that seemed to defy gravity and, who knows? We were talking about the Predecessors, so maybe they did. Globes and spikes rose on impossibly thin columns hundreds of meters into the painfully blue sky, connected by spider-web strands of silk, walkways perhaps, but nothing we could have built now or in a hundred years. Above the city, things floated free in the atmosphere, more than ships, less than skyscrapers, moving slowly as if with the wind, and I wondered if they were dwellings, some kind of equipment, or maybe even weapons of some sort.

It was easy to forget it was a city for people, to look at it from above and think it was a work of art. But as the view began to descend, the Predecessors themselves became visible. I suppose I should have called them Resscharr, but that would have been sullying these people by comparison with the Resscharr on Yfin-gam. These were *the* Predecessors, the legends, the gods some people worshipped, and they seemed to be worth the accolades.

Until the Skrela came. The video sped up, the tangible immediacy of the records losing something with the adjustment, as if I'd stepped back and realized I was watching something centuries old rather than standing on the living world and walking among the Predecessors. The sky darkened, lightened, then darkened again, and in that final darkness, the lights in the sky flashed, their fury apocalyptic.

I expected the view to move into orbit, into interplanetary space, to show us the details of the battle, but that didn't happen. It was as if whoever had recorded it wanted to demonstrate what the invasion was like from the ground, for the average person in the city. The view spiraled downward, closer to the street view, among the Predecessors, only a meter behind the feathered manes of hair, their sinewy muscles bare to the sun, their bodies covered by the briefest of garments.

"What recorded this?" Colonel Hachette asked, quiet and subdued, yet still his question breaking the immersion even more than the fast-forward. "Drones? Remote cameras on buildings? Or is this a computer simulation of some kind?"

"None of those," Dwight told him. "All of them. The process is complicated and involves technology you don't have, and it would take me long minutes to explain it. It is real. It happened. If you believe that, it doesn't matter how it was recorded. If you don't, my explanation will be useless."

Hachette scowled at the holographic representation of the AI, and I could tell he wanted to argue the point, but Top touched his arm and shook her head.

"Fine," he said. "Go on."

Wow. I knew Top was important, but I hadn't known she was *that* trusted by Hachette. It spoke of either uncommon good sense by the man, or else personal feelings I hadn't guessed about.

The recording continued, speeding up again, following the people as they hurried through the streets. I couldn't quite make out their faces. They always seemed to be turned away, and when one of them did turn toward the camera, it was from far away or just out of focus. I wondered if that was intentional. The eyes of the Resscharr I'd seen back on Yfingam were catlike, golden, utterly inhuman. If the purpose of this was to evoke our sympathy, maybe Dwight was doing what he could to keep them as humanoid as possible.

"Are they heading to shelters?" Top wondered.

"Not precisely. Physical shelters would not be adequate against the effects of the weapons the Resscharr would be employing against the Skrela. They're heading to sheltered areas beneath gravitic force fields. Those are used over the whole city, but these are more focused, stronger."

The air shimmered above the civilians as the footage looked up with them, behind their eyes, watching the fireworks. Ships were exploding, energies dispelling across defensive shielding, glowing red in some places, white in others. I had no proof, but I thought the white was worse, a sign that the shields were failing.

Vicky's hand sought out mine, her fingers squeezing out stress. I felt it too. It was as if we'd been running beside the civilians, like the enemy attack was coming down on *our* heads. And above all that, we *knew* what was going to happen to those people. We'd walked in their burned-out ruins.

High speed again, and I guessed the light show had gone on for hours. The civilians shifted positions in their shelter beneath the shield, some going to sleep, some taking a meal. It seemed ridiculous to me that they were sitting out in the open, but I sensed from the shimmering in the air that the gravitic fields keeping them safe were rising from multiple projectors. It was physically safe, but for me, it felt incredibly vulnerable on a psychological level. Still, it was clear they could ride this out there for the duration of the space battle...if the space battle had been all they had to worry about.

But despite the rain of debris from the thousands of Skrela

drop pods that the air defenses were destroying, some were getting through. From the view of the projection, their landing was invisible, and hope fluttered in my gut that they'd been taken out by ground troops. I smashed it with a surge of irritation, wondering why I was bothering to give place to hope in the face of hopeless foreknowledge.

As if mocking my useless optimism, a horde of scuttling, arachnoid shapes appeared at the end of the thoroughfare, looming large, even larger than I knew them to be. Each was the size of a draft horse, if you crossed a draft horse with a scorpion and an army ant and then bolted a plasma cannon to its shoulder. A Predecessor stepped to the front of the cluster of civilians and raised a familiar weapon, the same sort I'd fired on Yfingam. I didn't know what it fired, exactly, but I thought it had to be some sort of particle accelerator. The discharge was a coruscating wash of white fire, and when it touched a Skrela, they seemed not so much to explode as to come apart at the atomic level, their mass converting to energy in a concussive wave of heat and light.

The weapon was devastating, taking out two or three of the things at a time, but there was only one of them, and there were so many of the Skrela. Plasma tore the air to shreds, beat it into submission, and set it afire. The blasts of superheated hydrogen should have turned the Predecessor defender to a charred cinder in the blink of an eye, but he was shielded, though if it was from something he carried on his person or perhaps a field projected by the same machinery protecting the civilians, I wasn't sure. The plasma didn't exactly dissipate, nor was it shunted aside. Instead, it formed a glowing dome around the lone defender, yellow at first, then red, and finally, as more and more blasts struck it, painful white.

It couldn't last long under the unyielding barrage, and it didn't. The field collapsed, and when it did, the Resscharr disappeared. I couldn't say if he was atomized or simply vaporized by the heat, but there was nothing left of him, just a haze of white smoke. And all those civilians, screaming now, running. The sound was uncanny, inhuman, the kind of cheeping screech I would have expected from a bird being attacked by a raptor. When the Skrela reached the crowd, I looked away. Yes, I'd seen worse, but that didn't mean I wanted to see it again.

Mercifully, Dwight ended the playback there.

"This was one of the more advanced Resscharr outposts in the sector," he informed us, grim as a preacher at an atheist's funeral. "My brother, the AI for this world, told me that this outpost was one of the first and largest, an attempt to recreate what they once had back in the Cluster. They did that only too well. The Skrela found them several hundred years ago and wiped them from existence."

"Something about this doesn't make sense to me," Kyler Dunstan complained. I might have been projecting my own feelings onto him, but I thought he looked a bit green around the gills, as if the recording had hit him as hard as it had me. "Back in the Cluster, the Skrela traveled via seed pods. They sent them out like a shotgun blast, bits spreading everywhere, and when they detected a star-faring civilization, the pods opened, and they started reproducing drones and ships and such, right?"

"That is the usual pattern," Dwight confirmed.

"Then what's the deal here?" Dunstan spread his hands, his whole body wavering as only his ship boots kept him anchored to the deck. "The Skrela attack us right when we come through the gate, but this outpost..." He motioned at the display on the bulkhead of the Ops Center. "...is here for what? Thousands of years? And the Skrela don't get around to them until a few hundred years ago? I don't get it."

Dunstan wasn't always invited to the Ops Center for these inner-circle briefings, but he'd been the pilot for the mission, so

Hachette had given him the chance. I wasn't sure if he was regretting it now, since Hachette seemed to be annoyed whenever Dunstan spoke, but it was a good question.

"Maybe the ones who attacked us were in some sort of stasis?" I ventured. "Just waiting there for anything worth waking up for?"

"That is a distinct possibility," Dwight agreed. "We were never able to determine with any sort of certainty what activated the pods or how long the Skrela drone soldiers could live once they were produced." He shrugged, and might have been imitating Dunstan. "You must realize that out here is where they originally came from. For all we know, their pods are scattered around between the stars of the entire galaxy, waiting for a signal to pounce."

Dunstan grunted, but I didn't think he was convinced.

"Let's stick to the important part of the equation," Hachette interrupted, apparently having decided he'd cut Dunstan enough slack. "Does your friend have any clue about the gateway?"

"He confirmed it existed," Dwight said, and at this pronouncement, Hachette's shoulders shuddered with a sigh, as if the weight of the planet below had just fallen off his back. "He said it was not kept on this planet, but taken on to another, one he called Decision, roughly translated into your language, though he wasn't aware of the origin of the name."

"Does he know where it is?" Hachette asked, his tone sharp, not, I thought, with anger but instead with certainty. He'd been proven right, and now we all had to acknowledge it, that the way home *was* out here, and he'd made the correct decision to search for it.

"His name is Jozan," Dwight said, something sullen and stubborn in his tone. "Jozan gave me a Transition Line coordinate. He didn't travel with the Resscharr who took the Gate, but he was sure this was the direction they'd gone, and that it couldn't be too many jumps farther."

Hachette clapped his hands together, a manic fire behind his eyes.

"Captain fucking Ahab," Vicky murmured beside my ear, seeing the same thing I was. Hachette couldn't have heard her, but I saw the slightest narrowing of Top's eyes.

Shit.

"We have a course, ladies and gentlemen," Hachette went on. "And we have hope. Let's not lose sight of either." He nodded to each of us, even Dunstan. "Get ready. We break orbit in an hour."

We dispersed and I put a hand behind Vicky's shoulder, guiding her out as fast as I could walk in the ship boots, hoping Top wouldn't say anything.

"Alvarez. Sandoval. Hold up a minute."

Damn, damn, damn.

"Yes, Top?" I asked, all wide-eyed and innocent.

She waited until the others had filed out of the compartment, nodding to Colonel Hachette, then glancing up and down the passage before she pushed the hatch shut.

"Top," Vicky began, "I shouldn't have..."

"Shouldn't have what, Captain?" Top snapped at her. "Insulted your commanding officer, even under your breath? No shit. Listen, you two..." She jabbed a finger at us. "I know it's tough for you, being dragged into this when you thought you were civilians again, and twice as tough because of mission creep. We were supposed to neutralize the threat from Zan-Thint and now we're stranded in some distant part of the galaxy and if it's not bad enough that it's full of enemies and we might not get back, we're also burning up all our reactor fuel." Her eyes hardened. "And it's also a tricky situation since you're both captains and the only one in your chain of command who outranks you is the colonel. Which means there's no one who can kick your asses when you need it. Well, sir, ma'am, this sergeant-major is here to tell you, you both need it."

I realized I was trying to brace to attention, which was both inappropriate given our respective ranks and impossible in free-fall, and I stopped. I also stopped my instinctive reply. The relationship between a sergeant-major and a mid-rank officer like a captain is a complex one, which came down to the bottom line of: the sergeant-major has a huge edge in experience and authority and, most of all, political power and pull, and the captains should be very respectful.

"I shouldn't have said anything where someone could have heard," Vicky admitted, sounding honestly contrite to me, and I should know better than anyone.

"You shouldn't have said anything, *period*," Top interrupted, cutting the thought off with a sideways slash of her hand. "This isn't just a bitch session during off-time in a war. Remember what I told you about lifeboat ethics? This is a lifeboat situation, life or death every second. Not only should you not be talking shit about your CO, you shouldn't even be *thinking* it. Right now, he's on the ragged edge. You don't know him like I do. I served with him for over a year before you two chuckle-heads showed up. He's a good man." She shrugged. "Maybe a little full of himself, but that's a bird-colonel for you."

"He's going to get us all killed trying to get back to the Cluster, Top," Vicky blurted, and I winced. I believed the same thing, of course, but I didn't think Top was in a mood to hear it.

"He might. But he has more than just you to think about. Most of this crew has immediate family back on Earth or one of the colonies. About half are married, and half of those have children. Including the colonel."

"He's *married?*" I asked, disbelieving.

"Was." Top shrugged. "But he still has two children. Grown

now, but that doesn't mean he's okay with never seeing them again."

"Okay, I get that," I assured her. "And I'm not minimizing it. I know we're the outliers here." I thought of Vicky's mom back on Earth and shook my head. "Or at least I am. But our mission's *over*. Maybe Colonel Hachette has the authority to do what he's doing, but I'm not sure if those people with kids and wives are going to thank him if they're stranded in a lifeless system, or one with no other humans? Because that's what's probably going to happen if we keep chasing this gate."

"I thought he'd done the sensible thing when he made that announcement," Vicky added. "But now we have the report from this...Jozan, saying it's just around the next corner, I'm afraid he's going to keep chasing it until we've used the last metallic hydrogen fuel slug in the tanks."

"Maybe he will." Top didn't flinch, meeting Vicky's stare head-on. "And if he does, it's still our duty to follow him. And to make sure the people under us do the same."

"You mean the Vergai?" I asked her, trying not to scoff. "Because those are the only troops under us."

"They volunteered the same way you did. And maybe they didn't understand everything that meant, but you need to make sure they fight just as hard as anyone else."

"And you think that's fair?" This time, I couldn't keep the scorn out of my voice.

"I think," she replied, this time with the same iron in her tone that I remembered well from being chewed out as a private, "that it's been too long since you were a fucking street kid in the Underground, conning your way from one meal to the next, trying not to get killed by the gangs or nicked by the cops. Because that street kid would have never been *stupid* enough to stand here and insist to *me* that life is fucking fair."

I rocked back on my heels as if she'd slapped me. It had been a while since anyone had managed to shock me. I hadn't thought it was possible.

"Yeah, you're right, Sgt.-Major Campbell," I said, as stiff and cold as I'd spoken to her since I'd first reported for duty on Inferno. "I guess I *was* being stupid. I won't make that mistake again."

Her jaw worked as if she wanted to chew me up and spit me out, but Top just nodded curtly.

"I can't change how you think." She nodded toward Vicky. "Either of you. But keep it to your damned selves."

And she was gone, out the hatch, leaving us in the Ops Center, alone with each other and a shitload of resentment.

"That..." Vicky shook her head, unable to come up with a word.

"Yeah, nothing quite comes close," I agreed.

Anger roiled in my chest and wouldn't dissipate the way it usually did. I'd grown up with so much rage, so much pure hatred, that I'd either had to learn to channel it or let it consume me. I'd rolled it into cold, calculating thought, into swift, violent action, into resolute endurance. And it was easy, easy to forge it into a weapon and target it, because everyone was an enemy. It was so much more complicated now.

"What do we do?" she asked, and I wondered why she'd be asking me. What decision had *I* made since the end of the war that had been anything but a disaster?

"We keep going." The words were sour in my mouth, but unavoidable, medicine I had to choke down. "What else can we do?"

[7]

"This food is...interesting," Matis declared, picking at his lasagna without enthusiasm.

I barked a laugh, nearly choking on what I had in my mouth.

"You're very subtle for a farmer," I told him. "The food is shit. The only thing it has going for it is that there's plenty of it and the processors can make it look and taste like anything you want. Sort of. But when you scrape off the flavor and the consistency, at third and last, it's soy paste and algae powder."

"I know these things you gave us..." Matis tapped behind his ear, indicating the induction speaker fastened there with adhesive. "...translate your words. But there seems to be nothing in my tongue that resembles this *soy* you speak of."

"Lucky you," I assured him. Then I sighed, feeling Vicky's elbow in my side even though she wasn't eating with the Vergai. She'd offered, but I hadn't taken her up on it because I knew her well enough to understand she didn't mean it. "Soy is a bean. It's bland, but it has the advantage of being easy to grow and easy to store for a long time without spoiling. It has the same nutritional value as meat, but meat animals need a lot of resources and space."

"I've seen the machines you use that freeze food as if it is the deepest winter," Matis protested, shoveling down another bite, though he didn't seem happy about it. "You could freeze whole sides of beef and they would be as if a cow had died in the winter and thawed out in the spring, still good enough to eat."

"We could. And it would be enough to feed everyone on the ship for a few weeks. Or we can mash soy into a paste and compress it into cans and have enough protein to feed us all for months." I took another bite, trying to appreciate it. "But it won't last forever."

"You can get food from us," Matis suggested. "There is enough to trade, with the Karai and the Resscharr also working the fields."

"Yeah, that's a...possibility." I wanted to tell him that would mean us ever making it back there, but I wasn't interested in getting into another argument with Top. "But things could get complicated."

"Because of those other Karai," Matis deduced. "The ones you call the Tahni." I nodded. "How did they come to be your enemies?"

"That's a long story."

"We seem to have plenty of time," Matis said, smiling thinly.

I sighed, nodding, taking a sip of water to put it off.

"It all started when we first left our planet. We found a doorway to the nearest star, and there we found a map of those doorways and we began to spread out and send our people to the new worlds we found, to settle on them. But the Tahni were out there too. They'd found the doorways before us and it was their considered opinion that they were the rightful heirs to the Predecessors and everything in the Cluster, every world and everything on them, was theirs, and we were trespassers."

Matis laughed softly.

"So, they're not very different than the Karai at all."

"The thing is," I allowed, "they might have been right. What we've found out about the Predecessors in the last few months, it's likely that they *did* create the Tahni to be their children. Either way, we fought a war over it. They threw everything they had at us and we turned it back, but just barely. We didn't have enough left to finish them off." I shrugged. "Or so I'm told. Everyone went back to where they were before the war and both sides agreed to keep what they had and not take any more, and it seemed as if it might stay that way, but then someone went and figured out a way to create doorways to other stars ourselves, anywhere we liked." And yeah, I was simplifying things quite a bit, but he was a farmer, not a physicist. "That meant we couldn't control the doorways anymore, couldn't control who went through them, and anyone who wanted to could go make a home in any system. Including the ones the Tahni claimed."

"You broke your side of the agreement?" Matis seemed surprised.

"It's not like the government decided to do it." I was sounding defensive and tried to rein it in. "But the Tahni saw it that way too. They started the war again, even though they should have known better."

"Why? They matched you evenly the first time."

"They got to where they were because the Predecessors helped them. We got there because we tried to kill each other so often, we didn't have any choice but to get better at it. They hit us hard, rocked us back, but there was no way they were going to win. We beat them, invaded their planet, killed their Emperor, and most of them surrendered. But not Zan-Thint, not the ones with him. They couldn't accept living under human rule, and they made us think they were out to destroy the Commonwealth just to distract us from their plan to get out here and find a new home."

"Yes," Matis said, nodding. "You were correct. It is complicated. I don't know how you can trust each other enough to keep from killing each other."

"That's the problem. That's why we're out here, trying to find a way home."

I shut my mouth, realizing I'd probably said too much. It was too late. I could see it in his eyes.

"And when you leave, we'll be alone."

"If," I corrected, being honest rather than trying to comfort him. "There's no assurance that the way home exists. The last two systems we've hit, there's been nothing. Dead worlds as if there'd never been life. We don't even know if the Skrela killed them or there was just never anything there." I shook my head. "After we found the Predecessor outpost, a lot of people thought we were close."

"And now you don't?"

"I just hope we find out before it's too late."

"Attention all personnel." The voice over the galley loudspeaker was bland, as if they were telling us that we needed to get our clean clothes from the ship laundry. "Transition in one hour. You have thirty minutes to report to your duty station."

I sighed. I wanted so badly for there to be something at this next stop, and I believed so hard that it wasn't going to be there, I almost didn't want to Transition. As long as we were in T-space, I could still hold on to that hope.

But there was work to do.

"All right, Vergai," I said, pushing away from the table, "finish the food and get to your compartments, get strapped in. Let's see what fate has in store for us this time."

———

"Well, would you look at that?" Captain Nance said, arms folded across his chest, leaning back in his seat in a way that wouldn't have been possible if the *Orion*'s rotational drum hadn't been activated when the sensors hadn't detected any other spacecraft in the system.

I was glad of the gravity because I wanted to lean against the safety railing, wanted to let my mouth drop open at the images from the surveillance drones. The buildings were primitive compared to Earth or any of the core colonies, steel, concrete, and glass, the tallest maybe a hundred stories tall and most of them half that. The city itself wasn't that big, not even a tenth of Trans-Angeles in surface area, and even then, it didn't extend below ground. The roads were all surface streets and the vehicles driving them were manually guided, powered by fossil fuels, though there was ample evidence of electrical mass transport both within the cities and between them.

No, what was impressive about the place was that this wasn't the *only* city, wasn't one of a small cluster near the coasts or at a river junction. This was one of *hundreds* of cities on the planet, scattered between four different continents, the roads and rails stretching across them, ships powering through the oceans on engines fueled by coal or oil, propeller-driven airplanes and lighter-than-air blimps plying the skies.

And walking through those city streets, in the farm fields, and on the decks of those ships, were...humans. Their clothes were different from anything I'd ever seen, the men favoring loose, split-tail robes over broad-legged trousers, while the women were mostly in what I could only properly describe as kilts, and both sexes wore a cross between a turban and a fez as headgear. Their architectural style, the design of their vehicles, the layouts of their cities were all strange to me, but they were very clearly humans.

And that was just one continent, one culture. There were

others and just scanning the various views on the display was enough to reveal four or five distinct styles of dress and architecture.

"How many?" Hachette asked, and I thought at first the question was rhetorical, but Dwight answered it.

"One point three billion." The AI shook his virtual head in the projection. "It's quite incredible. I wouldn't have imagined that they could produce a society this populous and varied in only a few thousand years."

"I was a history major in the Academy," Hachette said. "That culture down there doesn't look anything like it, but the level of technology is on a par with Earth in the mid-Twentieth Century. Not exactly, not to the letter, but close. I don't see any sign of nuclear power or weapons, no rocketry, no satellites, but they have intercontinental air travel, widespread electrical power..."

"All fossil fuels," Wojtera contributed, pointing to a feed on the bottom left of the main screen, showing smoke pouring from the stacks of a power plant. "Oil and coal. Some natural gas."

"What's your estimate of their military capabilities, Mr. Wojtera?" Hachette asked the Tactical officer.

"It looks like there are a couple of low-intensity conflicts going on."

Wojtera touched a control and four of the drone feeds, which had been tiny fragments of the screen, zoomed to take up most of it, moving to the center. The lands in contention were both in the southern hemisphere, equatorial rain forests and tropical islands. I didn't see any shooting going on as we watched, but troops marched behind some kind of armored vehicles, patrolling the streets.

"Maybe even more primitive than mid-Twentieth Earth, sir," he went on. "No radar that I can detect, no armed helicopters, not even a lot of motorized infantry. Something like a cross between a tank and an APC, and the computer thinks it sees some automatic weapons, but most of the troops seem to be carrying manually-operated rifles."

"Any clue why they're fighting?" Vicky asked. *Nobody else would have. Maybe not even me.*

"I can't say for sure because we don't have a translation yet of their language..."

"You do now," Dwight corrected him. He smiled. "Sorry, it took a few minutes of auditing their over-the-air transmissions."

"Yeah," Wojtera went on, shooting the AI's hologram a side-long glare, "but like I was saying, the fighting is all fairly close to what looks like oil fields."

"Fighting the locals for control of resources," Top said. "Old story."

"But does that mean we don't want to go down and have a talk with them?" Hachette asked, looking around at us, Nance, Top, and even Dwight.

"What would we want to talk to them about?" Vicky asked. Top eyed her from beneath creased brows, a warning look, but Vicky ignored her. "There are no Resscharr here, and it doesn't look as if they have any leftover Predecessor technology. What would they know about the gate?"

"We won't find out unless we go down there," Top countered, not even giving Hachette the time to answer the question.

"It could be risky," I said, not wanting to get into it with Top but also not wanting to leave Vicky hanging. "If they're politically unstable, just us being there could cause a war. We might wind up having to shoot our way out. And granted," I added, "they don't seem to have anything that could touch us, but I'm not crazy about the idea of killing off a bunch of locals."

"You have a translation of their language now," Dwight pointed out. "And you have their public broadcasts on the electromagnetic spectrum. Surely you can find out if any of their national governments are stable and open-minded enough to handle contact with you? At the very least, if they are lacking even in basic radar, it should be possible for you to land in secret."

"You're concerned about us adversely affecting the population," Hachette said, looking at Vicky and me. "I respect that. Get with Lt. Plant, the junior Comm officer, and audit some of the audio and video transmissions. See if you can find the right government for us to make contact with."

Of course. That was Hachette's style. If you brought up a problem, you got detailed to solve it. Vicky made a face, but I just nodded.

"Yes, sir." Because honestly, I was curious as hell, and at least this way, we'd have some say in the matter.

"If nothing else," Hachette told me, a glint in his eye that could have been mischievous or could have been conspiratorial, "they're humans. If we wind up stuck here, it might be nice to have another option."

"Yes, sir," Vicky said, respect in her voice that I thought was genuine. "Another option that doesn't have a Tahni fleet hanging over it."

"Exactly." He smiled. "Maybe I'm not Captain Ahab after all."

I didn't remember the last time I'd seen Vicky blush. I would have resolved to give her a ration of shit about it later, but as fiercely as my own ears were burning, I was fairly sure my face was as red as hers.

[8]

"Tell me again why we can't be in our Vigilantes for this?" Vicky had to nearly yell the question to be heard over the roar of the drop-ship's belly jets.

She'd been asking me, probably looking for sympathy rather than an actual answer, since she knew I felt as naked as she did, both of us strapped into the cluster of acceleration couches in the upper tier deck of the bird while Solano and one of his platoons were anchored in their brackets down below. But we were tied into comms to the *Orion* in orbit, an unusual situation for us, since we were used to our signals being jammed or else restricted due to the possibility of the wrong people hearing them. And the wrong people were definitely listening.

"Because you're here to talk, Captain," Colonel Hachette replied, booming in my earbuds, "not blow shit up. You're our resident experts on the...what are these people called again?"

"The Vailoa, as close as we can translate," I supplied. "One of three major powers with the Sabanians and the Medini, as well as about twenty minor ones. They're the most powerful economically after the last big war about fifteen years ago, and they've been on the leading edge of technological advancement for this world. In this case, that means electric trains and radial engines in their airplanes, but it was enough to win that war for them."

"Yes, I read your report," Hachette said drily. "Very thorough. The two of you should consider working as Fleet Intelligence analysts."

"I'd rather go back to being a dirt farmer," Vicky retorted.

"You can ask if they have any openings," he said. "But you still won't be able to take your battlesuit with you."

The drop-ship thumped to a landing, the impact of the massive landing gear feeling so much more violent without the cushion of my Vigilante. The back of my head bounced off the pad behind it, my teeth clicking together on the rebound, and then we were down, and I was trying to shake off the crick in my neck as I unstrapped.

"Jesus, Duke," I muttered, knowing my throat mic would pick it up, "you not getting enough practice on this trip? That landing about smacked my ass up through my ribcage."

"Eat me, Cam," Fleet Lieutenant Duke Holland, the drop-ship's pilot, told me. "Orders were to keep our flight time as short as possible, which means your ass is the last thing on my mind."

"Thank God for small favors. You're not my type."

The metal grating on the steps down to the main hold rattled and shook under my boot soles, then thumped in a lighter rhythm to the beat of Vicky's footsteps behind mine. Top wasn't along for the ride, which I thought showed uncommon trust in our diplomatic abilities.

"Anything heading our way?" Vicky asked, her tone a bit more serious and businesslike than mine.

"Oh, yeah," Duke assured her. "We got twenty birds in the air, and at least two of them are bombers. On the ground... there's six, maybe seven cars, plus twenty-five of those tanks or troop carriers, all coming in on the dirt road from the main high-way. They should be on top of us in five minutes, so you might want to get all presentable for them, straighten your collars and shit."

His last few words were almost inaudible over the rumble of the huge belly ramp lowering and the metallic clunks of the Vigilante platoon pulling free of their cradles.

"Captain Solano," I said, "get your platoon arrayed in a 360-degree defensive perimeter around the drop-ship. Weapons down, but keep your backpack missiles targeting the aircraft overhead. Nothing they're carrying can touch you or this ship, but I'd rather not have one of the damned things drop a bomb on the two of us while we're playing at being ambassadors."

And yes, I *could* have called him by his first name, and yes, I *was* ordering him around despite the fact that we were the same rank, but I'd been given the command of this mission and it didn't hurt to remind him of that.

"Copy that, Alvarez. We'll try to keep you two crunchies safe."

I grunted but didn't say anything. *Crunchies* was how Drop-Troopers referred to anyone on the ground not in a suit, and it was most definitely being used as an insult in this case. I sighed. My stint as mission commander wasn't starting out well.

The blood-red rays of dusk flooded in through the opening belly ramp, the shimmering orb low enough that it didn't *quite* blind me as I stepped off onto the packed dirt, but it sure as hell blurred out the details of the approaching vehicles. I blocked the primary star out with my hand and squinted at the cloud of dust crawling toward us across the fallow field from the main highway. On the horizon, the glint of the setting star was just visible on the high-rise buildings of the city the Vailoa called Giatti Matti. It was a good twenty klicks away and I think they would have had us land even farther from it, except they wanted us close enough to get the military forces stationed there out to our landing site to meet us.

"Aren't they worried about someone seeing us land?" Vicky asked, shoulder up against mine.

"No one lives out here," I pointed out. "The nearest farm-house is at least ten klicks away, and if anyone was outside looking this way, all they'd see is the sunset."

"They're not stupid," she agreed. "For all that they haven't managed to make it past the whole propellor-plane stage."

"You with us, Dwight?" I asked, looking up as if he was an angel hovering over my shoulder.

"I will translate for you," the AI confirmed. "Your external speakers are in place?"

"Yeah, and I feel like a complete idiot wearing this shit on my belt," Vicky said, tapping the cylinder affixed to her gunbelt next to her sidearm. "They're going to think I'm talking to them through my stomach."

"The alternative is strapping it to our foreheads," I pointed out.

"No, the alternative would be using our damned suits and letting them do the talking for us."

"The suits are the stick, Captain Sandoval," Hachette piped up again, and if Dwight was the angel on my shoulder, the colonel was the devil on the other one. "You're the carrot."

"I'm not any damned carrot. And stop backseat driving, *sir*."

The caravan of vehicles was upon us now, the armored cars spreading out around the drop-ship, surrounding it, gun turrets mounted at the top spinning to cover us. They might have been primitive projectile weapons, but the muzzles were damned big and they could turn Vicky or me into a red mist, no matter that the battlesuits would kill them a second later. Hatches popped open on the sides of the armored cars, and troops piled out, taking up positions between the tanks and forming a guard for the passenger vehicles still approaching.

They weren't much to look at, the soldiers. All men from what I could tell. They wore no body armor, just camouflaged jackets beneath their load-bearing harnesses. Their rifles were some kind of bolt action, though nothing like the ones I'd seen in the Marine Corps Museum, their stocks polished wood, metal peep sights extending over the rear of the action. Open-faced helmets hung down to protect their necks, revealing pale skin and almost universal beards and mustaches, red and blond and brown. And wide, disbelieving eyes, fingers twitching far too close to the triggers of their weapons.

"Solano," I growled, "don't fucking move. Tell your Marines not to move a centimeter. These assholes are scared shitless, and it won't take much for them to shoot us."

"Copy that."

A passenger car pulled up only a few meters from us, throwing up a cloud of dust in its wake. The vehicle was ugly as sin, bulbous and black with doors that opened upward, disgorging four men and three women, all dressed in what was considered formal wear for the Vailoa, sterile, white, and baggy, like they were all researchers in a lab somewhere. One of the women took the lead, approaching not me but Vicky. The woman looked to be well into middle age, with grey streaking her long, straight brown hair and lines of experience etched into her face.

She spoke, the language almost musical, with tongue-twisting clicks at intervals, something I'd only heard once before from a Marine NCO born and raised in South Africa, who'd been raised speaking Xhosa. Not that this language was that similar to Xhosa, not any more than English was similar to Hindi, though they were both from the Indo-European family. When Dwight translated, the simulated voice retained the melodic tones of her natural voice, though the cadence of the English was familiar.

"I am Brinsel of Vailoa, designated speaker for the Assembly. How are you called?"

Vicky hesitated just for a moment, probably not having intended to say anything, but she recovered quickly.

"I'm Captain Victoria Sandoval of the Commonwealth Marine Corps, assigned to the starship *Orion*, and I speak for my commanding officer, Colonel Hachette."

"You are from another star, so your message said," Brinsel declared, "and I would not doubt that, given the ship on which you've arrived." She glanced at the battlesuits, eyes narrowing. "Curiosity bids me ask you why you've brought statues with you. Are they part of some ritual you must complete when you land on another world?"

This Brinsel seemed fairly blasé about the idea of visitors from another star who looked just like her and could translate her language, though I wasn't sure if that was because of any national character or just her own personality. The others who'd come out of the passenger cars with her didn't give anywhere near as confident an impression, and I guessed if they'd been given the choice, they would have stayed back in the city, where it was safe.

"Those are your soldiers?" Vicky asked, nodding toward the armed men surrounding our drop-ship. Brinsel gave a toss of her head that Dwight had assured us was the equivalent of a nod. "These are ours. What you see is their armor."

Now, for the first time, Brinsel showed disbelief.

"How could a man move armor so thick?" She gave a gesture I couldn't decipher. "I would see proof of this."

Vicky shot me a look and I shook my head, hoping Brinsel wouldn't know what that meant. I touched a control on my 'link to turn off the automatic translation. "Those idiots will shoot us the second one of the Vigilantes scratches its fucking nose."

Vicky nodded, then turned back to Brinsel.

"I would be pleased to demonstrate them for you," she offered, "but first, I am forced to ask that your soldiers lower their weapons and that you order them not to fire, though what they see might scare them."

Brinsel didn't reply at once and I thought Vicky might have offended her by the insinuation that we could frighten her troops. I also thought it was interesting that she was obviously in charge and well-respected, yet they had no female soldiers, though I had to admit that might be a result of their primitive weapons. Physical strength differences were a lot more important when you had to haul around heavy weapons and ammo with just your muscle and bone.

When Brinsel did speak again, it wasn't to us. She shouted an order to the soldiers, and they were in motion almost before the translator told us what it meant.

"Troop Commander Link! Tell your men to safe their weapons and keep their muzzles pointed at the dirt until I order otherwise! Any of them who disobey this order will be up on charges...if he lives that long!"

"One tough lady," Vicky murmured aside to me.

I scanned the troops, though I couldn't see the ones who were around the other side of the shuttle. Those didn't matter so much, I guessed, since they couldn't hit Vicky or me from over there, and there was nothing else out here their rifles could hurt except each other.

"Solano!" I barked. "Have one of your Marines step forward three meters and fire their plasma gun into the dirt fifty meters out. And *don't* hit any of the locals!"

"Copy that. Three meters forward, one shot, fifty meters out, don't hit anyone."

At least he wasn't a smartass about it this time.

I didn't watch the Marine who stepped forward. Instead, I watched Brinsel and the other Vailoans, and knew when the Vigilante moved from their reaction. Brinsel, to her credit, managed to control her shock at the echoing thump of metal footpads on the packed dirt, but the others were more open in their amazement...and terror. One of the older men, a wizened greybeard wearing what looked for all the world like a golden shower cap, actually dove back into the open door of the car.

No one fired, though, which I considered an unadulterated win. I finally glanced aside at the Vigilante, saw its right arm raising, the maw of its plasma gun pointed over the top of the vehicles. I squinted my eyes and turned my head and so did Brinsel. She'd been watching us and was smart enough to imitate us, even though she had no idea what was coming. Even with the precautions, the plasma blast was punishing, the actinic glare causing afterimages in my vision, the thundercrack of the blast battering my ears through my issue earbuds and their built-in protection. Worst of all was the wave of heat, washing backwards and turning the air around us into a convection oven, taking my breath away.

The plasmoid impacted nearly a hundred meters out, farther than I'd instructed, but I didn't blame Solano for adding a little fudge factor. The dirt erupted where the coherent packet of hyper-ionized hydrogen hit, the water trapped in the soil exploding into steam, the edges flash-heated to glass. Grass fires burned two and three hundred meters away, sending whispers of smoke into the purple sky.

Oaths and profanity traveled back and forth through the lines of Vailoan soldiers, some dropping to their knees, covering their eyes or their ears or both. Others stared at the Vigilante suit as if it were some ancient god, not even touching their weapons, realizing how useless they would be, which was the reaction I'd been hoping for.

"Are you certain that was a prudent course of action?" Hachette asked.

"Backseat driving, sir," Vicky said through clenched teeth.

"Captain Victoria Sandoval of the Commonwealth Marine Corps," Brinsel said, once the final echoes of the roar had died down, and the cries and curses of her own people had subsided, "would you and your subordinate..." That was to *me*, and I didn't miss the snicker of amusement Vicky tried to conceal. "...do me and the Assembly of Vailoa the honor of joining us in the Palace of the Administrator for a ceremonial feast to discuss how we may serve you?"

"Speaker Brinsel," Vicky replied, her grin very smug and self-satisfied and deservedly so, "it would be our pleasure."

[9]

"For a bunch of primitives," Vicky told me, "these people really throw a mean party."

I hoped both she and Dwight had been smart enough to keep that out of the translators, but I found myself nodding in agreement. I'd seen the massive rotunda of the Palace of the Administrator from our drones, but even the external view of the burnished bronze dome and white support columns three meters across didn't do the place justice. Inside, it was as opulent as any Corporate Council Executive's penthouse suite but a thousand times larger. Art of every sort imaginable lined the walls—paintings, frescoes, sculptures, carvings—though I couldn't vouch for the quality of any of it. We'd been escorted in by armed guards wearing rainbow-colored uniforms, their marching stride long and stiff-legged and slightly comical, though their faces had been deadly serious, and they'd taken us down broad hallways packed with more of the stuff, as if the Vailoans thought they could substitute quantity for quality.

We'd been late to the party, or so it had seemed from the hundreds of people already well on their way to a monumental drunk when we'd arrived. Alcoholic beverages had been floating around from one high-top table to another, with no chairs to be had, the red, blue, and sometimes yellow liquids served in earthenware punch bowls into which everyone felt free to dip their mugs. I'd been a little leery of that, but Vicky had convinced me by the sound, logical, reasoned method of accusing me of being a wussy. The red and the blue stuff was good, but I wasn't going to drink the yellow stuff again, at least not before drinking a hell of a lot more of the red or the blue stuff first.

The people were friendly and varied and their best trait was that they pretended not to notice that we were visitors from another planet who had no idea how things worked here. They told us jokes we couldn't understand even with Dwight around to provide context, most of them seeming to involve religion or ethnic slurs about the other nations on the world. I tried to listen in to the conversations, but there were simply too many going on at once for any one of them to be intelligible, and everything faded into a dull, background roar.

Until *he* came. I'd expected this fabled Administrator to be a woman, given Brinsel's high position, but no, he was a man, and not as old as I would have figured. There were a few grey strands through his hair and his mustache and beard were different shades of red. He was also a full head taller than me, and together with his wild hair and long beard, I couldn't help imagining him as a Viking.

"I am the Administrator," he'd told us as if that was his name and not his title, then he'd embraced each of us, laying his hairy cheek aside ours, and I'd had to force myself not to rub my face afterward to scrub off the head lice I'd imagined he was carrying.

Oh, and that was the other thing, the big negative amid all the hard-partying, hard-drinking government functionaries and their wild dress...they stank. Not like they hadn't bathed. They were a little primitive, but they weren't nomads living on horseback on the steppes, letting their old clothes rot away underneath their fresh ones. But they ate different food than us, used different colognes and perfumes, greased their hair with something that smelled like the ass-end of a cow, and the alcohol only helped so much. I couldn't let myself get too drunk because I was still carrying my sidearm.

That was another cool and possibly odd thing about the Vailoans—though there was armed security in the hall, none of them seemed to care that I had a gun, which might have been because the story of the Vigilante firing its plasma gun had spread and they didn't consider our sidearms much of a threat compared to that.

Certainly, the Administrator didn't. He'd circulated away from our table, the one we stood at with Brinsel and some other, younger woman wearing makeup like a clown at a child's party, but after Vicky's remark, he wound his way through the crowd back to us, as if he felt he had to make sure we were entertained.

"My friends!" he boomed from somewhere over my head, motioning broadly with his mug of whatever. "Have you tried the roast bush-boar?"

To emphasize the question, he reached over the shoulder of one of the servers, grabbing a handful of something that looked very close to pork and stuffing a piece in his mouth. As it turned out, I had, in fact, tried the bush-boar and it was delicious, but to be polite, I took another piece and gnawed a few bites in front of him to display my pleasure with it.

"You know," he said, leaning in conspiratorially, "I always thought the legends of the Predecessors were superstitious nonsense."

The words sent the hackles rising on my neck and I wondered if Dwight was providing an accurate translation.

"You know of the Predecessors?" I asked him.

"Who doesn't?" That shrug gesture again. "Are we not

raised from the cradle with the tails of the ancient beings who brought us here in the days of our ancestors?"

"Though as the Administrator says," Brinsel interjected, always the pragmatist apparently, "it's never been something we could prove. There are histories written thousands of years ago telling of the Exodus, but some people believe it to be nothing but a myth. It's true, of course, that the first evidence of civilization was ten thousand years ago, when the legends say the Predecessors brought us to this place, but all that means is that the first of us to build cities came up with a story to explain how they got there."

"Except there's you now," the Administrator pointed out, gesturing with his mug before taking a long pull from it. He wiped his chin with the sleeve of his dress jacket and regarded the two of us carefully. "There's you and your airplane that flies in space and your moving statues that can breathe the fires of hell, and your radio that can translate our language. And what is this if not a miracle, proof that the legends are true?" He cocked an eyebrow at us. "Or are they?"

I hesitated, mouth dry. We'd gone over this with Hachette, yet still I wondered if it was a good idea. And if he didn't like what we had to say, could we get out of here before they decided to have us burned at the stake as heretics? Sure, Solano and his platoon were just outside the building, ruining their lawn, but getting in here and getting to us would take minutes we might not have.

As had been demonstrated before, though, I wasn't alone.

"Tell him," Hachette urged in my ear.

"The legends *are* true," I said, following orders despite my misgivings. "You were brought here from a planet called Earth, the same place we came from."

"And you are here now as their emissaries?" the Administrator asked, leaning forward across the table. "You've come to tell us their will?"

"No," Vicky chimed in, taking back her role as the leader of our little expedition. "We've come to follow the path they took when they left us, to find them and seek their wisdom. That's why we've come here. You're like us, from our home. We figured you would be willing to help us, to share with us anything you know of where they went."

"Incredible," Brinsel said, the word breathed out like a silent prayer. "And you've managed to do this, to follow in the steps of the Predecessors and journey through the stars, with their help?"

"No." This time, I answered, not waiting for Vicky.

Hachette might not like this part, might have wanted us to lie and say we knew the Predecessors and were working on their behalf...no, there was no *might* about it; that was what he'd told us to say. But I had a sense about these people, and I didn't think that was the way to go.

"We were left to ourselves after the Predecessors took you and some others. They gave us no writings, no legends, not so much as a hint they existed...until we traveled to the nearest star on our own and found a map to the ways between the stars that they'd left behind. We've been looking for more signs and messages from them ever since, and only since we've come this far have we seen their wonders and found the path they took. What have you, our brothers and sisters, been told of where they went when they left here?"

And that *still* sounded unbelievably stilted. I felt like a first-class douchebag saying it, and I hoped the translation could turn it into something less pretentious. The Administrator and Brinsel didn't speak for a moment, but I couldn't read their expressions. They might have been in awe, or they could have both been thinking I was the biggest bullshit artist ever to darken their door.

"You were able to reach the stars without the aid of the Predecessors?" the Administrator asked, and this time, I was sure it was awe. "This has been our dream, though we are far from it. Even those of us who have come to think of the Predecessors as only myths still strive to use them as an example. Vailoa is the strongest nation on this world, and it has been my dream since I was but a young local Assemblyman that we would be the first to step off this world, to perhaps even visit Damarran."

"Damarran?" Vicky repeated.

"That is our word for the second world out from the sun," Brinsel explained.

"That one is habitable as well," Hachette supplied, as if I wouldn't remember it from the briefing. "We didn't detect any signs of civilization on it."

"We have seen it through our mountain-top telescopes," Brinsel went on, not hearing the kibbitzing in my ear. "There is extensive cloud cover there and many of our storytellers spin tales of alien life hiding beneath them."

"Like Venus in the early days of the Twentieth Century," Hachette cut in, and I ground my teeth so I wouldn't yell at him to shut up and wind up causing a diplomatic incident. "Except in this case, they're right and there is life down there."

"I saw in your broadcasts," Vicky said, seemingly unfazed by Hachette's interruptions, "that you've experimented with rockets for transportation."

"Yes," the Administrator enthused, "and our best engineers have drawn up ideas of mounting a rocket-driven plane on a balloon that could take it to the edge of the atmosphere and then launch it into orbit. We're very confident we can get this to work, but the damned Sabanians keep stirring up trouble in the

Vallin oil fields." His mouth twisted into a scowl beneath his beard. "Without those oil fields, our economy wouldn't last a year. Bastards know it too. If we could get them out of the way, we could accomplish so much. The Medini wouldn't cause trouble for us if the Sabanians were out of the picture." A glint in his eye that I might have called sinister in an uncharitable moment sent a shiver down my back. "I don't suppose I could convince your people to help us with that little problem?"

I froze at the question, though I shouldn't have been surprised. We knew they were having international conflicts. We'd seen the propaganda broadcasts that they called news. We'd dropped a high-tech military force into their laps and the second thing that was going to come into their minds right behind the awe and disbelief was going to be the idea of us solving all their conflicts for them.

"Don't promise them anything," Hachette warned me, "but don't stomp down on the idea. Let them think it's a possibility if they help us."

Or maybe just don't give them the idea that we've come here to fight their wars for them.

"I'll have to speak about that with my commander," Vicky told him, and it's a good thing she said it because I wasn't about to. "For right now, though, we'd be very interested in what your legends say about the Predecessors."

The Administrator tossed his head in assent, but Brinsel's look was more pensive, discerning. The figurehead was used to people agreeing with him, but she was a diplomat and knew double-speak when she heard it.

"I'm hardly an expert on ancient folklore," the Administrator demurred, "but I can have copies of the manuscripts from the era and scholarly treatises brought to you at your ship. I'll put someone on it tonight."

"We'd be very grateful," I told him.

"Of course." He waved it away as if it was barely worth mentioning. "Tell me, though, when do you think I might be able to meet with the commander of yours, this Colonel Hachette you've spoken of? I understand you've come as his emissaries, but surely he'll wish to speak to me himself."

"I'm sure he will," I said, speaking quickly before Hachette could reiterate the answers we'd already gone over in one rehearsal after another. "We'll have to send the drop-ship back up to transport him, and I'm sure he's going to want an in-person briefing from Captain Sandoval and myself in order to be better prepared for the meeting."

The idea being that we would hop on into the drop-ship with all the intelligence we'd come to collect and bid them a fond farewell from orbit, where they couldn't touch us. And the canny set of Brinsel's eyes told me she'd already seen right through it.

"We should prepare as well," she suggested. "If one of you were to stay with us, we could discuss our cultural differences, make sure no unintended offense was given when your commander joins us. Don't you agree, Administrator?"

"That's an excellent suggestion, Brinsel," the bearded man said, slapping his palms on the table hard enough to rattle the dishes. "Might you be able to radio your commander and see if he's amenable to such an idea?"

"Do it," Hachette ordered. "We don't want to alienate these people. We have more questions for them."

"I'll stay," I offered before Vicky could volunteer. My smile at her was genuine, though the one I offered the Administrator and Brinsel might have been less so. "Captain Sandoval is in charge, and I'm sure Colonel Hachette will require her to report personally."

Vicky didn't have much of a poker face, but she somehow managed to control the frown quivering its way out along the straight set of her mouth. I'd hear about this later, but the bottom line remained—there was no way I'd leave her with these people alone. Not that I particularly wanted to be here either, but I was a damn sight more comfortable with that than the alternative.

"Excellent!" Brinsel said, putting a hand on my arm, her grip stronger than I would have guessed. "We have so much to talk about."

[10]

"It's not the worst place I've ever slept," I murmured, rolling into what might generously be called a bed.

There were a lot of those cultural differences Brinsel had mentioned between us and the Vailoa, but the one that concerned me right now was the fact that they considered a flattened cushion laid out on the bare floor to be the height of sleeping comfort. Not to mention that there was no way to turn off the pale blue nightlight hardwired into the wall near the door.

I was getting soft. Once upon a time, back when I'd spent most of my nights curled up in a corner next to a waste-heat vent in the fabrication districts of the Trans-Angeles Underground, a private room with any sort of bed would have been a luxury. I lay down on the cushioned pad and tried to get comfortable. *That* wasn't happening, so I tried to just ignore it and go to sleep.

That wasn't happening either. I played the last thirty hours or so over and over in my mind, wondering if there'd been anything I could have done differently. Vicky and I had spent the first night on the drop-ship, convincing the Administrator that we were required to by custom, and I'd made what I thought was a pretty convincing argument to Hachette to just take off and to hell with a bunch of old books that probably wouldn't have anything useful in them anyway.

Vicky had agreed, though that might have been the only thing she agreed with me about at the time. No dice. Colonel Hachette had been firm in his conviction that the intelligence we were gaining was worth the risk, and anyway, spending a night or two as the guest of the Vailoan government wasn't a grave danger.

"Hell," he'd said, "they even let you keep your gun."

The next day had been pretty much as the Administrator had promised and a truckload of books had been delivered to the drop-ship. Well, I *guess* you could still call them books. They were bound from the top with metal rings and each page was folded to the back after reading it, but the material was paper, real paper made from wood pulp according to Dwight. I hadn't actually handled too many physical books in my life and the only ones that had been made from actual paper were the family Bible and prayer books my mother had kept in our house in Tijuana. I hadn't been allowed to handle those and couldn't remember what the pages felt like. The covers had been real leather, though, smooth and surreal and probably worth more than either of them made in a year, passed down from mother to daughter for generations.

Sensations flooded my memory. The smooth leather of the Bible cover, the warmth of my mother's hand, the way my father's beard had tickled my face when he hugged me. The cool breeze through our bedroom window at night and the way my brother would laugh at the chill. Something warm and wet trickled down my cheek and I brushed it away impatiently. It was stupid to cry about things I'd lost so long ago.

Vicky admonished me in a more recent memory, telling me

that I had to deal with the memories, the feelings, that refusal to deal with them was what had sent me on that downward spiral, and she wasn't going to tolerate it happening again. I could either act like a real human being or she was going to take off because she refused to watch me die. I'd done the best I could, was *doing* the best I could.

I considered wading back into the memories and letting my emotions flow free just for practice, but the realization that I was consciously wallowing distanced me from the feelings and exhaustion replaced grief, pulling me back to the cushion. I resolved that if I had to stay here another night, I was going to demand that they make me a pillow. What the hell kind of human civilization wouldn't have pillows?

The question drifted through my mind lazily, like a cloud, and sleep finally beckoned.

The knock on the door didn't register at first, muffled by layers of impending unconsciousness, but it was annoyingly insistent, raising in force and volume until I couldn't ignore it anymore.

"Shit," I mumbled, grabbing my shirt and slipping it back on. "Hold on, dammit."

The speaker was on my belt, sitting atop a small pile of my gear, including my sidearm. I hadn't grabbed it first, which bothered me, but either I trusted these people or I was dead. The translation of my reply to the knock was a wavering tone punctuated by clicks, and I winced, wondering how the cursing would go over with them. Boots, belt, gun, speaker, and then I was at the door, yanking it open. It hadn't been locked, and they could have barged right in, but I suppose manners here forbade it.

Brinsel was on the other side of the door, hands on her hips, and if she was from another culture on another planet, impatience still showed through the same.

"Sorry," I told her, running a hand through my hair. It wasn't the three-centimeter buzz it had once been and I wanted to make sure it wasn't standing up. "I was asleep."

"I apologize for visiting this late," she said, along with a slight bowing motion, her hands facing me, palms-out. She straightened and glanced around behind her before shooing me back into the room. She shut the door before she switched on the light. It was way too bright, and I shielded my eyes as she pushed past me.

Confused, I retreated into the bedchamber and watched in bemusement as she checked every corner of the room, running a finger along any seam in the wall. Finally satisfied, she faced me.

"This is the palace," she explained. "I made sure the electronic listening devices were shut off before I came, but there's always the possibility of ears behind the walls."

"Wouldn't anyone listening be working for your government?"

She rewarded that with a smirk.

"Somehow, I doubt you're naïve enough to believe that everyone in a government bureaucracy is working toward the same end, Captain Alvarez. I've been working for the Vailoan Union for nearly thirty years, and I left that sort of conceit behind quite early on."

"Maybe," I allowed, "but thirty years wasn't long enough to keep you from thinking my wife was in command of this delegation."

She laughed and it was nice to know that some things were universal.

"I not only knew you were in command," she corrected me, "I knew you two were married...and I knew if I acted as if she was in charge, you'd go along with it."

"Why the deception?" I spread my hands.

"Two reasons." She paced back and forth along the far wall. "First, to give you a sense of being in control, so you wouldn't be on your guard." A shrug, or the local equivalent thereof. "You controlled the translation so you could steer the conversation. I had to have some advantage. And second...well, you looked like someone uncomfortable being the spokesman for your people. I sensed letting your wife do the talking would put you more at ease."

I was still exhausted despite the adrenaline rush of the unexpected visitor, and I pulled a stool out from the S-curved table against the wall, fell into a seat there.

"You're a very perceptive woman, Brinsel. So, tell me why you're here."

"You've listened to our broadcasts," she said, taking one of the other stools. "And presumably those of the Sabanians and the Medini. You know this world has seen war in the recent past and likely will again."

"I have. And I'm going to be honest with you right now and tell you we have no interest in using our weapons to conquer the Sabanians." I shook my head. "I'm not sure if we have enough troops to make a difference in a full-scale war. From our estimates, there are 800 million Sabanians, and quantity has a quality all its own."

"You're wise. But I would expect that from a people who found their own way to the stars. Assuming you're telling the truth about that."

"It's complicated," I admitted. "We traveled through space on ships of our own design and making, but we reached the stars when we found a...gateway left by the Predecessors. We figured it would be better to keep things short and simple while talking to your leader."

She laughed sharply.

"Ganko is well-meaning, but he's far from our *leader*. He's the Administrator, our figurehead, the face we put to our government for the public."

I cocked an eyebrow.

"Your broadcasts sure tell a different story. Listening to them, I thought he was a cross between a general and a national hero."

"That's what everyone is *meant* to think. It breeds confidence in the populace." Her smirk told me she didn't believe it. "That's why we picked a tall, good-looking, hard-drinking man for the job. People either love him or hate him, but no one is bored by him."

"His name's Ganko? The way everyone talked, I thought his name was The Administrator."

"That's a custom. Once a man is elected Administrator, they give up their former life and devote themselves to the state. But I knew him before. I helped recruit him."

"You're the real power behind the throne?" I asked. I didn't believe it. The power behind the throne wouldn't be the one talking to me, wouldn't have met us in that field.

"I'm the strong right hand of the power behind the throne." She waved her hand in what I thought was a gesture of dismissal. "There's no one person, of course. The men and women who control the economy control the government. Is it any different where you're from?"

"Not at all," I admitted, perhaps a bit too loose with my words because we were alone, and I wasn't being monitored by Colonel Hachette. The man had to sleep *sometime.* "In fact, the president of the Commonwealth was chosen for about the same reason as your Administrator. But in my home, they're a bit more...open about it. They try to make themselves look like the good guys, but they're not shy about saying who's really in charge."

She looked at me with a sly tilt of her head.

"You sound as if it bothers you. Do you think it's any different where more than a dozen people live together? Someone is always going to have more power, more control."

I rested my chin on my fist and tried to formulate a reply that didn't sound childlike.

"It's always been the same way, but a lot of things used to be. We used to have slaves, used to torture prisoners as punishment, used to assassinate the children of deposed rulers because we were afraid they'd attract followers to overthrow the new king once they were older. We used to let soldiers take their pay out of looting and raping the peasants in a conquered country. We stopped. We did things better, even if they weren't perfect. I have to think we can keep doing better."

"Well, I would make fun of you for being unrealistic," she said, "but you came here in a ship from the stars and we've yet to fly higher than the upper atmosphere."

My eyes felt like they were full of sand and rubbing only made them worse.

"Brinsel, can you tell me why you came here? Because I feel like we still haven't gotten to it."

"For a soldier, you're very perceptive." There was humor in her tone, if the translator was accurate.

"I'm a Marine." The correction slipped out before I thought about whether it would carry over into her language. If it confused her, she didn't let on.

"It's simple, Captain." She speared me with a glare. "I don't believe you. You aren't on some spiritual quest to find the will of the Predecessors. You're too pragmatic a lot for that, despite your optimism about human nature. You're here for a reason and, as a loyal servant of Vailoa, I want to know why."

I closed my eyes, both to think and because they were starting to hurt from the light. Telling her the truth was against explicit orders from Hachette. But lying felt wrong. Lying *always* felt wrong to me, which made me a terrible spy and a terrible choice to lead this mission.

"It's a long story," I warned her, "and I'm not going to share all of it with you because it's irrelevant. But the bottom line is, we're from a place so far away from here, we could never get back on our own. And to get back, we need to find the Predecessors. We're not here to conquer, we're not here to scout for an invasion force, and we don't want your resources, your people, or your world. We just need information about the Predecessors, and you were the next link in the chain."

I wasn't lying, but I also wasn't telling her everything. Because if we couldn't get back, this would be the best place for us to settle...and those weapons I'd sworn to her wouldn't turn the tide in a war might work very well in a short, sharp revolution that put us in charge of one of these governments. I wanted to think Hachette and Top wouldn't resort to that, but despite what Brinsel thought, I wasn't *that* much of a starry-eyed optimist.

She fell silent, eyes clouded in thought, and I wondered what I'd do if she didn't believe me. For all that she insisted she wasn't the HMFIC, I didn't doubt she could summon a full platoon of infantry with a yell, for all her show of making sure we weren't being monitored. But when she focused on me again, I was sure she'd decided I was telling the truth. Still, there was something grim behind her eyes.

"In that case, you should know, you may not be entirely safe here."

Now, I was wide awake. I leaned forward, the oddly-shaped table creaking under my weight.

"Not safe from who?" Or was it whom? I could never keep it straight.

"The Sabanians aren't content to simply arm and encourage local malcontents in our oil fields." She shrugged. "Although we do the same to theirs, and who can say which of us started it? But they have eyes and ears everywhere in the capital and they'll have heard of your arrival by now. It's not possible to keep something like this a secret."

Which made her more sensible than most of the conspiracy theorists I'd run into over the years.

"You think they'd do something that overt?" I wondered, remembering the reports I'd seen and read of their cold war. "Wouldn't that be risking open conflict? You guys just had a war fifteen years ago."

"It would be, and we'd respond exactly that way. But think about it from their point of view. You're from the stars and you came here. They'll assume you mean to aid us against them militarily, just as the Administrator wants. And if that were so, it would mean the end for them. Their only hope is to nip this in the bud, to convince you that we're too weak, that we can't even protect you in our capital."

And we sent all the Vigilantes back upstairs...

"Shit," I muttered. "And you can't protect me?" I winced inwardly. That sounded cowardly, impotent. Even if I was just one guy with a handgun, I was still a Marine. I didn't need anyone to protect me. "I mean, you can't keep the Sabanians out of the capital?"

"We can try. But if they're desperate, which they may be, they'll be willing to take the losses and burn their whole network of operatives they've spent the last fifteen years getting into place."

The light bulb came on and I sat back, nearly falling off the stool when I forgot it had no back. What did these people have against chairs?

"You knew this was what would happen. *That's* why you wanted one of us to stay. You knew they'd come after us, and when they did, you get to destroy their covert resources." She stayed calm and silent and my eyes narrowed, the gears inside my head starting to grind. "But why would you tell me now? You know I could just call for an immediate pickup and they'll be down here in a shuttle in a couple of hours."

Brinsel smiled thinly.

"Then you'd better hurry."

Oh, shit.

I scrambled on my belt for my 'link and touched the call button.

"This is Alvarez, calling for *Orion*," I said, trying not to sound panicked. "Come in, *Orion*."

"This is *Orion*." It was Lt. Plant, one of the Comm officers, the junior one, which was why he was on duty now. It was a coincidence, but the on-board duty schedule had this as the sleep period for the primary shift. "Go ahead, Captain Alvarez."

"I need dustoff ASAP," I told him. "We have enemy forces inbound and imminent."

"Wait one, sir."

There was silence for the space of about a minute, and while I waited, I watched Brinsel's eyes. She'd pushed away from the table and was pacing the tiled floor, watching me watching her. I'd made my living reading people once upon a time, but those days were long gone, and even at my best, I don't think I could have read her.

"Cam," Colonel Hachette said, his voice hoarse and gravelly, as if he'd just woken up. I was gratified that someone else's sleep was being interrupted besides mine. "What the hell's going on?"

"Sir, Brinsel, the Vailoan representative, has informed me that an attack on the capital by the Sabanians is..." I glanced at her. She wouldn't have come to me with this now unless the wheels were already in motion. "...under way. They're intent on taking me out because they're convinced we're about to ally with the Vailoans and take them out." I scowled at Brinsel. "And I wonder where they got that idea."

"Goddamn it," Hachette hissed. "All right, I'm sending down a drop-ship with a Vigilante platoon. Stay where you are, if possible. We'll come to you." A pause. "And you know Captain Sandoval is going to have your ass in a sling for this."

"You can tell her for me, sir," I assured him. "I wish she was here as much as she does."

Maybe she could have thought of a better way out of this.

[11]

Gunfire echoed across the courtyard, a *snap-snap-snap* of high-pitched cracks that seemed to come from every direction, and the floodlights shining from the roof of the palace didn't reveal anything but flitting shadows. I assumed the Vailoan Guard could see what they were shooting at because they were firing nonstop from dug-in positions around the courtyard, their muzzle-flashes a chain of firefly flashes.

"Don't worry," Brinsel told me, leaning against the wall beside the window overlooking the courtyard, a glossy blue steel revolver held at the low ready. "The Palace Guard companies down there are the best troops we have."

I wondered what that said about the ones clustered behind us, rifles pointing down the stairwell. Second-rate? I wasn't counting on them for protection, though they'd probably do better than I would with my handgun, for all that it was a couple of centuries ahead of their technology.

You're a Marine, whether you're in a battlesuit or stark naked with a fucking knife. That was what our unarmed combat instructor in Boot Camp had told us. I'm not sure if he envisioned this particular set of circumstances.

But maybe she was right. The troops down there had machine guns—or crew-served automatic weapons of some sort, though the brief glimpses I'd had of them didn't remind me of anything I'd seen in the museum. They had dug-in, fortified positions, armored cars, spotter planes overhead. There was no way the Sabanians could come up with enough troops from their covert force to take on that many soldiers.

"Where's the Administrator?" I asked, raising an eyebrow. "Surely he's out there leading his troops?"

Brinsel snorted a laugh.

"Oh, that'll be the story by tomorrow, with plenty of pictures and movies of him walking triumphantly through the battle zone, rifle in hand. And every soldier who knows what's good for him will tell that story for the rest of their lives. However long that might be."

A cynical bark of a laugh escaped my lips, unable to be contained, and I was about to say something very unflattering, but I didn't. I didn't say anything.

I was on my back. I hadn't been on my back before. And the windows hadn't been shattered before. Brinsel was down as well, her mouth open in shock, face covered in tiny cuts from bits of flying glass, and I wondered if that was what I looked like. I tried to feel at my cheek with my right hand, but something cold and metallic got in the way and I remembered I was holding my pistol. At least I had held on to it.

I repeated the attempt with my left hand and felt trickles of blood, wiping them away with a profound sense of gratitude that I could still see. I knew it had been a bomb. My ears were ringing, and I'd heard this tune before. An explosion, and one to shatter the windows, it had to have been either very close or very big.

I rolled over, shaking my head clear of the haze, then real-ized some of the haze was smoke drifting in from the courtyard.

The troops who'd been guarding us were down as well, none killed, but a couple of them rolling on the floor with shards of glass sticking out of their arms or legs, blood pooling around them.

I should check on them. It was a noble thought, but I pushed it aside. I needed to check on something else more urgently.

I didn't want to stand up. My instinct was to low-crawl, but a floor covered in glass made that impractical, so I ran in a crouch to the window, putting my back against the wall beside it. The window itself was gone, nothing left of the frame or the glass. And edging out to take a glance below, I could see why. Where the defenses had been in the courtyard was a series of craters, each two or three meters deep and ten across, overlapping like the Olympic symbol.

It hadn't been a bomb, it had been a dozen of them, twenty maybe...and they'd been dropped from the air. The Vailoan air forces couldn't drop ordnance or strafe the palace grounds for fear of hitting their own troops, but the Sabanians had no such qualms. They'd wiped out any of their people who'd been engaged with the Palace Guard, left the bits and pieces of their remains irretrievably mixed with that of their enemies. Brinsel had been right about them. They were panicked and desperate and willing to do anything. She just hadn't realized how desperate.

Brinsel was beside me, not seeking cover, just staring out at the carnage below. Most of the floodlights were out, but the fires licking the sides of overturned armored vehicles lit the night, funeral pyres for hundreds of men.

"No radar," I murmured. "No lidar. They just flew their bombers at high altitude, and you never saw them coming."

I could hear myself talk. That was my first clue that my ears weren't too bad off. The second was when I heard Brinsel.

"They've killed all their troops. They had to have. They're insane."

"No," I corrected her, pointing into the darkness of the road outside the palace grounds, where streetlights had recently lent a golden hue to the pavement.

The lights were gone, either knocked down or broken by the concussion of the bombs, but there was enough ambient light to catch the shifting shadows, the flitting figures running from every direction, grouping together and advancing on the ruined courtyard and the battered palace buildings.

"They only sent enough to keep your men engaged," I told her. "Enough to draw them out and reveal their positions, then they bombed them. Sound familiar?"

I shouldn't have felt any satisfaction at this. Hundreds of men were dead, probably men whose only sin had been unquestioning loyalty to their government, their nation. And hadn't I been guilty of the same thing? But Brinsel had been so damned smart, so sure this would work.

"We have troops in reserve," she said calmly, though I could see the flare of anger behind her eyes at the dig. "They're already moving up from their holding positions a few blocks over at the Assembly Hall."

"And that'll take what?" I guessed. "Half an hour? Fifteen minutes? Just how long do you think we have?"

I could see them now. They were no longer spectral shadows; they were men and women in black combat gear, running across the courtyard as fast as the craters and debris and fires would let them. Here and there, surviving Palace Guardsmen fired on the incoming enemy, but each pocket of resistance was quickly overwhelmed, taken out in a volley of gunfire. More loyal soldiers losing their lives for Brinsel's scheme.

"Do we have a shelter of some kind?" I asked her, watching them getting closer, moving to the main entrance.

Gunfire greeted them there, automatic weapons. I couldn't see the clash, as it was directly below me, but I heard it. Gun emplacements by the front entrance, which had to have been installed after I passed through the day before. Preparations for the anticipated battle.

"Yes," Brinsel answered after ten seconds of staring at the destruction. "Down in the basement...the Administrator is there along with his advisors and the chiefs of the assembly." She locked eyes with me and her expression was haunted, horrified. "They weren't supposed to get this far."

"On my world, we have a saying," I told her. "The road to Hell is paved with good intentions." I didn't wait to see how the translator would handle that, just motioned toward the stairs. "Let's get to the shelter."

Brinsel nodded to the commander of the troops who'd accompanied us and they led the way down the stairs. Their faces were pale, eyes wide, just as shocked and unprepared for this as Brinsel, and I guessed they were relieved to get the order to run for shelter. Downstairs, the automatic weapons fire had fallen silent, and Brinsel paused at the railing for the stairwell, listening.

"Maybe they've been driven off," she said, a light of hope brightening her expression.

A shout answered her optimism, and the first shot killed it, as well as the lead guardsman in the file heading down the stairs. He was young, as young as I'd been when I'd joined the Marines, and his high-pitched cry drowned out even the staccato beat of the shot, the smack of bullets into plaster.

I should have been scared. Maybe these people weren't the Tahni, maybe they didn't have electron beamers, battlesuits, and fusion reactors, but just one lead bullet mined by a forced laborer with a shovel, smelted in a foundry, and fired from a hand-tooled rifle by some kid who'd never even been up in an airplane could kill me just as surely as any energy weapon.

But it seemed so absurd, that I should survive a war with the Tahni, multiple battles with Zan-Thint's renegades and rampaging alien drones hatched out of a seed pod, just to die at the hands of another human so far from home, I couldn't even see the Sun with a radio telescope, that I just couldn't accept it. Maybe if Vicky were here, smacking me on the back of the head and telling me to take it more seriously, it wouldn't have felt so unreal.

"I don't think we're going that way," I told Brinsel, grabbing her arm and pulling her away from the stairwell.

The soldiers were backing up toward us, another falling on the edge of the first step, blood pouring from his mouth in an oxygenated froth, his lung pierced. This one was older, a streak of grey in his beard. He reminded me of Captain Covington. I wanted to take the time to grieve for these men who were dying to try to save me, but I couldn't spare it.

"*Orion*, this is Alvarez. Check my position on my 'link's locator. I'm on the second floor and we have enemy troops advancing up the stairs."

Two commandos clad head to toe in black rushed up the steps, the only ones to make it past the protective barrage from the Guard troops. I don't recall aiming, never made a conscious decision to pull the trigger, but the 10mm service pistol bucked twice in my hand and the first Sabanian up the stairs slumped forward, something that might have been a short-barreled pump shotgun clattering to the tile from his hands.

I did consciously decide to target the second, but he went down before I had the chance, the light revolver in Brinsel's outstretched hand cracking spitefully. The Sabanian's head snapped back, and from the lack of an exit wound, the round stayed inside his brain as he collapsed on his side.

"If you don't have something inbound now, you may as well take off and not worry about me."

"Hold your horses, bud."

"Dunstan?" I blurted, looking around as if he was going to step out from the corner. "Is that you?"

"Damn right it's me. Hold on a sec, I need to dispose of these antique airplanes." It was more like ten or fifteen seconds, but I could hear his work overhead in the night sky. A long, sustained sonic boom and the tell-tale *crack-crack-crack* of a Gatling laser turret. I wasn't going to stick my head out the window to check, but I was pretty sure if I did, I would have seen the burning wreckage of the Sabanian bombers falling out of the sky.

"Okay, try to hold out for a few more seconds. Gonna clear the yard for the lander."

"Copy that. We'll do the best we can."

Another of the protection team went down, not dead but clutching at his leg, a red stain already spreading down his pant leg, and a few seconds might have been longer than we had.

"I'm a fucking Drop-Trooper," I muttered, "not Force Recon."

But nobody wanted to hear me whine, and I hadn't been wasting my time on board ship reading romance novels like Top. The ship had a ViR tactical range and I'd been running the shoot house with Vicky—we had a running bet involving a set of restraints and who was going to wear them. I ducked around the edge of the stairwell railing, catching a glimpse of a full platoon coming up, firing timed volleys with sawed-off shotguns and short-barreled carbines, the sound a hammer against the inside of my head.

There was glass littering the floor, but I didn't have the luxury of being careful and I ignored the sharp edges digging into my shoulder through my utility fatigue sleeve, laying out flat, the pistol locked out in front of me. The pistol thumped, barely a whisper compared to the ear-blasting gunpowder rifles, but the miniature rocket motors built into every round kicked in just centimeters from the end of the barrel and the warheads detonated automatically on contact with their target, sintered metal ignited by a bursting charge that turned each bullet into a tiny spear of superheated plasma.

It wasn't quite the plasma blast from a Vigilante main gun, but none of the Sabanian commandos complained about the lack of respect. Or anything, ever again. I emptied the weapon into the front rank of them, then rolled to the side and dumped the spent magazine, grabbing at my belt for another. But the thing about ViR simulators was they didn't seem to take into account the fact that your fingers might be slick with your own blood. It only cost me a second or two, but that was long enough for the second rank of Sabanians to scramble past their dead and dying compatriots.

I was staring down the muzzle of a shotgun and it looked about as wide as the fusion drive on a cruiser from where I sat.

This is going to be the last thing I ever see.

But the next sound I heard wasn't a shotgun discharging; it was the hum-snap of Gauss rifles firing, and the sound came on the heels of the sight of the Sabanians falling, the tungsten slugs bursting out the front of them as if they weren't there and slashing through the ceiling. Plaster dust rained down amid a shower of sparks from the light fixtures shattering and I hoped to God no one innocent had been in the floor above us or they were in for a very unpleasant surprise.

What came up the stairs behind that deadly hail of slugs was not a surprise, but it was far from unpleasant. It was Force Recon, a platoon of them, and at their front was my old friend Sgt. Motte. He charged up and stood over me, covering the Vailoan troops but not opening fire on them.

"You about ready to get the hell off this rock, sir?" he asked, offering me a hand. I took it and let him pull me to my feet. "Because Captain Sandoval is outside in a Vigilante battlesuit, and it was all I could do to convince her not to smash right through the wall."

"Believe me, Sergeant, I am very ready to be anywhere else."

"Captain Alvarez, please wait."

It was Brinsel. She looked a bit the worse for wear, her face covered in tiny cuts, her clothes spattered with blood and now covered in plaster dust. But worse than the injuries was the look on her face, a look I knew well. It was that look that said *I fucked up.*

"I'm sorry. I didn't want it to happen this way. Don't let them blame this on the Vailoan government. This was all my fault."

I regarded her coolly, thinking not about the danger to me but about all the dead people in and around this building, all those people who didn't have die. They'd died because some government hack had decided that they were cleverer than anyone else, surely than their enemies. And I'd been there before.

"I don't give a shit about blame," I told her. "And I don't think my boss will either. We're not interested in blowing up your capital to punish you or any other such bullshit." I speared her with a glare. "But I think we might have tried to help you. I would have argued for it if you'd been honest with me. Not weapons, but there's a lot else we could have done for you." I gestured around at the devastation. "Enjoy your victory. Because you're never going to see us again."

I hope.

[12]

"You've got to be kidding me." Dunstan had said it, but any of us could have. It sure as hell echoed what I was thinking, staring at the screen. "Why did we even bother to send drones to this world again?"

It wasn't a bad question. After what had happened with the Vailoans, I'd been more than ready to get out of this system and move along, but Hachette had insisted on poring over the books they'd given us before we Transitioned out. And while that was going on, he'd ordered Vance to micro-Transition over to the second planet, the one the Vailoans had called Damarran. It was wreathed in thick, white clouds with brief glimpses of blue in the rare gaps between them, and it had, I supposed, been a pretty background to have up on the viewscreens while we waited for Dwight and the ship's techs to find anything action-able in the books.

"It's habitable," Hachette told the pilot. He must have been warming to Dunstan—this was the second Ops Center meeting Hachette had invited the man to attend. "Tell me if I'm wrong, Dwight, but I don't think the Predecessors waste habitable planets."

"They don't," Dwight agreed. "They considered the engineering of living worlds their sacred duty, their reason for being. In fact, their name for themselves, the Resscharr, means Lifebringer in their language. They saw themselves as bringing life to a lifeless universe, and if they could bring two living planets in the same system, it was seen as a miracle. They wouldn't ignore it."

"And they didn't." Hachette nodded toward the images.

This wasn't the Vailoans, with their concrete and glass cities. It wasn't even the feudal fortress and farms of Yfingam. No, this was more like the Islanders, with their small, dispersed communities, though these seemed to be farms rather than fishing villages.

And they were Tahni. Every one of them. Oh, the clothes were different, the hair almost unrecognizable, with no sign of the Mohawk and queue of the Tahni I knew, but there was no mistaking the ridged brows, the flattened nose and ears.

"Here the humans are," Top mused, rubbing her chin thoughtfully as she looked at the images from the remote cameras, "with cities and guns and airplanes...and there are the Tahni, just one planet away, like this." She shot a look at Hachette. "Any geological explanation? Lack of heavy metals?"

"Not according to the spectrographic report," he replied, tapping a control on his 'link to bring up the report on the main screen. The colored graph of minerals seemed out of place beside the images of the primitive Tahni farmers staring up in alarm at the unfamiliar lines of the observation drones. "There's plenty of iron ore, copper, bauxite...hell, even uranium if they ever found a use for it. Not even far from the biggest settlements, just a few klicks away in the hills above the river. They just haven't bothered with them. As near as we can tell from the drone footage, they don't even use plows for farming."

That had to be rough, I assumed. Everything I knew about

primitive farming came through the eyes of a six-year-old. The farming I'd halfway learned involved autonomous harvesters and planters and more mechanical maintenance than I ever wanted to do again.

"Okay," I said, hesitant to speak up after the knock-down, drag-out row the two of us had indulged in behind closed doors after I'd returned from the Vailoan debacle, "so we know that there are primitive Tahni there, living off the land. That can't be why we're in here watching this. If that was it, you would have just made a note of it in the log and we'd have moved on."

Vicky shot me a warning glance, but Hachette didn't lose his shit at the question, which I think meant he'd realized I was right. Either that or he'd decided to space me at the earliest opportunity and the knowledge had brought him enough peace of mind that he could stay calm no matter what I said.

It had started harmlessly enough, just a standard debrief. I'd been a little nervous that he might think I told Brinsel too much about us, but he'd seemed very pleased at the whole mission.

"I think we've laid a groundwork here," he'd enthused. "The Vailoans feel indebted to us and they probably also have a sense of shame for deceiving us, which would make them even more inclined to help us should we need it."

I'd been confused, and since it had been just the two of us in his office, I hadn't hesitated to admit it.

"Why would we need anything from them? True, they're more advanced than the humans on Yfingam, but they still couldn't make metallic hydrogen for us." I'd snorted a humorless laugh. "Hell, they could barely manage *liquid* hydrogen at their tech level."

"Not *now*," he'd agreed. "But as you're so fond of reminding me, we may be here for a long time." He'd shrugged and settled back in his chair. "Which is why I had my staff prepare a technological development package and handed it over to them when we picked you up."

I'd goggled at him in disbelief, and the only reason I'd taken a few seconds to comment was to keep from sputtering.

"A *what?*"

"A technological development package." He'd shrugged. "Okay, so I gave it that designation myself, but it's not as if the possibility had come up before. It was a printed collection of design specs, engineering principles, basic computer designs, practical physics...basically everything they needed to take the next step, become a space-faring civilization."

I'd tried to hold it in, I swear to God, but I just couldn't.

"Are you *nuts?* Sir," I added too late, but pressed on. "You saw what just happened! They're about two centimeters from *another* world war! And you just gave them the how-to they need to make long-range missiles! Maybe even with nuclear warheads!"

He hadn't lost his cool. Not yet. But there'd been icicles hanging off his words when he'd replied.

"A commander is often forced into decision where there's no perfect answer. I made a call and you don't have to agree with it, but you *do* have to respect it...and me."

My brain had been a pot left too long on the stove and my temper was at a rolling boil, the lid clanking as steam pressure built up.

"You say I should respect your decision, but you didn't even respect me enough to wait and hear my report before you handed over the secrets for building nuclear missiles to the people who almost got me killed."

"Why should I value your intelligence estimations? Aren't you the one who keeps telling everyone that you're a Marine, not a spy? Have you suddenly become an expert on the political machinations of pre-spaceflight human societies?"

"I don't know if I'm an expert on anything except running a Vigilante," I'd ground out, "but of everyone on this ship, I *do* know more about the Vailoan government than anyone here, because I spent more time with them. I think that has to be taken into consideration." A deep breath. "I also think by giving this sort of technology to one side in what's essentially a war is irresponsible. We're playing with millions of lives."

Hachette's icicles had quickly turned to steam.

"They're not *my* people, Captain, nor are they yours, and they're also not our responsibility, neither should their welfare be our biggest concern! If I have to sacrifice their political stability to even *possibly* benefit us long-term, then it's my duty to do it!"

"Well, Jesus Christ!" I'd exploded, throwing up my hands. "What the fuck makes us better than the damned Tahni in that case?"

"You think I *care* if we're better somehow?" He'd leapt to his feet, squaring off as if he were about to take me on. I'd found myself in a defensive stance, scanning his guard to calculate where I should hit him. He was a big man, but I'd spent my life taking on bigger guys. "You think this is some kind of game where everyone has to play by your rules? We didn't beat the Tahni by trying to be moral! We beat them because they were so concerned about not breaking their own religious restrictions, they forgot they had to win a Goddamned war!"

And that had been it for me. I'd given no more thought to rank or decorum, just gone nose to nose with Hachette.

"We beat the Tahni," I'd bellowed right back in his face, "because people like me, Vicky, and Top *died* by the thousands for people like *you*! Do you have any idea how many friends of mine died because of bad intelligence and half-assed battle plans drawn up by idiots who'd never once stepped foot on enemy territory? Do you know what it did to us? Do you know what some of us turned into because of it?"

"Oh, I read your fucking file, Alvarez. I knew about it long before Cunningham recruited you." His sneer had just begged to be wiped off his face. "I read about you nearly getting court-martialed because you were so damned concerned with Tahni civilians that you disobeyed a direct order."

My voice had been a low, cold growl, so much less ferocious than the fury roiling in my gut.

"Then you know what happened to the lowlife piece of shit who thought his rank meant he could do whatever the hell he wanted, and the UCMJ be damned. He blew his fucking brains out because he wound up showing everyone just what kind of a cowardly, selfish prick he was. And it's a damned good thing for him that he did, because I don't think Top would have been as gentle with him as that." My lip had twitched, baring teeth. "And if she hadn't done it, I would have."

"Get the fuck out of my office."

And I had, and we hadn't talked again for the last twenty-four hours.

"You're right," he said, and maybe I was just imagining that he meant more than me being right about the importance of this planet. "It's not just that there are Tahni—and *only* Tahni—on this planet. It's this."

The screen shifted from the wattle huts and ox-driven carts to...something else. It was a dome, and from the comparative size of the Tahni wandering in and out and around it, I estimated it was at least thirty meters tall and nearly a hundred meters in diameter and made entirely of hand-cut stone blocks.

"There is no fucking way," I said, "that dirt farmers who don't even have iron tools made that thing."

"That was my first instinct as well, Captain Alvarez. Which would be intriguing enough on its own. But it also brings up the other question. If they *did* build it...why?" He raised his eyebrows. "Let's go find out."

———

Vicky slumped to the bed, wiping sweat from her eyes, breathing hard, and I rolled onto my back beside her, equally spent.

"Why are we waiting so long to put together a landing party?"

I squinted aside at her, frowning, though I wasn't sure she could see my face in the darkness of our compartment.

"That's not really the sort of pillow talk a man likes to hear from his wife under these circumstances."

She laughed and smacked me on the shoulder hard enough to sting.

"If it wasn't mil-spec, don't you think I'd be complaining about it?" she pointed out.

I couldn't argue with that, and it wouldn't have done any good if I had, so I sighed and considered the question.

"From what Top said, they're still going over the books from the Vailoans. She said Dwight is talking about how they might be significant, and Hachette doesn't want us to go down there blind."

She rolled over and I could just barely make out the whites of her eyes.

"I don't like what's going on with Hachette. I feel like we're just rolling downhill, like this is all an avalanche building as it goes, and eventually, it's going to squash us all flat like some old mountain village back in the day."

I didn't bother to point out that she was calling us both the avalanche rolling downhill *and* the village that was going to get squashed by it. Yes, we had just had sex, but I kind of wanted to do it again someday.

"Did Top say anything to you?" I wondered.

"Not a word." Vicky shook her head, her hair teasing my arm. "If you hadn't told me, I'd never have known."

"She didn't say anything to me either," I confessed. "And that worries the hell out of me."

"Maybe he was embarrassed. Maybe he didn't say anything to anyone because he doesn't want it to get out."

"That sounds...far too reasonable." I rolled my eyes. "This is Hachette we're talking about. But yeah, I was thinking maybe he decided he'd pushed things too far. The question is, do I try to...I don't know...say something? Try to smooth things over? Or do I pretend it didn't happen? Do you think he'll let it go?"

"Of course not! You said it yourself, this is Hachette we're talking about. You're just going to have to keep your head on a swivel. He can't do anything drastic like relieve you, but he'll do what he can to make your life miserable."

"What do you mean, he can't relieve me?" I asked, sitting up. "Why the hell *couldn't* he? I thought Top was pretty clear about the fact that both of us could be relieved."

"She was bluffing. You may not..." She paused, chuckling. "No, let me rephrase that, you *probably* don't know this, but you're something of a legend with the crew."

"A fucking *what*?" I nearly yelled, stopping myself at the last moment before I got too loud.

"Oh, for God's sake, honey...these people are all *Intelligence*. They've all seen your file. The ones whose job didn't require it did it anyway out of curiosity. I know you think you're just good in a battlesuit, but the only reason you didn't win the Medal of Valor is that incident with Captain Cronje. Everyone here knows it."

Well, maybe *they* knew it, but it seemed distant and unimportant to me.

"The upshot is," she went on, "it would be...dangerous for him to act against you."

"Why?" I spread my hands. "What are they gonna do? Mutiny?"

"You don't think that's a possibility? We're pretty far beyond mission parameters. And as dedicated as the crew is, none of them signed on for life. And neither did we." She grabbed my hand and squeezed it. "Oh, don't worry, they're not going to shoot Hachette in the back of the head and dump him overboard. But he has a lot riding on making this trip pay off. He's got half the crew who'd do anything to get home and half who're afraid we'll die trying. Right now, he's got the half who want to go home on his side and the other half doubting. If we don't find the gate, or something that tells us where it is, then he's going to have everyone angry with him and they'll be looking for someone else to lead them."

"You mean like Captain Nance?" I could see that. Nance was a loyal officer, but at third and last, this was *his* ship and I always sensed a little resentment that Hachette got to be the one to put her in danger.

"Maybe," she acknowledged. "But Nance only commands the loyalty of the ship's crew, not the Marines. They might be looking to *you*."

I barked a laugh, sitting up in bed and switching on the light just to make sure she could see my face. She squinted, staring up at me. I let my eyes travel up and down and nearly forgot what I'd meant to say. I shook my head, trying to reassemble my thoughts.

"I don't *want* to lead these people. I don't even want to lead a company, and I'm damned happy Solano is there so I don't have to."

"You know that, and I know that." She shrugged. "And I

think Hachette knows it too. Which is why he can't come down on you too hard."

"Can you explain that part to me very slowly?"

"Hachette told you he read your file. And as much as I think he's an asshole about half the time, he's very good at his job. He knows you. Not as well as I do, but close. And he's got Top advising him. And both of them know that you're very loyal as long as you feel like someone's being straight with you. But when they're not..." She smiled and grabbed my shoulder, pulling me back to the bed. "He doesn't want to piss you off," she finished the explanation as a whisper next to my ear, "because he knows you don't want his job. And he doesn't want to give you a reason to change your mind."

[13]

"We are honored to be assigned to this mission with you, Captain Alvarez," Matis said, sounding as earnest as the translation program allowed.

He and the other Vergai looked out of place stuffed into body armor and strapped into the troop seats of the lander, but I don't know that I felt any less so. I was getting damned tired of being sent down to unknown planets basically naked and unarmed. Well, okay, the locals down here didn't seem to have any weapons more sophisticated than *atlatls*, but it's the principle of the thing.

"I'm glad to have you and your people with me, Matis," I assured him.

Though the others didn't seem quite as enthusiastic as he was about the shuttle ride. The trip through the cloud layer had been rough, tumbling and shaking us a bit, and more than one of the platoons of Vergai had taken advantage of the spacesick bags provided at every acceleration couch. We were through the worst of it now and the air was smooth, but some of them still gripped their armrests with white knuckles.

"Is it true that there are Karai down here?" Matis asked me, fascination in his tone and his expression.

"Not quite. They're related to the Tahni and the Karai, but they're very..." I hesitated, not wanting to call them primitive, since I didn't want him to get the idea we thought of him and his people that way. "They don't have metal-working or guns. They farm with stone and wood."

"Which is why you allowed *us* to guard you," Matis deduced, a knowing grin twitching through his beard.

"It's why Colonel Hachette allowed me to use you when I asked," I corrected him. "He's a cautious man. He wouldn't have allowed me to bring the Vergai as my security detail if he didn't think you could handle any threats down here."

"And I suppose he let me come," Vicky suggested from the seat on my other side, "because he knew I'd be nudging his elbow in the Ops Center if I wasn't along."

"Probably." Personally, I was wondering why the colonel had okayed the mission so quickly. He'd said he was waiting on further data from the manuscripts the Vailoans had provided us, but I hadn't heard anything on the subject before he'd told me it was a go. "Dwight, are you there?"

"As long as there are communications, I am here, Captain Alvarez."

Great. Now the AI is copping an attitude.

"Were you able to find anything significant in the Vailoan manuscripts?"

"The Vailoans have a very extensive history of the Predecessors ferrying their ancestors to their world six thousand years ago. The descriptions of the ships are quite detailed, their account of the appearance of the Predecessors is accurate, and they even have a tradition of their forebears being adjured to make themselves worthy of the honor they'd been given, to be part of spreading human life to a new world." There was a shrug in his voice, even if I couldn't see him. "Ironically, the Vailoans have relegated these records to legend and myth, but I am convinced they're mostly history."

"Okay, but did they give us any clues as to where the Predecessors went? Or if they had a gateway device?"

"Not as such. If I were to infer anything from their records, it is that they were, of course, quite impressed with the Predecessors, but the opposite was not the case. The sense these legends gave me was that the little they were told was mostly of how they were unworthy and needed to improve. They were given nothing; no technology, no token of the Predecessors, just the world and their domination of it. But." Dwight loved drama. He was becoming a bit too human for my tastes.

"But what?" I pressed him.

"The legends also featured Damarran as being critically important to the Predecessors, as if it was of more interest to them. According to the oldest documents, there was a tradition that the Predecessors had left *their children* there."

"The Tahni," I guessed. Vicky was shaking her head.

"Why the hell did the Predecessors have such a hard-on for the damned Tahni?"

"Trust me, Captain Sandoval," Dwight assured her, "that is a question I have asked many times."

"Captain Alvarez, two minutes 'til we land," a female voice buzzed in my ear.

"Thanks, Chief Lawrence. Have they noticed us yet?"

"Oh, yes, sir," the chief petty officer said, chuckling. "They're in quite a tizzy down there, running around and looking at the sky. A few are doing this weird thing where they throw their bodies against the ground with their hands spread out...well, you're just gonna have to see it."

"I know what this is," Dwight told us. "I have absorbed the information from my duplicate who was loaded into the Tahni destroyers on gateway. It is a traditional Tahni greeting...for the gods."

"Well," Vicky said dryly, glancing around at the interior of the lander, where one of the Vergai was upchucking into a bag, "I hope they won't be too disappointed."

Damarran, or at least the major eastern island chain where the dome was located, as it turned out, was damned hot. Not quite Tartarus-in-summer hot, but it seemed an inescapable fact of life in systems where there were two habitables that one of them would be temperate and the other would be a humid, tropical hellhole.

Why the hell can't I be in my nice, air-conditioned battlesuit?

Technically, I should have let the Vergai go first down the ramp, but the Tahni-ish looking people here on Damarran hadn't seemed that violent on the drone footage and I didn't want to take the chance of alienating them with the wrong optics. Still, my right hand hovered over my sidearm and I scanned the sky for falling *atlatl* darts as I stepped out of the lander and into the constant, bright haze of the afternoon sky.

There were no darts nor other weapons, though there *were* Tahni.

We'd landed in a clearing between their largest village and the dome, a flat, grazed-out plain at the edge of the hills where we guessed that the stones for the dome had been mined. The village was barely visible through the trees, just a glimpse of a collection of wattle huts gathered around a central hall. But the dome...

I was a big-city kid, raised in the massive megacity of Trans Angeles, so I wasn't easily impressed by architecture, but the contrast of the dome to the village where these people lived made the dome more incredible. It wasn't just the size and scope of the structure, but its provenance. Who here would build it even if they could? And why? A grain storage area? A religious artifact?

God alone knew, and He wasn't talking. Hachette could have found out if he'd been willing to send a drone into the building, but he'd decided against it, figuring that the locals would see that as provocation and we would wind up unable to approach these people.

Which would be fine with me.

"Matis," I said, trying not to bark the commands. What would work on a platoon of Marines wouldn't necessarily work on the Vergai. "Deploy a security perimeter around the shuttle and wait for my instructions. Do *not* fire unless you receive a direct order from me, even if you're attacked first, am I clear?"

"Yes, Captain!" He turned and began chivvying his people into place, having to physically guide some to the position where he wanted them.

There were a score of Tahni gathered around the dome entrance, a few more who had been caught in the open on the way there from the village, and all those were prostrate, flat on their faces as Chief Lawrence had said, arms in a V, fingers splayed. Not one would look up at us, and I walked within five or six meters of one of them, wondering how we were going to talk to these people if none of them would even look at us.

"Dwight," I told the AI, "try the Karai language from Yfingam first."

"Yes, Captain."

I was wearing that stupid speaker on my belt again and I made sure the volume was turned up before I started.

"Greetings," I told them. "We come seeking peaceful discussion with you. Is there anyone who can talk to us?"

The translation from the speaker was typical, sing-song Tahni and I couldn't tell the difference between that and what the Karai spoke on Yfingam, though Dwight assured me it was significant. Tahni was, I had been told, a very stable language, and there was a chance that even after several thousand years, they should be able to understand some of it.

One of the Tahni males closest to the shuttle rose up from his impromptu faceplant and raised his arms in a V over his head. His words had the same sort of vague familiarity that Italian had to a Spanish-speaker, not quite the Tahni I'd grown used to during the war, but close. Apparently, close enough for Dwight to interpret it.

"Greetings, lords of the stars and the sky. I am your servant, Kotin-Joni. What manner of creature are you? For you are not the gods, yet neither are you the People."

"The People," Dwight added editorially, "seems to be their name for themselves."

"How original," Vicky commented. "And I suppose his name for this planet is 'the world.' Because that would be just right for this bunch."

I shot her a glare. True, her translation circuit wasn't turned on, but there was a chance my microphone could have picked up her comment and then this guy Kotin would have thought I was the one who'd said it. Behind Kotin, the other Tahni who'd thrown themselves down stood slowly and carefully, eyes fixed on us, tensed as if they might run at the slightest provocation. Two or three who had been near the dome were running back to the village, and I hoped that wasn't a prelude to a mob carrying torches and pitchforks.

"You say we're not the gods," I replied to Kotin-Joni, moving closer to him and farther away from Vicky. "How do you know that for sure?"

Not that I intended to pass myself off as a Predecessor, but if these guys knew what one looked like, that was probably significant.

This close to the Tahni, his stench was overwhelming. It wasn't noxious or even particularly unpleasant, but it was strong, wafting off him like he drenched himself in some kind of musk. And he might have. I'd been far too close to a lot of Tahni in my life, and whatever this was, it wasn't their natural smell. I noticed a slight gleam to his skin and it might have been some kind of coating...maybe a guard against the ultraviolet damage from the primary star.

"I know the gods as well as I know my own children, stranger," he told me. "For are we not the children of the gods?" He made a motion with his arm and wrist that I couldn't have duplicated, lacking Tahni joints. "Is this not their house that you have come to in your flying ship?"

"Is that what this is?" I asked him, pointing at the dome. "That's why we're here. We're trying to find out where the gods went when they left here. Do your people remember when you were brought here?"

"And do your people have shade?" Vicky put in *sotto voce*. "And maybe a few chairs?" She wiped sweat out of her eyes.

"We remember as if it was yesterday," Kotin told me, the set of his shoulders and the motion of his hands a Tahni gesture expressing joy, "for all that it was one hundred and seventy-two generations ago."

"Assuming he's using the typical Tahni measure of a generation," Dwight supplied helpfully, "which is approximately thirty-five of your years, that would be over six thousand years ago."

Kotin's head tilted to the side. "Yet you have not answered my question, stranger. I have told you who I am, and now I tell you that I am Keeper of the House, the one who is told the histories of it to pass on to others. You are not us and you are not the gods. Who are you?"

"My name is Cameron Alvarez and I'm from a world called Earth." My mouth was dry and I hesitated, trying to work up some moisture. I wasn't expecting violence, at least none we couldn't handle, but I was much more afraid of fucking up. "We come from the homeworld of the gods."

I couldn't read his expression, but it seemed as if he rocked back, either in surprise or horror, or even joy. Then, as if the backwards motion were part of a dance, Kotin-Joni surged toward me, and out of the corner of my eye, I noticed Vicky and Matis both taking a step my way, Vicky's hand going to her sidearm. I stopped them with a raised palm, not one hundred percent sure he wouldn't attack me, but totally certain that if he wasn't, shooting him would send the wrong message. He put a hand on each of my shoulders and leaned his head forward, touching his forehead to mine, which would have been much more emotional if it hadn't been for that damned smell.

"It was said you might come. We were told."

The passive voice was annoying, and I wondered if it was an artifact of the translation program.

"You were told," I repeated. "Who told you?"

"The scribes," he said as if that explained everything. "Come, I'll show you."

He turned to the other Tahni still gathered around the ship, staring like tourists, and began shouting to them and gesturing. There were, I noticed with a start, *females* in the crowd. I'd thought, at first, that the slighter, shorter Tahni had been juvenile males, but now that they were standing, I could see obvious proof that I'd been wrong.

That shook me. Tahni males and females of breeding age *never* mixed socially. They lived in separate societies, the males in the cities, running the government, the military, and the priesthood, most living above fabrication shops where they made machinery and electronics. The females stayed segregated in their communes, working in shops to mass-produce clothing, or sometimes on farms where they grew the staple of the Tahni diet, a root that provided all their dietary needs. They met only as negotiated, to mate and produce children.

The reason for this was biochemical since the pheromones the females produced were impossible for the Tahni males to resist, and when the females were ovulating, the males would lose control of their actions. It had taken them thousands of years to come to an accommodation with this biological inconvenience, and the odd direction it had taken their society had been one of the reasons we'd beat them in the war. Both wars.

And yet, here they were, and none of the males seemed to even make note of their presence.

"Go back to the others," Kotin-Joni called to those gathered around him. "Tell them we have visitors from the home of the gods, the prophesied ones. Prepare a feast and make sure all know these are our honored guests."

Well, *that* was a relief.

"Would you walk with me now," Kotin asked, "to the house of the gods?" He was motioning toward the dome. Even nearly a kilometer away, the thing was huge, looming over us like a mountain. I didn't especially *want* to enter it, but this was why I'd come.

"It would be my pleasure." I gestured to Matis. "Keep your people here, and stay in touch with me on the comms. *Don't* forget you have them. Anything happens, you *call* me. No one shoots, no one does a damned thing unless you call me first."

"Yes, Captain Alvarez," Matis said, nodding firmly. "You can count on me."

And I really hoped I could. Despite the fact that I'd been opposed to the Vergai coming along on this trip to begin with, I knew Hachette would find a way to blame it on me if they fucked up.

"Vicky," I said, "you want to come along?" I wasn't sure if I wanted her to say no, to stay and keep an eye on the Vergai...or to say yes and back me up inside, so I wouldn't be alone in there.

Her smile gave me her answer before she spoke.

"I wouldn't miss it for the world."

[14]

I'd expected something eldritch, something from a horror story, an altar stained with blood at the feet of twisted, monstrous statues of the Predecessors. What I *hadn't* expected was an art gallery.

Yet that was what the dome was, a gigantic art museum. Beneath the shade of a capstone that had to weigh tons, lit up by the reflection of guttering torches and bonfires tended by devoted acolytes, were images painted on stone, carved into it, shaped from colored stones. No statues. I should have known, because the Tahni didn't do statues on their homeworld. But this was representative art, something I'd never seen on their homeworld either, and some of the Tahni tending the fires were adult females, so maybe sculpture wasn't such a huge reach.

But even without it, the art told a story.

"Where does it start?" Vicky asked. I was going to repeat the question to Kotin, not knowing whether Dwight was translating from her or just me, but the speaker on her belt jabbered in sing-song proto-Tahni.

"Here," Kotin replied. "At the entrance."

I wasn't sure, mostly because I couldn't be certain he'd react the same way as the Tahni I knew, but he didn't seem stressed or bothered by our presence, despite the fact that this place probably felt like a church to him. Instead, he might have been...proud?

As for me, I was speechless, unable to form as simple a question as the one Vicky had asked.

At the entrance, the images were familiar, not too different from the village outside, though on a different world. The sky could have been anywhere, but the arrangement of the mountains and the moon over the bay called back a memory from years ago, an image I'd never forget. It was Tahn-Skyyiah. Six thousand years ago, I assumed.

The next images were closer in, Tahni in clothing similar to the rough, hand-spun wear of the locals here. They were looking up, pointing at the sky, and as the three of us walked slowly around the curve of the dome, I could see what they were looking at. I'd seen them before, at Yfingam, the cylinder shapes surrounded by a green glow, and I didn't need Dwight to tell me what they were. He did anyway.

"Those are Predecessor ships," he said, and if his voice sounded wistful, I had to believe that was how he consciously intended it. He was an AI speaking an alien—to him—language. He wouldn't be giving any signals he didn't mean to. "This had to be one of the last stops they made before they left the Cluster forever."

"Here," Kotin narrated, pointing to an image built up from layers of colored rock, of Tahni lying prostrate at the feet of a handful of Predecessors, "is where our ancestors were given the everlasting honor of meeting the gods face-to-face. They came to us and told us that we were meant for more, meant to do something greater. And they took our fathers and mothers in their ships, far away from our home."

"They brought you here," Vicky said. "But why here? What made this place any better than the one you left?"

A fair question, one that had been nagging at the edges of my consciousness since we'd found Yfingam. The Predecessors had been forced to leave for fear the Skrela would devastate everything they'd built back in the Cluster, I got that. But why bring Tahni with them? And why humans? If the Tahni were right, we weren't their intended heirs, nor had they helped us along as they had their chosen children.

"You can read the story in the pictures if you know how to see them," Kotin replied, sweeping a hand across a series of them, which, to me, seemed to show random images of Predecessors, Tahni, starships, and what might have been their representation of stars and planets. "They told us all, held nothing back. We knew of their great enemy, of their decision to flee from them, to take the fight somewhere else, to a battleground of their own choosing. They said that leaving all of our people back there, in the place they left, would be foolishness, as if a farmer left all his roots in the same cellar for the winter. Rot could take them all and he would starve. But if he were to spread them out amongst many, if one went bad, he might still live off the rest."

"They were afraid of the Skrela..." I paused, not knowing if they would have been told of that name. "...of their great enemy wiping out those of you they left behind?"

"Not their enemy, but whatever else might befall them," he corrected me. "Plague, war, disaster. The gods told us that the universe is a dangerous place and that fate itself had been responsible for more deaths than any devil of war or enemy demon. And there was more." Another image, this one of what might have been stars or planets, spread out along lines emanating from somewhere outside of the picture. "Where many are given the chance to make their own way, each may contribute something to the total knowledge."

"Experiments," Vicky said. She tapped a control, and when she spoke again, her speaker didn't...she'd turned off the mic. "They're experiments. All of them. Put into separate little Petri dishes, set up in different settings, different resources. They were trying to find the optimal configuration, right? Decide if they'd done right giving the Tahni so much help or if they should have left them alone, or maybe trusted them and told them everything."

I turned off my speaker before I replied.

"That makes sense. Dwight said that the Tahni were an experiment to begin with, while we were the control group, left alone to see what happened. They moved out of the Cluster, but they didn't want to give up on their program, so they brought the subjects with them."

"How obsessive do you have to be to worry about shit like that when the Skrela are hunting you down in every one of your systems?" she wondered.

"The Resscharr," Dwight said, though I'd thought the question was rhetorical, "could be quite obsessive. I would not have been surprised if they'd let their belief in their purpose overwhelm their good sense."

The more I saw of the Predecessors, the less I thought of them as gods and more as people...people given too much power and with way too much time on their hands. I switched my speaker back on.

"Kotin-Jani, I've met your people before, the ones left behind when the Predecessors left and also some who were brought here at the same time as you. They all have...a problem with the males being around the females. They keep adult males and females separate so the boys won't kill each other over the girls. You don't seem like you have to worry about this? Did the gods do this for you?"

"That is here as well," he promised. We followed him around the curve until we found a painting of a Tahni male and female standing before a pair of Predecessors. I don't know why, but I felt they were supposed to be male and female also. "It was shortly after we were brought to this place, this paradise, that the gods gave us our purpose. We were told that it was not our calling to learn their magic, to fly among the stars, or make light out of the darkness. Others had been given that task."

"And what were you supposed to do?" Vicky asked, addressing the Tahni male for the first time. "What magic were you to master?"

"We were to master...ourselves." Tahni didn't smile the way humans did, which was just as well given the steam-shovel horror show of their jaws, but I knew that the stance he was taking meant the same thing for them. "We were to tame the demons within to make the best version of us that we could."

I stared at him in disbelief, then glanced at the females.

"You're telling me," I said slowly, "that you were able to conquer your...urge to mate?"

"We were. It took us hundreds of generations, yet we did as the gods instructed. Here." Kotin pointed again, this time at images of Tahni males kneeling, arms and hands in some intricate arrangement no human could have duplicated, gathered around a fire. Another sat before them, some kind of leader or shaman. "We meditated, we prayed, and we found a root here that we crushed and smoked, and put in our food. And eventually, we were able to live beside each other as equals."

Kotin stretched out an arm and one of the females tending the central fire came to him, her hand going around his waist.

"We no longer live apart, nor must we negotiate through the elders for bearing sons and daughters. Now we meet each other as partners, and when we have children, we agree to it because our families are compatible and wish to become one. It is the true miracle that the gods have given us, the more so because we achieved it of our own will. Which is why we expected you."

"Us?" I said, a paranoia creeping up my back that the Predecessors had foreseen me, personally, making it to this planet.

"You, the stepchildren of creation. The weeds among the flowers, hardy and refusing to die no matter how badly the owners of the land treat you." Kotin took us farther around, nearly to the other side of the dome now. "This is the oldest image in the house of the gods. Two thousand generations ago."

Two thousand Tahni generations ago. Seventy thousand years.

The images were no longer of the Tahni, no longer of this hothouse they called paradise. These were of Earth. The planet from orbit was easily recognizable, despite the thousands of years that had elapsed since the image had been taken and passed along. The humans in the next picture were wearing nearly the same thing as the early Tahni, though perhaps more of it. And they, too, were pointing at the sky.

"How?" I choked the word out, unable to come up with more, though Kotin was able to decipher my question.

"We were shown these events as if they happened before us, though the gods insisted they were shadows of things from before, happening again through their magic."

"The Predecessors showed them video recordings," Vicky said, her voice flat, neutral, like none of this affected her, though I knew it did, just as it affected me.

There was a thing I studied, very briefly, in OCS in an accelerated science class, called the genetic bottleneck. Sometime around 70,000 years ago, the entire population of humanity was reduced to a thousand mating pairs. Scientists used to think this was from an eruption of the Mt. Toba supervolcano, but later studies had proven that the eruption 75,000 years ago hadn't significantly changed the weather in Africa. Various other theories had arisen—plague, meteor strike, drought. None had ever been proven.

But I knew now. In the pictures and engravings, the story became clear. Those humans were looking up, pointing at the sky for the same reason the Tahni had...Predecessor starships. But these glowing green cylinders weren't coming to have a conversation, to leave advice and a statement of purpose.

They were coming to kill.

Green-tinted rays stretched out of the sky, and where they touched, the land parted beneath them in clouds of smoke and dust. After they left, bodies littered the ground, rendered quite realistically, with generous use of red ochre to represent the blood. I could barely make out the translation of what Kotin was saying over the roaring in my ears, had to concentrate to focus on his words.

"They tried once, long ago. They said you were not developing how they'd imagined when they'd chosen to leave the homeworld in order to give the life there a chance to evolve on its own. You were violent and sadistic just as your ancestors had been, not improving, not working together beyond your family groups. They decided the best chance intelligent life had on your world was to do away with your species and wait for something to take your place. There were other candidates." He motioned to the next image, of shorter, thicker-bodied humanoids, huddling in furs in snow-covered Europe. Neanderthals. "And yet, after the culling, you *didn't* die. You weren't wiped out. Like a weed, you returned from the barest of leavings, and when the gods returned, you were again the dominant species."

I wasn't one hundred percent sure of the accuracy of the translation when it came to things like tone and emotional content, but I could have sworn Kotin sounded proud of us, as if we'd personally accomplished something by the survival of our distant ancestors.

"Dwight," I ground out, not caring if the Tahni heard it, or had the words translated for them, "did you know about this?"

He didn't respond immediately, and I wondered why an AI would hesitate. He could think faster than us, could calculate all the possibilities in fractions of a second.

"You ask a complicated question, Cameron," he finally said. "Did I have access to this data? Of course. I have access to all of Resscharr history for *millions* of years. Yet I sense that the real question you're asking me is, why didn't I tell you?"

"Yeah," Vicky agreed, staring up at the ceiling of the dome as if she could see him through it, floating in orbit. "That one."

"Because I wasn't aware I should. It would be as if I asked you why you didn't tell me about the purge of all sentient AI projects on Earth after your Sino-Russian War. You neglected to tell me because it happened so long ago, it has lost meaning to you."

Okay. I could buy that. Maybe. But it didn't change what I'd seen here, or what it had done to my image of the Predecessors.

"You told me Resscharr meant 'life-bringer,' didn't you?" I reminded the AI. "How did they reconcile that with trying to commit genocide on another sentient species on their own homeworld?"

Kotin was staring at us and I wouldn't have blamed him if he thought we were insane, talking to the air.

"They are not gods, despite what our Tahni friend believes," Dwight replied. "They were, and are, living beings plagued with the same flaws and vulnerable to the same changes in ethical standards and societal mores as your own culture. Should I demand of you how your people tolerated slavery for thousands of years? They acknowledged what they did as a mistake later, but at the time, they considered it what you would call a command decision. Leaving you alive would mean, as it finally did, the end of the species you refer to as Homo Neanderthalensis, one just as intelligent and self-aware as your own. They *knew* this, as surely as you know the speed of light in a vacuum."

That was harder to argue against. I exchanged a look with Vicky and we agreed silently to leave it for now.

"I am not human," Kotin admitted, "nor am I an expert in reading your moods, but I sense this has upset you. This was not my intent and I regret that it is the result of me bringing you here. But you must understand, the gods knew after you survived the culling that nothing would stop you as a species. That is why they told us you would come someday, either the selected few who were brought with them when they fled their home, or even, as turned out to be the case, you from their homeworld."

"Did they say this was a good thing or a bad thing?" Vicky asked.

"Is the sun rising and setting a good thing or a bad thing?" Kotin answered obliquely. "Is the rising and falling of the tide a good thing or a bad thing? It just is. It's inevitable, a result of the way of the universe. And so was your arrival. You are what we are not. Aggressive, adaptable, determined to shape the universe to your liking rather than accept it as it is. This is what the gods feared in you, I think. I believe, after much consideration and drawing on the wisdom of those who have held my position before me, that we here are the attempt of the gods to perfect their creation before allowing us to join them among the stars.

"But you...you didn't need to ask permission, and yet, here you are."

"Here we are," I agreed. "The gods told you about us...but

did they tell you anything about themselves? Where did they go once they left you here?"

"They said if you came, you'd ask that too." He waved us away from the wall to the center of the dome, where the eternal flame burned.

A twist of smoke curled upward to the hole in the ceiling, the seam where the stone slabs came together. I was no sort of architect or structural engineer, but I had no idea how the hell this building held itself together. The fire had no sort of chimney, but it did have a stone slab set in place at one side of it, and carved into that flat stretch of stone were what could only be star charts.

No, *not* just star charts...

"Are those Transition Lines?" Vicky asked, tracing with her finger the faded striations between the representations of solar systems.

"I believe you're correct, Captain Sandoval," Dwight said, his voice quavering with excitement.

"Alvarez," Hachette said, the first time I'd heard his voice since we landed, "get me a clear shot of that."

No, I thought I'd ignore the thing and hope I could memorize it.

"Got it, sir." I pulled my 'link off my belt and made sure the video pickup captured a full image of the engraving. "Kotin, where are we on this map?"

"You," he told me solemnly, pointing at the bottom of the carving, "are here."

"And where did the gods head off to when they fucked off and left you here?" Vicky asked. I winced, wondering how Dwight was going to translate that.

If Kotin was offended, he didn't show it, or at least, he didn't show it in any way I could interpret. He put his finger beside Vicky's along one of the striations representing Transition

Lines, and traced upward to the top of the carving. There was a system sitting there apart from the others, nothing remarkable from the representation, just a single star with six planets and two asteroid fields.

"Here. The gods went here."

"And that," Hachette buzzed in my ear, sounding disgustingly self-satisfied, "is where we're going."

"Not yet," I told him, feeling a perverse need to undercut his dramatic moment. I nodded toward Kotin. "We have a standing invitation for dinner."

"Four weeks," Dunstan moaned, rubbing his hands over his eyes. "Four fucking weeks in T-space. I don't think I've ever been under this long without popping up for air."

I sloshed tequila around my cup and tried to ignore his whining, because it was way too close to what I'd been thinking myself. At least he'd smuggled aboard the booze, so I had to let him complain without telling him to shut up.

"Could be worse," Vicky opined, taking a sip of some mixed drink concoction Dunstan had dubbed the "Kyler Special." She shrugged, as if giving it her seal of approval. It was alarmingly orange, and I'd turned it down in favor of straight tequila. "We could still be wandering around blind, not even sure if we had a destination."

"You said I'm supposed to watch this door," Matis told me, his words slurred, the distortion passed through the translation program. He motioned at the hatchway to Dunstan's compartment with his cup and his Kyler Special sloshed over the rim, splattering his utility fatigues with orange splotches. "What, exactly, is this door supposed to do?"

"We're not supposed to be drinking on this ship," Vicky

explained...again. To be fair, Matis had been sober the last time. "We need you to make sure no one who shouldn't know we're drinking comes through that door."

"And what if they do?" He waved around him, thankfully with his free hand this time, at the compartment. "This room is small. There's nowhere to hide. Am I to subdue them? Beat them into submission?" He fumbled at his thigh pocket and pulled out a knife, flicking the switch to extend the blade. "Slit their throat?"

"No," I told him firmly, leaning over and snatching the knife from his hand. "And you shouldn't be carrying weapons when you're drunk."

"I would not have," he insisted, "if you'd warned me before we came here that I might be getting drunk." He shrugged. "Not that I'm complaining. It has been months since I've had a drink of anything but water or fruit juice. Do your ships serve nothing else? Not even beer?"

"Non-alcoholic beer," Dunstan told him, then made a face, and a shudder went through his shoulders. "But that's a fate worse than death, if you ask me."

I downed the last gulp of tequila and held my cup out to Dunstan. He sighed as he poured it full again.

"Dude, you need to try my special. Then you wouldn't be burning through my stash so damned quick."

"I do not complain," Matis said, voice too loud and a little unmodulated. "I am happy to be with you here. But if I can ask without being rude, why did you bring me to this gathering?"

"Because we need to talk," I told him, the alcohol loosening me up just enough to be honest. "And the people in this room are the only ones on the ship I can really trust."

"Does that include me, Captain Alvarez?" Dwight asked, his hologram snapping to life in the corner, projected by the compartment's small entertainment console.

"I hope." I shrugged, still feeling far too honest. "Though it might just be that I knew you were the one person I couldn't shut out or distract no matter what else I did."

"What do we need to talk about?" Matis asked, eyeing Dwight with distrust and perhaps a little fear. More than a little. The AI was too much like magic for the Vergai farmer.

"Everything," Vicky said. "Everything that doesn't make any sense, which is pretty much everything at this point."

"Could you be more specific?" Dwight requested.

"Okay, here's one thing." I saluted the AI's conjured image with my cup and then took a sip before going on. "We've stopped at quite a few planets now, and I've yet to see any life that didn't originate from Earth. And we haven't seen any sign of any intelligent life that's not either human, Tahni, or Resscharr."

"Or Skrela," Dunstan added.

"I'm not sure I count them. The drones aren't anything that evolved naturally. They're biomechanical, engineered by someone or something, somewhere. Maybe there's an intelligence out there that created them or maybe whatever it was died off a long time ago and they're all that's left. But that's all beside the point. There's a whole galaxy out here. You can't tell me there's no planet that didn't develop life on its own except Earth."

"What about the Tahni?" Matis asked, brows knit in confusion. "They aren't human, and from what you said, the life on their planet is different from yours."

"The Tahni are not human," Dwight agreed, answering for us, because if there was anything sentient AIs liked to do, it was talk. "But neither did their ecosystem originate naturally on their world. The Resscharr took genetic samples from Earth three million years ago and used them to engineer all the life on

Tahn-Skyyiah, their homeworld, as well as the ecosystems on the habitable worlds surrounding that system."

"Well, I didn't fucking know *that!*" Dunstan blurted, sitting up in his bunk, eyes wide.

"Neither did I," I assured him. "But it makes sense."

"So *all* of the life we've seen so far," Vicky said softly, staring at the orange hue of her drink as if the answer to all our questions were just beneath its surface, "originated on Earth. The Predecessors, the Tahni, us." She glanced over at Dwight. "Does that mean Earth was the *only* planet that evolved life on its own?"

"The universe is large," he replied, "and we have only experienced one spiral arm of one galaxy. It may be that the whole of it is teeming with life that we have yet to encounter. I cannot say. What I do know is that the records the Resscharr left behind for me indicate that when they took to the stars, they were sad to see that they were lifeless and cold. That was when they decided they had to populate them."

"That's *one* possibility," Vicky allowed.

"Or maybe there were other living worlds," Dunstan suggested slowly, his voice and his thoughts both sounding sluggish from alcohol consumption, "and the Skrela just wiped them all out."

"That's another."

"And of course," Dwight said, "the odds of life evolving at all are high, the odds of sentient intelligence developing on its own astronomical."

"What is it, Vicky?" I asked, eyes narrowing. "I know you've got something nagging at you."

"Well, you know, it's the victors who write the histories." She glanced at me sidelong. "After all, if you audited the official records of the Commonwealth government, you'd think that everyone welcomed them as saviors after the Sino-Russian War.

But we know that's not true. It's right there in our military history courses. The Commonwealth military was formed because it *had* to be, because there were separatists and nationalists and a shitload of other people who didn't want to be told they had to join with and contribute to a world government."

"Everybody knows that," I said, hearing a defensive tone in my words and not knowing where it had originated. "We're human, after all. It's impossible to get a thousand people to agree on the speed of light in a vacuum, much less how the planet's supposed to be run."

"My point is, the Predecessor records *say* they found a lifeless universe and decided to give it the gift of the very same life that evolved on Earth. But what if that's all feel-good bullshit? Just because a planet has life doesn't mean it's inhabitable by someone who evolved on Earth. Kyler, you went to the Academy. You must have read about all those ideas we used to have... life that could evolve on worlds with methane atmospheres like Titan, or floating high in the upper cloud levels of a planet like Venus. But worlds like that would be worthless to the Predecessors. Life like that would be impossible to exploit...and since it wouldn't have evolved from DNA, may be impossible for them to tinker with." She shook her head and sipped at her drink. "And they sure as hell liked tinkering with genes."

"No," Dwight said, and for once, I didn't get the impression that was affecting his hesitation and uncertainty. "I would know of such things if they were true."

"How would you?" I asked. "You were given records and you assume they're all accurate. We have a saying about computers on my world that applies to every human as well. GIGO. Garbage In, Garbage Out. If you're fed all your information from one source, you'd have no way of knowing if it's accurate."

"Hell," Vicky said, snorting a humorless laugh, "they tried to do it to *us*. Tried to wipe out a sentient species because they didn't like where we were heading. What makes you think they would have hesitated to do the same thing to an ecosystem so different from theirs—ours—that we would barely recognize it as life?"

None of us spoke, not even Dwight. His image was staring into nothing, so fixed and unmoving, I thought maybe there was a glitch in either his processing gear or the holographic projectors. But he finally moved, though still not looking at us.

"It is...possible," he admitted. "Or should I say, it is not *impossible*. But I do not want to believe it. Perhaps I am being...sentimental."

"It's hardly a mortal sin," I told him, shrugging. "Just means you're human. Sort of."

The knock on the door nearly sent me tumbling off the chair.

"Open up, you idiots."

"Shit," Vicky hissed. "It's Top."

"I can't hide all this shit," Dunstan said helplessly, looking around at the cups and the bottle. "I'm not sober enough."

"Fuck it," I said, pushing out of the chair. "I'm way past caring."

The door was locked, though I knew Top could override that if she wanted. That she hadn't was probably some kind of peace offering. I sighed and slid my finger across the control, freeing the electromagnetic seal, then pulled the hatch aside. Top was waiting, arms crossed, eyebrow tilted upward in that same disapproving glare I remembered from so many years ago.

"Come on in, Sergeant-Major Campbell," I invited her, not even bothering to set down my cup. "Can I interest you in a drink? Kyler has this weird orange thing I wouldn't touch, but I figure you're more adventurous than I am."

Top pushed past me and slammed the hatch shut behind

her, grabbing the bottle from Dunstan's hand with a move so swift, I doubt he could have avoided it even if he hadn't been well on his way to a good buzz.

"What is this shit?" she demanded, sniffing the opening. "Smells like death."

"It's the finest tequila within a thousand light-years," I told her, downing what was left in my cup. The amber liquid burned its way down my throat and settled in my stomach like a meteor burned up in the atmosphere. "Which isn't saying a hell of a lot."

She scowled and took a swig out of the bottle. The expression deepened and set, combined with a twist of distaste.

"You got that right." She handed it back to Dunstan and her eyes settled on Matis, who had jumped to attention and was swaying back and forth, sweating profusely. Top had been a combination of God and the boogie man to the Vergai during training. "I see you're corrupting our allies already."

"No, Sergeant-Major!" Matis insisted with a parade-ground bark. "I was already corrupted!"

And that was more than even Top could take. Her shoulders shook and she couldn't contain the laugh that burbled out of her.

"Oh, Jesus, this is like every nightmare I ever had as a young NCO." She plopped down on the bunk beside Dunstan and he stared at her, gobsmacked. "Close your mouth, Dunstan, before something flies into it."

"Top," I blurted, "has something changed? Because the last time we talked, you had some very specific *suggestions* about our dealings with Colonel Hachette. And the last time I talked to *him* alone, things..." I shrugged. "...didn't go so well. So why are you here and why aren't you, like, I don't know, *arresting* us or something?"

She laughed again, this time less uncontrolled and more calculated.

"If I was here to arrest you, boy, I'd have a few Force Recon types with me."

"What?" I asked her, grinning a challenge. "You don't think you could take me on yourself?"

"You?" She shrugged. "Probably. The Force Recon goons would be for *her*." She nodded toward Vicky. "You're stronger than her, but she's more vicious. Isn't that right, dear?"

"You said it, Top." Vicky saluted her with her glass.

"As for why I'm here, and what's changed, well…Jesus, boy, everything. We know where we're going, and well…" She sighed heavily, sinking back against the bulkhead. "You were right. He was wrong. He knows it."

I was, for once, speechless. I stared at her, and she waved it off.

"Come on, Hachette's many things, but he's not an idiot or a martinet. He's a proud man, of course, and has something of an ego. I mean, he's a colonel, for Christ's sake. You don't get to be a colonel without thinking pretty highly of yourself and your judgment. But he realizes he fucked up by giving the technology to the Vailoans… realizes it more now after what we found with the Tahni colony."

"If the Vailoans start building interplanetary rockets," Vicky said, an acerbic tone to her voice, "they'll slaughter the Tahni. Or just take over their land and shunt them aside somewhere where they can barely grow food."

"Yes, they will. And he knows it now. He was acting out of desperation, trying to lay the groundwork for a backup plan, in case things didn't work out. But he's not going to act again on a decision this important without at least getting the opinions of the rest of his senior officers, and that includes you."

"And he sent you here to tell us this?" I asked, unable to

fight the skepticism crawling all over any optimism I might have been inclined to feel.

"He did."

"Why didn't he come himself? Why didn't he call me into his office and talk to me in person?" I hadn't meant it to sound that hostile, but I couldn't help it.

"Because he figured you wouldn't believe him." Top grabbed the bottle from Dunstan and took another slug, her scowl of distaste not as profound this time. "You'd figure he was conning you, playing Mr. Intelligence Spook to try to get you on his side." She speared me with a glare. "Tell me I'm wrong."

"You're not," I admitted.

"And he knew you'd trust me. Despite everything, you know I wouldn't lie to you."

"No," Vicky agreed. "You wouldn't."

"Here's the thing," Top went on. "We're sailing into some Odyssean shit here. We don't know if we'll be talking or fighting or both. He needs you either way. All of you."

"Even me?" Matis asked, looking as if he'd been smacked between the eyes with a mallet.

"You," she told him, "should probably just pretend none of this ever happened."

"I can do that," he promised, nodding.

"This hasn't been easy on him." Top squeezed her eyes shut as if they were irritated, rubbing at them with thumb and forefinger. "He's an Intelligence officer, not a troop commander, and what's happened here..."

"I don't think any of us expected it," I agreed.

"I sure as hell didn't," Dunstan put in. "But then again, it's not like I had anything back there holding me down. I was a dumbass working for the Corporate Council as a mercenary pilot, with no idea what I was going to do next. As fucked up as all this is, it's still probably more interesting than anything I would have done with my life."

Vicky laughed softly.

"I think that pretty much sums it up for us too."

"Tell the colonel that we have his back," I assured Top. "Just as long as he doesn't do anything else monumentally stupid."

"I can't promise that," she said, grinning crookedly as she stood and headed to the hatch. "He is a colonel, after all. But thanks." She nodded. "From both of us."

I said nothing, just watched her close the hatch behind her. But then I looked at Vicky and she nodded, confirming my suspicion. Top wasn't just an NCO looking out for her officer. She and Hachette were involved.

As if things hadn't been interesting enough.

[16]

I suppose it was some demonstration of goodwill between Hachette and us that Vicky and I were invited to the bridge for the Transition into what everyone had taken to calling the Predecessor system. I thought that was counting our chickens before they hatched, but everyone needed some hope and I wasn't going to make a big deal about it. Hell, even Hachette seemed upbeat and hopeful, though the half-hidden smiles he and Top were sharing was enough to turn my stomach. It was like thinking about your parents having sex.

"Transition in thirty seconds," the Helm officer warned. "Prepare for free-fall."

I yanked at my seat restraint, making sure it was tight. God knew what we were going to find. If anything.

"Gonna be a stone-cold bitch," Vicky said softly beside my ear, as if reading my fears, "if we get there and the whole place has been burned to a crisp by the Skrela."

"Let's keep the good thought."

"All combat spacecraft," Hachette said, touching a control at his command chair to reach the correct net, "are you ready for emergency launch?"

"Intercept Two ready." That was Major Brandano, who I had talked to exactly twice on this whole mission and could barely have picked out of a crowd, mostly because he and Dunstan did *not* get along, and since I was usually hanging out with Dunstan, Brandano avoided us both.

"Intercept One ready." The fact that Brandano disliked him was just fuel for Dunstan, which was why he waited so he could go last.

"Drop-ship One ready for launch."

"Drop-ship Two ready for launch."

Solano was in the first drop-ship with half his company, and if anyone would have asked my opinion, Vicky and I should have been in the second with the other half. But Top had convinced me that snubbing Hachette's peace offering would have been a bad first step in mending our fences.

"If there are Predecessors here," Captain Nance said, his gravelly voice harsh, "I sure hope the bastards have metallic hydrogen for sale. Because right now, I can barely guarantee we have enough to get back to Yfingam."

I whoofed out a nearly-silent breath, surprised. Nance was not the type to make small-talk on the bridge, usually leaving the strategizing and the bullshitting to Hachette. The fact that he was mentioning the fuel situation was either a commentary on how bad it was or how frustrated he was, or maybe both.

"Transitioning now," Yanayev reported, interrupting whatever retort Hachette might have had.

Reality jerked and sputtered around us and the main screen went from a sterile star map to the inky blacks and glaring whites of realspace. A hesitation rocked everyone, a pause for breath as if we'd all jumped off a two-meter drop and had to suck the breath back into our lungs before anyone could speak.

"G-class star," Wojtera said, his clipped, professional voice stepping into the silence as if he was dragging us all back to reality. "Nothing too remarkable about it. Six planets—two terrestrials, two gas giants, two ice giants. Asteroid fields between the outermost terrestrial and the first gas giant and another between the outer gas giant and the first ice giant."

"Just like the representation in the dome," I noted. "And if the map was accurate..."

"So is everything else they said," Hachette agreed.

"Wojtera," Nance said, eyes glued on the main screen, "I'm not seeing anything. What have we got?"

"Not much," the Tactical officer admitted, shaking his head. "Not getting any fusion drives, no reactor signatures, no thermal..."

"The second planet out is habitable," Yanayev added. "I can tell from the spectrography."

"Yeah," Wojtera said, "but there's nothing I can see in orbit...well, nothing that's producing anything on thermal like I'd expect from space stations or orbital factories." The man shrugged. "At least nothing I can make out from this far out. I think we're going to have to micro-Transition and get closer if we want any more details."

"Nance," Hachette said, "Alvarez, Sandoval...opinions?" He glanced up at the holographic projection. "Dwight?"

I kept my eyebrows from shooting up only by an effort of will. I guess this was a concerted effort to live up to the new and improved Colonel Hachette that Top had promised.

"I don't see any reason not to," Nance replied. "No navigational hazards, no static defense platforms. In my opinion, this is going to be another dry hole, but as long as we don't use too much maneuver fuel, it couldn't hurt."

Dwight didn't wait his turn, perhaps because human manners weren't something he considered important, or maybe because he considered his opinion more likely to be valuable than ours.

"I see no signs that the planet has been devastated by a Skrela attack, which is a good sign. Even if there are no Resscharr there, we may find a clue of where they went when they left...perhaps even the gateway itself, if they left it behind."

I didn't even try to stop from rolling my eyes. Dwight was blowing sunshine up our asses, though why he'd want us to keep going, I wasn't sure. Hachette looked to Vicky and she spread her hands.

"It couldn't hurt. We're here to scout and this is our target. I don't see anything to be gained by sitting out here for hours or days, waiting for answers we won't get until we get closer."

And then it was my turn. I think Hachette said my name, but I didn't hear. I was staring at that planet, so far away, we couldn't see it as anything but a slightly brighter star on optical, though the computer had simulated it with a blue and green globe that could have been any of a hundred habitables I'd seen. Possibilities ran through my mind, not on any conscious level, more along the lines of the way they did during combat, just a stream of images passing by too quickly to make out the details until just one emerged clear as day.

"What I think is going to happen," I told Hachette, "is that we're going to micro-Transition to minimum distance and then we're going to find ourselves too close to react to whatever happens. If there's nothing down there, then we're fine. If they've left some kind of trap, maybe for the Skrela, or if there's a threat we can't see, then we'll be well and truly fucked. I think the smartest thing to do would be to come in slower, more cautious. Maybe halfway in and then boost the rest of the trip. That gives us the option of jumping back out if we see any warning signs."

"But we can't fucking well *do* that," Nance said, aggravation scratching at his words like sandpaper. I blinked. I'd never heard Nance curse once on the bridge, and now he'd done it twice in one conversation. Top was right, the tension was getting worse. "We don't have the fuel. We boost that far, we won't even have enough to achieve a stable orbit back at Yfingam."

"Skipper's right about that," Yanayev piped up, though no one had asked her opinion. "Our fuel stores can handle a few more Transitions, but one long boost, or a sustained, high-G combat burn..." She shook her head. "We're driftwood."

Hachette looked back at me with a question in his eyes, as if giving me a chance at a rebuttal.

"I don't deny the fuel situation," I told him, "but it doesn't change my assessment, sir."

Hachette considered the mysteries of the deck, eyes fixed downward, either debating the input he'd sought or trying to give the impression that he was. When he looked up, there was a decisive set to his face.

"We're going in," he said. "You're right, Cameron, that it's a big risk. But we can't turn around and leave this system without investigating, and there's just not enough in our tank to do it the slow and careful way. Captain Nance, I want our backup capacitor banks charged. If we see a threat, I want us ready to jump back out to at least the outer system." He shook his head. "That's the best I can do."

"Yes, sir," was all I gave by way of reply, because what else was there to say? He'd asked for my opinion and I'd given it to him.

"Take us in, Nance."

"Helm," Nance said, nearly stepping on Hachette's command, "plot me a micro-Transition to minimal safe jump distance and execute."

"Aye, sir." Yanayev's fingers flew over the haptic hologram of her control board and a green line connected our position on the computer layout to one just outside the orbit of the second planet's single moon.

"Another moon," I murmured, and Vicky glanced over at me. "All the habitables we've ever seen have moons."

"They do now," Dwight said, hearing our conversation better than anyone else around us. "The Resscharr determined long ago that a large moon was necessary for sustained life. Any of the worlds they terraformed that didn't already have moons, they brought one in from one of the gas giants."

"They moved *moons*?" Nance asked, his bushy eyebrows shooting up. "Moons?"

"It was...energy intensive," Dwight admitted. "But necessary."

"Energy intensive, he says," Nance repeated, snorting in what I took for disbelief. "They moved *moons*."

"Micro-Transition warning," Yanayev announced, sounding a klaxon that bit through the conversation, warning everyone on the ship that we were about to undergo two Transitions within a few seconds of each other, which could be uniquely unpleasant. "Ten seconds."

I gritted my teeth. Regular Transitions were bad enough, the vague sort of discomfort of a chill down the spine with no recognizable source. Micro-Transitions were like snapping a rubber band, and I had no confidence that any of us could react quickly enough if there was an unknown threat at the other end of the jump.

Yanayev didn't bother counting down the seconds, bless her. It was bad enough without the anticipation. Something twisted deep inside my gut and my vision shrank to a dark tunnel before light flashed out of it and smacked me in the face.

I blinked as if I'd just woken up, and looking around, saw a dozen other faces doing the same thing.

"Maneuvering thrusters," Nance rasped. "Get us into a stable orbit here." I understood the order despite my lack of shipboard experience. We'd jumped into the general area of the

Lagrangian points between the planet and her moon and we could either shift into one of them or start getting pulled around at random until we were in orbit around the moon.

"Aye, aye, sir," Yanayev replied, and within a second, sledgehammers banged against the hull as the steering jets took us in the right direction.

"Tactical," Hachette said, clearing his throat halfway through the word, trying to shake off the micro-Transition like the rest of us, "report."

Wojtera didn't have the opportunity...and in a moment, we didn't have the need.

We could all see it on the main screen. Cylindrical shapes, flattened at the ends like a cigar, glowing green. Where they'd been before, I couldn't say, and I would have been willing to bet our instruments and sensors couldn't either.

"What the fuck?" Wojtera blurted. "They're...I don't see them on the sensors."

"You would not," Dwight confirmed. "They're not using fusion power, nor are they emitting heat. All their thermal output is shunted into another dimension."

"Might have been good to know that a few minutes ago," the Tactical officer ground out, then shook it off. "They're surrounding us."

"I'm picking up some strange gravitational readings," Yanayev reported. Which she would, rather than Wojtera because there'd be no reason for the tactical sensors to detect gravitational readings. That was a navigational matter...until it was Predecessor starships.

"It's their drives," I suggested. "Dwight said they were based on microscopic black holes or something, right?"

"They are," Dwight confirmed, "but that isn't what your instruments are detecting. I'm afraid that is a buildup of the external field, used to project the gravitational waves as weapons."

"Transition, Helm!" Hachette snapped, not waiting for further explanation. "Get us out of here!"

Something hit us. Not like a laser or a particle beam or even a railgun round. The energy weapons wouldn't have moved the ship, and the railgun round would have been more a vibration through the hull, the ringing of a giant bell. This was as if the *Orion* were a giant bone and the biggest dog in the universe had just grabbed her in its teeth and shook her. I cursed incoherently, my head whipping back and forth against the padding of the acceleration couch, and then nothing. I looked around, expecting the ship to be coming apart, the air gushing out through a dozen gaps in the hull, but just...nothing. The only stars I could see were the ones in front of my eyes from hitting my head.

"We're..." Yanayev began, then seemed to lose focus and had to shake her head. "We're stopped."

"We were already stopped!" Hachette said, panic fraying the edges of his voice.

"No, sir, we were under maneuvering thruster boost. We weren't accelerating quickly, but we were moving, both under our own power and from the gravity wells of both the planet and the moon. And now...we're not." She touched a series of controls, then swore and did it again. "The maneuver controls are dead. It's as if the computer has shut off the connection from my board to the steering jets or the main engines."

"We can't Transition?" Nance demanded.

"No, sir. The capacitors are drained and they're not recharging." Yanayev shook her head and spread her hands helplessly. "The reactor's still up, but the power won't go anywhere except life support and comms."

"Weapons controls are down too," Wojtera confirmed.

I put my feet on the deck and sagged in my chair. And then I realized, I'd just *put my feet on the deck and sagged in my chair.*

"Why do we have gravity," Nance asked before I had the chance, "if we're not under boost?"

"Dwight?" Hachette asked, with the sort of tone an adult might use when an unruly child has gotten into trouble one too many times.

There was no response. The holographic image was gone from the projection screen.

"Dwight, are you there?" I asked, pulling the quick-release on my restraints and looking around as if he might be hiding. It was stupid. We were being held by alien gravity beams in space and they could easily have shaken us again just for the fun of it and broken every bone in my body. But why would they when they could just rip us to pieces?

"Intercepts One and Two!" Hachette called, smacking his fist down on the comm control. "Can you launch?"

There was a long pause and I wondered if the intercom system was just as useless now as the drives.

"No, sir," Brandano finally said. "Our maneuvering thrusters are not responding and neither is the main drive."

"And even if they were," Dunstan cut in, "the launch cata-pult is down. No power going to the electromagnets."

Vicky was out of her seat now too, though she kept a hand on the safety railing.

"What the hell are they going to do to us?" she wondered. "I mean, they've got us frozen with that gravity beam shit, they've cut our power, won't let us jump out...why don't they just kill us? Why are we sitting here?"

"And what happened to the AI?" Top added. She hadn't unstrapped from her seat, ever the cautious one, but she was leaning forward, feet flat on the deck as if she were ready to spring into action if the need arose. "Why would they take out the AI? How would they even know about it?"

"We're moving," Yanayev said, her voice thick with disbelief.

"I thought the drives were dead," Hachette protested, his eyes going from her to the main screen.

The Predecessor ships were still out there, still at the same distance from the *Orion*, but the moon was drawing away on one side of us, and the planet was racing up to meet us at a ridiculous speed, the acceleration fast enough that it would have mashed us all into a thin, fine paste on the deck.

"They're towing us, somehow," Nance guessed, fingers gripping his armrests so tightly, I was surprised he didn't snap them off. "With those gravity drives of theirs."

"Towing us where?" Hachette demanded.

The answer came with the fading of the blackness of space around us, its replacement with the dazzling blue of a daylight sky. We were in the atmosphere, yet the ship wasn't overheating, and no wind buffeted the irregular lines of the *Orion*, shielded somehow within the grasp of the gravitational beams.

"Down," I supplied. It was obvious. "They're taking us down." I waved at the screen.

"This ship is landing."

[17]

The *Orion* was never meant for an atmosphere.

That thought ricocheted from one side of my head to the other as we descended through the cloud layers over the planet's northernmost continent. I kept expecting flames to begin creeping up around the edges of the superstructure and from the sweat beading on Captain Nance's brow, I was betting he did too.

But it didn't happen, and the only flame I could see was a faint green glow surrounding the ship.

"What the hell is that?" Hachette asked, so quietly I wasn't sure if he meant anyone else to hear it.

"It's their gravity weapon, I think," I told him. "I remember seeing something like that from the ships back on Yfingam. I think besides pulling us, it's protecting us."

"I'd like to do more than think when it's the only thing between this ship and burning up." I didn't take offense. He was keyed up, and I could identify.

"They aren't going to kill us," Nance said. "They would have done it already. They want us down there to talk to us."

I wasn't sure if he was trying to convince us or himself, and I wasn't going to be much good to him. I held on to the railing with one hand and Vicky's hand with the other, as if one of those was going to keep me safe from what was coming.

"Sir," Top said, sounding as if she were asking Hachette about the latest training schedule, "do you want me to have the Marines ready to deploy once we touch down." She shrugged. "Assuming we do touch down."

"No, Sergeant-Major," he replied tautly, as if he was having to exert every bit of self-control not to scream the answer. "I think they've shown us quite graphically that they can dispose of us at their leisure. I'd rather not give them a reason to do it." Hachette sucked in a deep breath, closed his eyes, and visibly calmed down. "Get everyone out of the drop-ships and the Intercepts. I don't want them to see us as a threat."

"They disabled our drives, our reactor, and our weapons remotely," Nance told him, eyes fixed on the screen. "They're lowering a ship the size of a destroyer to the planet with gravity beams. Somehow, I don't think they see us as a threat, Marcus."

I raised an eyebrow. I don't think I'd ever heard Nance call Hachette by his first name.

"If the descent stays at the current velocity," Yanayev said, "I estimate touchdown in two minutes."

"What's down there, Tactical?" Hachette asked.

"Sensors are inoperable," Wojtera told him, "but going from the external cameras, it looks like there's a pretty good-sized city down there, at least ten klicks on a side."

"Are there any other cities down there?" Hachette threw off his restraints, apparently as convinced as I was that a survivable crash was unlikely, and leaned over Wojtera's station to get a better look at the multiple views from the external cameras. "Eight klicks on a side could have a population in the hundreds of thousands, but if they've been down there for thousands of years, that seems low."

"We don't know how quickly they reproduce," Top pointed out. "The Resscharr back in Yfingam still had a small number, though that might have been a result of all the wars they fought and the limited technological resources they had."

"I didn't see any other cities," Wojtera told them, "but I'm just going by visual and there was a lot of cloud cover."

"Touchdown in one minute," Yanayev said.

"Oh, my God," Vicky breathed, staring at the main screen, at the image of the city below us. "Look at it."

It was, I thought, everything I would have expected from a Predecessor city, nothing at all like the primitive palace at Yfingam. It was a Moebius strip, constrained and finite, yet unending, without any coherent beginning or end. There were bare spots that I thought of as courtyards, and some of them were hundreds of meters across, but there was nothing I could have labeled a street or a sidewalk. Nor could I determine the function of any of the structures by sight. These had been designed by an inhuman mind, for all that we'd been told the Predecessors had evolved back on Earth.

They were humanoid, terrestrial, air-breathing, built from DNA, yet they were this different. I tried to imagine what a truly alien mind could be like, something akin to whatever was behind the Skrela, and failed miserably. Maybe that was the reason even the Predecessors had never figured out who had made them, or what their final goal was.

"There," Wojtera said, pointing at one of the courtyards, this one a kilometer long. "That's where they're taking us."

I peered at it and caught a hint of movement.

"Are those people down there?"

Hachette looked from me to the screen, then reached into his command console and zoomed in even more. The square was occupied, though we were still far away enough that we couldn't make out any details. But we were coming down fast, and as we grew closer, the nature of our observers became clear. I'd seen their like before, in Yfingam, but there was a qualitative difference between those debased Resscharr and the Predecessors below.

Their body design was the same, of course. Three-toed feet, knees bent backward, digitigrade. Deep chest and long arms, terminating in a three-fingered hand. Long neck and a flattened face with the skull stretching back, seeming even further elongated by the mane of feathery hair at its crest. The clothes were different, which was no surprise...the Resscharr we'd met before had sunken to what was basically medieval feudalism, while these clearly had not. These wore sleeves of multicolored cloth that looked like nylon or maybe even neoprene on their forearms and thighs, and separate squares of the same material over their pelvic area and chests.

Did that mean they had some sort of nudity taboo? Or was the clothing purely decorative? *And why do I care?* I guess I cared because figuring out something about their mindset might be the only thing that kept us alive...and I was hoping they were different enough from their devolved relatives that they wouldn't think of us as lowly slaves.

They were certainly interested enough in us to crowd the edges of the landing area almost right to the outline of the *Orion*, which I thought was reckless. This was a fusion-powered starship, and even with all their almost-magic technology, being that close to it was dangerous. Maybe that was another piece of the puzzle I could use to figure them out.

"We're landing," Yanayev said, two seconds ahead of a jolt that nearly threw me off my feet. The safety railing bit into my fingers and I spread my stance wide, barely able to stay standing. Vicky went down to a knee, steadying herself with a palm flat against the deck, while Hachette held on to the back of his command seat, lips moving in what might have been a silent prayer.

Creeks and groans and crashes echoed through the ship, noises never heard in the vacuum of space, never *meant* to be heard on a ship this size. Even after the craft settled against the ground, the metallic shrieks carried on and I looked around the bridge, expecting it to collapse around us, expecting the ship to break into pieces.

"Damage control?" Nance asked, his voice anguished, as if he felt the pain of the ship's distress. "What's our status?"

"We've got some minor structural damage on support struts for the comm antennae and the port weapons pod," Lt. Landry reported, his tone neutral and professional for all that his face was three shades paler than it had been a minute ago. "The dorsal railgun mount is cracked in three places and the weapon's unusable. But the superstructure is stable. There's strain, but nothing the ship can't handle."

Nance sighed and settled back in his chair, like a man whose job was done. Hachette didn't seem anywhere near as relaxed.

"Captain Nance," he said, supporting himself still against his chair, though less for balance, I judged, and more for an emotional anchor, "how the hell do we get off this ship and down to the ground?"

Nance laughed, a tinge of hysteria in the sound.

"It's not something I've ever considered before," he admitted. He tapped a control on his station, bringing up a schematic of the ship. "Here." He pointed to a spot just below the hangar bay. "There's a maintenance lock right here that should be low enough on the superstructure to get you to the ground safely."

"What the hell are we going to do out there without Dwight?" Vicky asked. "We won't be able to talk to them."

"I am here."

I couldn't help it; I jumped at the words. They weren't accompanied by a holographic projection and they seemed weaker, less self-assured than before, but it was Dwight.

"What happened to you?" Hachette demanded.

"I was...suppressed. Analyzed." If Dwight had been a human, I would have said he was morally offended, violated. "They went through my short-term memory, what I had stored in your computer systems. It wasn't everything, just the most recent, and I think they were mostly interested in where you were from. They have your language now and I think they're waiting until their translation systems are ready to speak with you."

"Can you tell us anything about them?" I asked the AI. "Besides the obvious."

"They're as advanced as the Resscharr who constructed me. I do not see any indications that they've regressed at all, technologically. The size of this city, and the fact that you didn't notice indications of any others, tells me they've restricted their population growth purposefully, either to conserve resources or to keep from attracting attention."

"Humans of the Commonwealth vessel *Orion*, we require you to send representatives to speak with us."

If Dwight had startled me, the voice of the Predecessors poured ice water down my back. It was a computer simulation— it had to be. There was no way a non-human throat could have pronounced the words that perfectly. But it didn't *sound* like any computer simulation. It sounded even more natural than Dwight, though I couldn't have sworn as to why. And yet, at the same time, it was so utterly *inhuman*, not from the intonations or the pronunciation or the cadence. It was the utter lack of emotion, or at least the emotion I would have expected from the demand. It had taken Dwight a while to perfect his understanding of the emotional content of conversation, and it was obvious the Predecessors weren't there yet.

I stared at the overhead where the voice had come from the speakers, but said nothing. None of us did for several seconds. It was Hachette who managed to shake off the fugue first, clearing his throat and speaking clearly, with a steady voice.

"We'll be sending out four individuals," he told the Predecessors. "They'll be unarmed."

"One or a hundred," the Predecessor replied, "armed or unarmed, or in one of your powered war suits, it will not matter. Just come."

"Confident sons of bitches, aren't they?" Vicky mused. No one but me would have detected the nervous flutter in her tone.

"I'm going out," Hachette declared. Top started to object, but he cut her off with a slashing gesture. "Don't bother telling me it's a risk. They could kill all of us at their leisure. It's my responsibility."

"Yes, sir," she grumbled.

"Don't be so glum. You're going with me. You too, Alvarez, Sandoval." His eyes turned upward, like a prayer. "Are you going to be with us, Dwight?"

"If they allow me, Colonel Hachette."

Hachette grunted at the comment and waved for us to follow him out of the bridge.

I'd never taken this route through the ship, down the central hub on the fold-down steps because we didn't trust the lift system after the landing. I tried to picture the *Orion*, sitting on her drive bell, like some orbital rocket from the Twenty-First Century, with us picking our way down her, bypassing the rotational drum, locked into place since before our Transition.

"Thank God they landed us on our tail," Vicky said, speaking up to be heard over the clomp of our boots on the metal grating of the steps. "Can you imagine what a bitch it would be with the ship sitting on her side and us trying to climb over the furniture?"

"Yeah, thank God our alien overlords were merciful to us puny humans," Top retorted, barking a laugh.

"God," Hachette snorted. "It sounds to me as if the Predecessors thought they *were* gods until the Skrela came along and taught them otherwise."

"Maybe that was the point," I suggested. "Maybe they played god once too often and the Skrela were sent by someone who didn't like it."

"I have nothing in my records about the Resscharr ever encountering another intelligent, star-faring race," Dwight objected. "Of course, as has been pointed out to me, I am relying on the Predecessors who provided me with those records."

"You're learning, buddy," I told him.

The final exit from the central hub came out in engineering, but just before that hatch, there was another; narrower, not meant for general traffic. A warning label was slapped across its grey metal, promising an Article 15 non-judicial punishment for any unauthorized personnel who went into the area.

"What?" I asked Top. "You get people trying to sneak down here to drink or have sex or something?"

"Something like that." She eyed me over her shoulder, scowling. "Not everyone has their own compartment where they can drink booze against regulations."

Squeezing through the narrow passage beyond the hatch, I was honestly surprised they had any trouble with people coming back here. It didn't bother me, but I was a Drop-Trooper, used to tight spaces. I couldn't imagine most Fleet personnel braving the passage just for some illicit drinking or sex. Past the squeeze point was another hatch, this one set in the deck and sealed with a security lock. Hachette pressed his palm to it and the hatch opened with a pneumatic hiss. The opening was barely big enough for a grown man in a pressure suit, which was exactly what it was designed to accommodate. The bow maneuvering thrusters were mounted just aft of the hangar bay, and this was the only access to service them apart from a drydock.

"I understand the concept that this is the lowest external egress on the ship," I said, watching Hachette descend into the shadows of the tunnel, "but that's still gonna be like fifty meters above the ground, isn't it?"

"It is," Top confirmed. "You don't have any problems with heights, do you?"

"They aren't my favorite thing in the whole world." I sighed and clambered down the ladder.

It went on for twenty or thirty meters before the tunnel opened up on a compact airlock, the gateway to the outside. It opened at a push on the control panel, since there was no need to cycle it, pressures on both sides already equal.

"It's true no one ever imagined a ship this size landing on a planet," Hachette said, reaching through the outer lock hatch to twist a physical lever downward, "but some visionary team of designers did anticipate the possibility of the ship's main drive going down away from a drydock. And gave us a way to get to it."

I leaned over the edge of the lock and saw the telescoping pole lowering out of the rim of the outer hatch, the grinding hum of long-disused motors echoing up through the hull. As each section of the pole extended downward, hand- and footholds unfolded from its surface at one-meter intervals. I thought the thing would keep going all the way through the grassy field below us, but it stopped a meter or two up, and it still seemed to go on forever.

"Fifty meters down that thing?" I asked, staring at Top in askance.

"You want to go first?" She grinned a challenge.

"Oh, hell," I murmured. "Fine." But I only volunteered because I could sense Vicky was going to do it if I didn't.

There were handholds recessed into the walls of the airlock, but finding them while I hung down from the rim of the hatch was beyond tricky, and I could barely hear the wind whistling by outside the hatch over the drumbeat of my heart. My palms were sweaty by the time I reached the first protrusion past the hatch, and I paused for a second to wipe them off on my pants before I continued.

A gust of warm wind hit me about two meters down the pole and my fingers nearly cramped from gripping the handholds so tight, but I kept going, keeping my eyes level and not looking down. It was too far down to look, and the damned pole was swaying back and forth in that wind. The climb down took years, or at least that was what it felt like to me, and I only began to breathe normally once I reached the junction of the drive bell and the ship.

That was when I saw the buildings surrounding us, let my attention drift to their mind-twisting curves, trying to make sense of their shape. There didn't seem to be any practical reason to them, as if the whole city was a work of art. I was still staring at them when I felt for the next rung of the pole ladder and felt nothing.

"Shit!" I exclaimed, finally looking down.

The ground was a meter below me. I chuckled softly and jumped down.

The gravity here was close enough to Earth normal that I didn't notice the difference when I landed, absorbing the shock with my knee, not feeling any twinge of pain. I looked up and found Vicky only a couple of meters above me, scrambling down so quickly, I had to step out of the way before she landed on my head. She shot me a tense smile and grabbed my hand, looking over my shoulder in the direction I'd avoided. I waited until Top and Hachette came down beside us before I let myself look at them.

This close, they towered over us, as intimidating physically as the Resscharr we'd seen before, but much more so for the technological superiority they'd shown. The energy pistols the Yfingam Resscharr had wielded were deadly, but they hadn't scared me any more than a plasma gun. The *Orion* sitting on her drive bell, stretching five hundred meters into the sky, scared the shit out of me.

The Predecessors gathered around the ship were all adults, from what I could see, and I wondered if they'd kept their children out of sight to protect them from possible danger or to not let them see what they planned to do to the tiny, ugly humans. A group of them stepped out of the press, walking our way with odd, bounding steps.

No, not a group...*two* groups. The separation between them was clear, right down to how they dressed and even how their manes of feathery hair were arranged.

"What's with this shit, Dwight?" I asked, hoping he could hear me. "It looks like they're dressed differently?"

"I can't say for sure," he answered in my earbud, "but I believe the clothing is a sign of different schools of philosophy. I don't know the significance." I could almost hear his shrug. "All my information is a few thousand years out of date."

Right down the middle of the two groups walked an individual, a female I believed.

She approached within a few meters of us and made a sign with her hand that I couldn't interpret.

"I am Lilandreth," she said, and there was no lag, no speaking of the Predecessor language followed by a translator repeating it in English. Somehow, she was able to communicate in English just minutes after getting the details of the language from Dwight. "I would welcome you to the world we call Decision."

Hachette stepped past Vicky and me, and he looked very confident except for the tremor in his hands.

"I'm Colonel Marcus Hachette of the Commonwealth Fleet Intelligence Service. We've come here to ask for your help."

"We know why you've come. You must speak before the Council of Elders. We must decide your fate."

And *that* didn't sound ominous at all.

[18]

I still didn't know what a Council of Elders was, and Dwight had been no help in that respect, still claiming ignorance of the local culture, but at least I knew *where* it was. We'd been led through the crowd of onlookers, their ranks parting before us like the Red Sea, to one of the entrances into the city. I thought of it that way instead of "into a building" because now that I looked at it from ground level, the city was all one building. And not in the sense that the housing blocs back in Trans-Angeles were one building, either It was more as if the whole city was one *room*, with no real separation other than the curving sightlines. And somewhere amid those curves, I became so lost that I couldn't have made it back to the outside without a Predecessor guide, or a GPS signal from my 'link. We wound up in a high-ceilinged area, surrounded not by walls, but *waves*, low curved partitions sometimes rising nearly to the ceiling, sometimes only a meter high, but separating the sections of the building not so much physically as psychologically.

We weren't surrounded anymore, not like we had been outside. That is, I *knew* there were other Predecessors around us —I'd seen them on the way in—but the sight lines kept them in the background, out of mind. For all I could tell, it was just the four of us and eleven of the Predecessors, five from each of the two factions we'd met outside, along with this Lilandreth. She hadn't said another word to us on the way in, nor had we been offered introductions to any of the others. I wanted to ask Dwight if that was a bad sign, but I knew they could understand me, and I didn't want to do something they might perceive as rude. And God alone knew what a race of intelligent dinosaurs who'd lived in another part of the galaxy for the last several thousand years might consider rude.

The Predecessors offered us no chairs because they used none themselves, simply squatting on their backward-bent legs. My own legs were pretty damned tired after climbing down the ship and walking all this way, and I stifled a curse.

"We want you," Lilandreth said, standing at the center of their group once more, as if she was the referee, "to tell us where you're from, how you came to be here, and who you think we are."

"I thought you knew all that already," I said, ignoring the sidelong glare from Hachette. If he hadn't wanted me to talk, he shouldn't have brought me along. "You scanned the memories of the AI who came with us, so you have to know exactly who we are and where we're from."

Lilandreth turned and spoke to the two groups, finally lapsing into the same sort of harsh, buzzing language I'd heard among the Resscharr before. They replied, taking several minutes, and I wondered what the hell they were talking about. Again, I wanted to ask Dwight, but... Finally, the spokes...*person?* turned back to us, and if my question had upset her, well, I had no way of knowing.

"What we know," she said, "has come to us from the computer you call Dwight. He is an artificial intelligence." She stopped there as if that was enough, and I figured she wouldn't be able to read our faces enough to tell it wasn't.

"He's *your* AI," I pointed out. "Why wouldn't you trust him?"

"We utilized artificial intelligence when we had no other option. For those circumstances, they are useful, but we prefer living minds."

Well, wasn't *that* all sorts of interesting? It made me glad I hadn't spoken to Dwight openly. I expected him to say something in his own defense, but there was no voice in my ear. Hachette had apparently had enough of my improvisational skills and took the conversation back over.

"We are from the same place as you," he told them, his tone making it sound like it was something we should be proud of, something we had in common with the Predecessors that elevated us to their level. "We understand that you left the world when you deduced other intelligence would arise, but we also know you visited sometime in our past and took some of our people away to seed other worlds, just as you did with the Tahni." I frowned but said nothing. He was drifting already. He should have answered the questions as they were asked.

"We're here because we passed through one of your gateways back in the Cluster, the section of space you closed off to protect us from the Skrela. We didn't intend to get pulled through it...that was the decision of one of the AIs you left behind. We've been trying to track you down in the hopes you might have access to another of the gateways to get us back home."

Vicky nudged me, frowning, and I nodded agreement. Hachette was smiling like a salesman, looking self-satisfied and righteous, but he was leaving out too much. They *knew* what had happened, knew about the war, and Zan-Thint and Yfin-gam, about what had happened with the Resscharr there. By not explaining it, he was going to make them think we were lying to them to make ourselves look better.

Lilandreth turned from Hachette and toward me.

"He has told me who he is. Who are you?"

"Cameron Alvarez. I'm a Drop-Trooper in one of those powered battlesuits you told us we could bring if we wanted to. I kind of wish I had."

"And if I were to ask you the same questions, what would your answers be?"

Oh, wonderful. Now, I could either repeat the sunshine Hachette had been blowing up their asses and make us all look not just like liars but *stupid* liars, or I could tell the truth and risk the colonel and Top getting royally pissed at me again.

Tell the truth and shame the devil. Mama had always said that. Of course, Mama had barely known aliens existed much less suspected her younger son would ever be standing in front of them.

I gave Hachette a second to see whether he'd order me not to say anything, but he and Top just stared at me in expectation. Vicky squeezed my arm.

"What I would say," I told Lilandreth, "is that we're the red-headed stepchildren, the ones you didn't want to be here. We were the control group in your experiment, the results you compare to the ones you were actually trying to study. We found your wormhole network, the one you left for your children, the Tahni. We found it and we used it to build our own interstellar civilization, and when the Tahni came along and told us we were playing in their sandbox, we kicked their asses because you handed them everything they had, and they weren't ready to stand on their own two feet."

Hachette was staring at me in horror, his face gone pale, but from the twisted grin on Top's face, she was enjoying it. She understood. We were at the mercy of these things, but kissing their asses wouldn't work. That was what you might do to a *human*, but these weren't humans. We kept forgetting that with them *and* the Tahni.

"We didn't wipe them out." I shrugged. "Maybe we should have. Maybe then we wouldn't have had to deal with General Zan-Thint when he decided to run out of the Cluster. Only, along the way, he found a few Skrela seed pods and he set them loose to try to wipe us out, or at least distract us. Which meant we had to chase after him, and we chased him here, whether we wanted to or not. Now he's right where he wanted to be, away from us humans, but we're stuck, and if we stay here, we're going to wind up fighting him the same way we wound up fighting his people back in the Cluster."

I spread my hands.

"That's who we are and what we're doing here. As to who we think you are, well, a lot of people from back where I'm from think you're gods. They think you were part of some golden age that they can bring back again by trying to be like what they believe you are. They worship you. The Tahni think you're angels, not the same as them but sent by their version of God to help them along, that you left them the Cluster as their birthright."

"And what do *you* think we are, Cameron Alvarez?" Liland-dreth wanted to know. She wasn't human, and the voice she was using was an imitation of ours, devoid of much of the emotional content it should have had, but if I'd been tasked with judging her mood, I would have had to guess it was amused. Like we were monkeys doing tricks for her.

"I think," I told her, "that you were lonely. Like in a lot of our myths, where God is lonely so He creates man, I think you were born into a galaxy with no life, and something in your nature couldn't let that stand. You decided that you wanted to change that, but the only source you had for doing it was Earth.

You moved off the planet because you couldn't risk contaminating that one source, and you started the long process of transforming the worlds around other stars into habitable ones."

I wasn't pulling this out of my ass. I'd been putting it together for months now, from what I'd learned about the Predecessors talking to Zan-Thint and Dwight. Of course, I'd been assuming neither was lying to me, which might not have been the smartest move.

"And I think by the time you were done, by the time you were ready to seed those planets with life, you figured out that sentient life was going to evolve on its own on Earth, not just once but multiple times, from those little monkeys skittering in the trees. Right? I mean, I know from Dwight that you have an understanding of biological evolution that's as predictive as our knowledge of physics, so you must have seen what was coming. And I bet I know just what you thought."

I paused, looking around for something, *anything* I could sit on.

Fuck it.

"My legs hurt and it's been a hell of a day," I told her, "so I'm gonna sit down."

I plopped down right there on the floor. It was cold and hard, but it was still better than standing. I folded my legs into a lotus position and looked up at the others expectantly. Vicky chuckled as she sat next to me, putting a hand on my shoulder. Top sighed, but squatted beside us before shooting a "what-are-you-waiting-for" expression at Hachette. He took a knee, stiff and awkward and looking as if he'd rather be just about anywhere else.

"Anyway," I went on, picking up some steam, "I know just what you were thinking. You were thinking, if it's possible for sentient life to develop multiple times just in this one ecosystem, then it should sure as hell be possible for you to engineer it yourself. And once you'd finished terraforming those other worlds and putting ecosystems in place with life you transplanted from Earth, you got to work at playing God."

I tilted my head to the side, regarding Lilandreth as if she personally had been the one to make the decision.

"I'm no expert on genetics or evolutionary biology, but I've read enough to know that we've determined Tahni genes are as different from ours as monkey DNA. That's a pretty big gap, so I'm betting you started this from some early hominid, way before even apes evolved on Earth. But you kept your eyes on that control group, on *us*, and when you saw something you liked, you gave it to your pet project. And then you tried to clean the fucking Petri dish." I hadn't meant to sound quite so harsh, but it was hard to keep the vindictiveness out of my tone. "I figure this must have been about the same time as you reached the final stages of development on the Tahni. You had them just how you wanted, so you didn't need us anymore. We were just an unwelcome reminder of the fact that you couldn't improve on random mutation and natural selection. And I'll bet there was more. I'll bet you could see the potential there for friction with your chosen ones, the Tahni. So you tried to wipe us out, but we came back, like the cockroaches we are."

I laughed softly, leaning back on my hands.

"I've read about how people used to predict we'd kill each other off, that humans would die off from war, or sickness, or climate change. But humans have already come as close to extinct as you can get and still recover genetically, and came out the other side. Maybe you had a change of heart, maybe you thought you'd made a mistake, since you didn't try to wipe us out again, but I think there was something else involved. I think that was when the Skrela first showed up. I bet they weren't much trouble for you at first, not with the technology you have.

But you could see the writing on the wall, and you knew things were going to get worse."

I wagged a finger at Lilandreth.

"That's when you started planning to seal off the Cluster, wasn't it? When you figured out that you couldn't beat them. And once you started settling out here, *some* of you didn't want to give up on the old experiments. That's why you brought us and the Tahni along. Because you still wanted to see if you could make the Tahni better." Hachette might have been about to pass out, but Top was nodding. "Who do I think you are?" I repeated, regarding them without fear or intimidation this time. "I think you're like every scientist and researcher who forgets they're part of the experiment too. You thought you were gods until the Skrela came along and reminded you that someone else can play god too." I folded my arms across my chest and looked into Lilandreth's huge, liquid eyes. "How'd I do?"

More chitter-chattering between them, arms waving, feet shifting. They might have been trying to decide how to respond, or they might have been discussing whether to eat us all fried or grilled. Whatever the nature of their debate, it ended with a sharp chirping sound from Lilandreth, as if she'd cut off their argument with a reminder of who was in charge.

"Cameron Alvarez, you are remarkably intuitive," she said, her hands stretching out toward me. "You've done well for what you know, though I sense that your opinion of us may have been colored by your association with the AI."

"Dwight actually has a very high opinion of you," I interrupted her. And yes, I know I was being foolish and impudent, but I'd never been able to control my anger around bullies. "He tried to explain to us how you tried to commit genocide on our species because you were concerned we would wipe out the Neanderthals or some such shit. Maybe because that was what he'd been told. Now, I know you're not humans, but you had a big hand in creating the Tahni and their culture, and what you left them with is one of the most cynical, unfeeling con jobs I've seen in a life full of cynical, unfeeling con jobs." I raised my hands in a gesture of dismissal. "I don't really care. Maybe I'm wrong about this too, but that wasn't you. That was 70,000 years ago and I wouldn't expect you to accept responsibility for that any more than I would take the blame for the Sino-Russian War. But you asked who I thought you were, and that's the last I know about you." I cocked an eyebrow. "Tell me what's changed."

Lilandreth's eyes were alien, catlike, but they were also incredibly expressive, and I thought I saw a flare of emotion in them. If she was anything close to human, it might have been annoyance, since that was the emotion I seemed to inspire the most in authority figures.

"If you had made these accusations ten thousand years ago," she said, "there would have been much truth in them from your point of view. But many things have changed since we were forced to leave what you call the Cluster. Prior to that, when we were faced with the threat of annihilation by the Skrela, we were unified in thought and intent. It seemed there was only one moral way out of our situation and no one questioned it."

"Lifeboat ethics," Vicky murmured beside my ear, and I nodded.

"Things changed on the other side of the gateway. Where there had once been one vision, now there were four. You've met one of them already. Some of our people wanted no part of the traditions and way of life we'd lived with so long. They'd grown tired of the constant battle, the constant retreats, and they decided to simply settle on the first habitable worlds on this side of the gateway. They kept little of our technology and none of our capability to produce more, though we left them one of the AIs to watch over them since it was all they would accept."

"It hasn't worked out so well for them," I told her.

"We never believed it would. What you see before you are two of the other three factions. Our names for ourselves do not translate well to your language, but the closest I can come is the Substantiation..." She gestured toward the group on her right. "...and the Denial." The one on her left.

"Are these like political parties," Vicky asked, never one to care about talking out of turn, "schools of philosophy, or religious sects?"

"You say that as if any of those differentiations mean anything to anyone who is not human. Yet I think the best answer to your question is that there are elements of all three involved. And more religion than you might think." Lilandreth inclined her long, top-heavy head toward me. "Cameron Alvarez, you referred to us as thinking of ourselves as gods, and that may be fair. We believed in no god greater than ourselves, for we couldn't believe that any creative being would leave the universe so empty. Surely, we had to be an accident, that one in trillions chance. Even when your kind evolved, we thought the Earth was the only home to life varied enough to produce intelligence. The attack by the Skrela changed that perspective, though it took much time for those changes to percolate through our species." I was impressed that she knew how to use the word "percolate" in a sentence. I mean, even the best translation programs usually don't handle words with multiple meanings well.

"And now they have?" I assumed.

"The one thing we all agree on is that there is a creative being, and that this being has a purpose for us. The Substantiation believes that the Skrela were a test, meant to ensure that we are worthy successors to the Creator, that we may continue the Creator's work of spreading life, but with more humility and a new sense of purpose. They believe that we must continue our efforts here, despite the risk of the Skrela finding us again. They welcome your coming as evidence that our efforts in the Cluster have borne fruit, even if there was conflict between you and the Tahni."

"And the Denial?"

"The Denial embrace the opposite philosophy. They think we failed as life-bringers, that we created conflict and war, that our engineering of habitable planets was unnatural and destructive. They see the Skrela as the punishment of the Creator, and our exile in his place as an opportunity to contemplate our sins and start afresh. They see you and your arrival as the personification of the blasphemy we committed and the judgment of the Creator, intended to bring the Skrela down on us and purge us from this galaxy as undeserving. This is the dilemma we face. Prior to your arrival, we believed we had millennia ahead to debate and decide which of these views was correct. Now, we must come to a conclusion immediately, for if the Denial are correct, you must be killed, your ship destroyed, and every evidence of your presence eliminated before the Skrela track us down through you."

"Oh," I said, swallowing hard before I could continue, "that's...interesting." And it was pretty much the nightmare scenario.

"What about the third group?" That was Hachette and he sounded steadier than me, less bothered by the news, as if he'd expected it. Or maybe it was just bluster, but either way, it was impressive. "You said there were three groups. Where's the third?"

"The Seekers. They refuse to accept the concept of a Creator. They believe that we are the ultimate arbiter of right and wrong, and that our destiny is to hunt down the Skrela, or rather, the race behind them because they believe the Skrela are a designed species that someone sent to destroy everything we built. They took everyone who would come and headed toward the galactic center where they believed the source of the Skrela is. They took a gate with them so they could return to the Cluster once they'd set things right."

A smile spread across Hachette's face, despite everything else we'd heard.

"That's it," he exulted, grabbing Top's hand and pulling her to her feet. "The gateway is out there. We just have to find a way to follow them."

"We don't have any fuel," I reminded him. "And our ship is sitting on its ass about a kilometer thataway."

"The Substantiation will, of course, support aiding you in your quest to return to the Cluster," Lilandreth said. "*If* they win the debate. If they don't, you won't have to worry about your fuel situation. Because you'll never be allowed to leave here alive."

[19]

"Why can't we go back to the ship?" Vicky asked, pacing across the...well, not *room*, since the Predecessors didn't have rooms to speak of. We were being detained in an enclosure with no closure. A section of the city separated from the rest of it by curving sculptures rising from the floor, arresting the sight lines, was the only thing imprisoning us.

That and the fact I didn't think we could find our way back out.

"What's the point in keeping us here?" she went on. "It's not as if we can take off into orbit and escape." She frowned and stared at Hachette. "We can't, can we? I mean, we can't just use the fusion drive?"

"Even if they hadn't frozen our controls," Hachette told her, chin resting on his hands, "the thermal blooming from the fusion blast would overload our shields and cook us all with radiation." He was sitting on something that might have been the Predecessor version of furniture or might have been a decorative sculpture, and he hadn't moved since Lilandreth had dumped us here and told us to wait. He cocked an eyebrow at her. "Now, there's a possibility we could get one of the Intercepts launched if we could figure out how to shut down whatever it is they used to take control of our computers."

"They won't even let us *talk* to the ship," I reminded him. I didn't trust the sculpture thing and I was sitting on the floor, which was a toss-up for which would be less comfortable. "If we can't figure out how to get a comm signal past their jamming, I don't know how the hell we'd be able to launch a starship. I mean, hell, we can't even ask Dwight since they cut off our comms."

"All I know," Vicky said, jabbing a finger at Hachette, "is that I have to pee, and unless one of those ostrich-looking freaks shows me to the evolved-dinosaur equivalent of a little girl's room soon, I'm going to find a corner—or as close to one as I can get in this madhouse—and do my business on the floor."

"Do your people require a special room for small females to urinate?"

I was on my feet, clutching at where my sidearm should have been before I realized it was Lilandreth, standing behind us as if she'd stepped through a portal in mid-air. I shouldn't have been surprised, but somehow I thought a two-meter tall talking dinosaur humanoid would make more noise when it walked.

"We usually go in private," Vicky replied, hands on her hips, staring defiantly at the Resscharr female, "in a room set up to recycle the waste."

Which was putting far too positive a spin on taking a piss, but I didn't try to argue. Lilandreth motioned around us with her multi-jointed fingers.

"We have no such space, but the floor is built to absorb all waste, both bodily and otherwise."

"Oh, that's just a great mental picture," Top said, still leaning against the one flat spot on the nearest of the half-partitions.

"How long are you going to keep us here?" I asked, trying not to think about the floor since I'd been sitting on it.

"The Council of Elders is debating now."

"And you're not with them?" Hachette wondered.

"I have no place there. I am with neither the Substantiation nor the Denial."

"Then what *do* you believe?" I asked.

"As a designated Mediator, I am not allowed a position on the matter." And she didn't sound as if it bothered her.

"You mean, you can't tell anyone what you think about it?" Vicky asked, looking as if curiosity had quelled the call of nature, at least temporarily. "You have to keep it secret?"

"There is no secret to keep," Lilandreth insisted. "I am not allowed a position. I do not consider the matter at all."

"How the hell do you keep yourself from thinking about the question?" Top asked.

"I think about it constantly. That is my job, to see both sides of the issue without coming to a conclusion."

"And you don't have a problem with that?" Top snorted. "My opinions are fairly well established."

"This is an argument with no physical evidence to support either side. To *not* come to a conclusion is as logical as to come to one. But that is what the Council must do."

"And how long is that going to take?" I pressed, trying to bring everyone back to the original question.

"Hours. Days, perhaps."

"You *do* know we're going to need food, water, rest," Vicky said. "Don't your people ever do *anything* quickly?"

Lilandreth regarded her silently for a moment, maybe with amusement, maybe with consternation.

"Why should we? We have no pressure of time. This world is comfortable, we live well." She straddled the same formation that Hachette had been sitting on, confirming that it was indeed

Predecessor furniture and not their idea of art. "If we make no decision at all and simply keep you here, then you will be treated well. You would want for nothing and, in time, would be given land of your own."

"Some of us have families back home," Top said, though her voice lacked the conviction I would have expected from one of the crew who actually *did* have a pressing reason to go back.

"You give much weight to this, still. Mating and offspring and their importance."

"And you don't?" I asked her, a little surprised. The Resscharr on Yfingam had lived in family groups.

"Neither will you or your people, in time. You still act on instincts gained when you were wandering the plains, hunting and gathering, honed when you worked the first farms, when the only guarantor against senescence was a large family to take care of you when you became old and feeble. But your technology is already such that you've extended your lifespans to centuries. The only thing standing between you and effective immortality is your memories."

I shook my head. I considered myself well-read, but I wasn't sure what she was talking about. Hachette, by contrast, obviously was.

"The human brain," he told us, either to show how smart he was or because he could tell how clueless we were, "can only record so much in its memory before the whole system starts to break down. We're seeing it now even, when the oldest people around are only two hundred years old. They're mostly very rich people, because they were the first ones to be able to afford the anti-aging treatments, so they've managed to cope by transplanting cloned memory cells and taking nanotech injections to repair the damage." He shook his head. "That's only a stop-gap measure, though. It'll get them another few decades, a century at the most. I guess they're hoping someone will figure something out before then."

"Or someone already has," Lilandreth suggested. "Being able to read memories into digital files and store them is something one of your researchers has no doubt perfected or will soon."

"That's what you do?" I blinked, considering the idea. "But what do you do with it once you record it? Keep it in a library and experience it when you get nostalgic?"

The sound she made was akin to a bird chirping, and I intuited it was the closest thing the Predecessors had to laughter.

"We implant the digital storage into our brain stems," she explained, tapping a long, dexterous finger against the base of her skull. "And not just our own memories. We can access the memories of others, or learn skills by uploading them to the storage devices. Which was how I learned your language, though I required a further enhancement to my vocal cords before I could actually speak it."

"They implanted something in your vocal cords in the time between us Transitioning into this system and our ship landing?" I stared at her in disbelief. I'd always thought of Commonwealth medical tech as nearly magical, but even a simple implant took days or sometimes weeks to heal and be useful.

"It's a comfort to have the memories," she went on as if she hadn't heard the question. "Even though they do lose the emotional attachment after a few centuries. I remember what it was like when we felt as if we had to fill the galaxy with life, like we were truly the lords of creation."

"Wait a second," Vicky interrupted, catching that at the same time as I did. "You were around before the Skrela? But that would make you..."

"Sixteen thousand years old," Lilandreth confirmed. "Those are memories I'm just as happy not to connect with emotionally, the time when the Skrela came. The fear, the chaos, the confusion. Those were dark days."

I didn't say anything, *couldn't* say anything. Sixteen *thousand* years old.

"Are all of you that old?" Top wondered.

"No, very few. Most of us who were around back then were killed in the war. And there were others who fled in the opposite direction, to the next spiral arm, determined to keep up our way of life. Many of the oldest of us went with them...though we had not yet developed the gateway then."

"Then how did they get there?"

"They took the Transition Line outward. Before they severed them."

"You can *do* that?" I blurted. "You can actually cut a Transition Line?"

"We can no longer," she admitted, "not with the technological tools left to us. To do so required creating multiple singularities and we have not the facilities left to even create the microscopic ones to power our ships anymore." She shifted her balance on the furniture and made a gesture I took for dismissal. "The rest of us...the old ones who survived...came out here past the dead zone in the Transition Lines using the gateways. And now, here on Decision, there are only three of us from that time. The other two lead the Substantiation and the Denial, and the rest, the younger...they follow them blindly, having never experienced a universe where we were the unchallenged masters."

"There's something I don't understand," Vicky said. "The other Resscharr, the ones who gave up and stayed on places like Yfingam...why haven't you done anything to help them? None of them were even as old as you. They probably don't have that digital memory shit you were talking about, so they can't live past a few hundred years, right? Why don't you go give them a boost? They're your people."

"The Substantiation wishes to do so, but they can't without the agreement of the Denial. We all took an oath when we arrived here, that none of us will take action that could affect all of us without the consent of all, unless our survival is directly threatened by the Skrela."

"And nothing forced you to do that until we got here," I put in.

"Which is another reason the Substantiation welcomed your arrival. And to some extent, so do I."

"I thought you weren't allowed to have an opinion."

"I'm not. But it has been too long and I would welcome a change. This planet is named Decision, after all. It would be pleasant if we made one."

"Can you let us speak to our ship?" Hachette asked her. "Or is that something both sides would have to agree on too?"

"That was done simply as a precaution. If you would give me your word that you won't attempt violence, I will allow you to speak to your vessel."

A muscle twitched in Hachette's cheek, perhaps a sign of internal struggle about whether he should promise anything of the sort. But finally, he nodded.

"You have my word."

Lilandreth said nothing, simply stared into the near distance for a moment, then turned her attention back to us.

"It is done."

Hachette's eyes narrowed, doubt written across his face, but he touched his earbud.

"*Orion*, this is Colonel Hachette." We couldn't hear the reply, but his eyes lit up. "Yes, Captain Nance, we're fine. The Predecessors are debating what to do about our presence." He snorted. "Yes, they might kill us. But they also might help us. I'm keeping the good thought, since there's not a damned thing we can do about it either way. Just sit tight, and if we're here much longer, I'm going to have you lower down some food for us."

Hachette turned back to Lilandreth, smiling.

"Thank you," he began, but she wasn't listening. Her eyes were unfocused again, as they were when she'd been asking to unlock our comms. I took that to mean she had some sort of implant communication device, either hooked up to her aural nerves or maybe just squirting information directly into her brain like those memory boosters.

She jumped up from the seat without warning, abruptly enough that I jumped as well, falling into a defensive stance out of instinct. Lilandreth looked around as if she'd forgotten where she was, or that we were there.

"Our early warning sensors have alerted us to multiple Transitions at the outer edge of the system."

My first thought was Zan-Thint. The nosy bastard could have followed us out here, maybe because he didn't trust us or maybe because he'd changed his mind and wanted to get rid of us away from prying eyes. If that was the case, he was in for a big surprise when the Predecessors got their hands on him.

"We can't be sure yet, but our initial readings indicate that it is at least a thousand Skrela motherships."

Zan-Thint faded from my thoughts, along with any worries I had about winding up stuck on this world forever or even the Denial killing us. They wouldn't live long enough to make their decision.

The Skrela were here, and we were all dead.

[20]

I didn't know the name of the Denial leader, wouldn't have been able to pick her out from any of the other Predecessors, but she was the first of them who spoke to us in their language. It was eerie, primal, sounds from a lineage no human had ever seen until the Predecessors had come along and scooped some of us up for their experiments. Hoots and high-pitched chattering, clucks, and other sounds I had no name for, directed at us though we couldn't understand them.

Dwight could, though.

"Her name is Porotel," he informed us, "and she's the leader of the Denial, the only one here older than Lilandreth. She's telling you that you can go. They're going to put your ship back in orbit and allow you to leave, since the damage is done. She says you brought the Skrela down on them by your presence, but there's no point in you dying as well."

The square where Lilandreth had brought us was within sight of the *Orion*...though given how tall the ship jutted into the air, almost anywhere in the city would be in sight of her. The primary star was setting, but the courtyard didn't seem dark and I couldn't have said why. There was a diffuse glow enveloping the city, not coming from any particular place, just everywhere somehow. It might have come from the surface of the buildings for all I knew. But the light cast no shadows, making the gathered throng of Predecessors seem ghostly and likely to fade away any moment.

Which was very appropriate given the circumstances. One thing had changed, though. The two groups no longer maintained a separation. They stood shoulder to shoulder, and I suspected that soon they'd be wearing identical clothing styles as well. There was nothing like a common foe and impending death to bring people together, even if those people weren't human.

"The computer has told you the truth," Lilandreth confirmed, as if there'd been a possibility Dwight would lie to us about the translation. "You will be allowed to leave us."

"We don't have enough fuel to leave," I blurted, earning a dirty look from Hachette. But hell, someone had to say it. I was as upset as anyone about the Skrela showing up, but if there was a chance we could get a tankful of metallic hydrogen out of these people, we shouldn't turn down the chance.

"We are aware of your fuel situation," she told me. "We can resupply you before we tow your spacecraft back to orbit."

"We're not going," Hachette declared, jaw set in the very image of stubbornness.

"We're not?" Top repeated, staring at him wide-eyed. I wasn't sure if I'd ever seen her shocked until that moment.

"I don't know whether the Denialists or whatever you call them are right about us bringing the Skrela to your system," Hachette went on, "but if there's a possibility that we're responsible, there's no way we're just going to leave you here to deal with them yourself."

I realized that my mouth was hanging open and I forced myself to close it.

"Your technology is primitive," Lilandreth pointed out. "You would not last an hour against the Skrela."

"Yeah, what she said," I echoed, still facing the colonel. "I've fought these damned things before, sir. That was just a few hundred of their foot soldiers against a couple hundred Drop-Troopers and we *still* lost people. She said there are a thousand of their motherships out there with God knows how many troops on each of them. What the hell are we going to do against *that* except get ourselves killed?"

"We've seen the defenses they have in this place," Hachette said with more confidence than he had any right to feel. "The Predecessors will thin out the herd. We'll take on what's left."

"It is true," Lilandreth admitted, speaking slowly and deliberately, "that our defenses will attrit their numbers considerably. But that has always been the case. The Skrela overwhelmed us because their numbers are nearly unlimited. They produce themselves with nanotechnological factories inside the pods they scattered throughout the galaxy and there are more such fabricators in each of their motherships."

"Then you need to go after the motherships," Hachette said. "If you destroy their fabricators, you cut them off at the source."

One of the others replied to that, apparently getting a translation in real time. His hooting and chirping went on for a good thirty seconds before Dwight relayed it to us.

"The male is Tamlannd and he's the Elder of the Substantiation. Apparently, only the Elders are allowed to speak. He says that committing their vessels to destroying the Skrela motherships would leave everyone on the planet open to attack by the Skrela ground forces."

"You can disable their drives," Top said, and I wasn't sure if she'd decided to take Hachette's part or if the logical part of her brain was rebelling against the train of the argument. "Just like you did to us."

"They don't need drives," Lilandreth said. "Their drop pods are designed to survive a fall from orbit. Of everyone here, only the three of us remember fighting them. If our technology alone could have defeated them we would not be on this world. and neither would you."

I was still pissed at Hachette for volunteering our services in a suicide mission, but what Lilandreth said pissed me off even more.

"So you'd rather just give up and let them kill you than try to fight back?" I demanded, spreading my hands. "Maybe we won't make a difference, but you said it yourself—only three of you have even been there when anyone fought a war. Every one of us..." I pointed back at the *Orion*. "...have been in the military for most of our adult lives. We've all seen war, all fought for our lives. Maybe we don't have the technology you do, but we're the best you've got."

"What the fuck are you *doing*?" Vicky hissed beside my ear. "We don't owe these assholes anything, much less fighting a whole army of Skrela for them!"

"I know that," I insisted, "but they're just going to lay down and die!"

"We came here for their help," Hachette reminded us, with the demeanor of a disappointed father. "Are we going to just take their fuel and run like cowards in the face of the enemy?" He jabbed a finger toward Lilandreth. "Fill up our tanks with metallic hydrogen and we'll take this fight to your enemies."

Maybe it would be letting down my self-appointed surrogate father, but I was half-hoping that Lilandreth would say no, tell us we had to leave. Instead, she hooted and chittered at the other two Elders for a good minute, and whatever she said left them quiet for a few seconds before they each replied in turn.

"Dwight?" I asked, impatient at his lack of a translation.

"They're discussing your involvement," he said, his sigh

affected, as if he was trying to convey to me what a stupid question it was. "Lilandreth is presenting the argument for each side. I believe the Substantiation is all for you helping out, but the Denial doubts you could be of any help."

Bastards. Not that I wanted to fight their battle for them, but I was pretty damned sure that, super technology or not, they didn't have any fighting force that could match the Fleet Marine Corps.

I was about to butt in and give them my opinion of their capabilities and leadership when the cacophony ended and Lilandreth switched back to English.

"It has been decided," she said, and I wondered if she meant the question of whether we could help in their defense or the bigger debate of whether the Creator had cursed them or was simply testing them. "Though your technology is primitive, your experience is unarguable...and our fate will be the same whether you are wrong and we follow you, or you are wrong and we ignore you. Therefore, logic dictates we only have one chance of survival—to behave as if you're correct and allow you to lead us in the battle against the Skrela."

"Well, shit," Vicky said, hopefully low enough that Lilandreth didn't hear it.

"Excellent!" Hachette exulted, clapping his hands as if he were huddling a sports team in the middle of the field. "I'll have my people prepare for refueling..."

"If you are fighting for us," Lilandreth interrupted him, "we must give you the best chance at victory. Our technicians will be installing a gravitic power source on your ship, one which will not requiring refueling, as well as scalar energy weapons. It is no guarantee that you will survive, but it's the best we can do for you."

"We have time for that?" Hachette asked, practically beaming at the thought.

"We have days," Lilandreth said. "The Skrela are in no hurry. They'll mass as many of their insertion ships as they can and attempt to overwhelm us." She turned to me. "You have spoken of your armored battlesuits. These are not something we have used, but if they take a power source, I am certain we could improve them."

Now it was my turn to salivate. A Vigilante with a Predecessor reactor and those energy beamers that the Resscharr on Yfingam had used was a prospect no Drop-Trooper could turn down. I looked a question to Hachette and he nodded.

"Tell Solano I said you're in charge of the upgrades." There was an indulgent twinkle in his eye. "And if you can think up anything else they can stick in the suits, make sure you ask."

I had to grin, despite everything. The thought of ordering Solano around was almost enough to make me forget we were all going to die.

———

"I feel like I'm watching someone else have sex with my wife," Warrant Officer Frank Spagnuolo said, hands running through his short-cut hair as he watched the Predecessor technicians take apart *his* Vigilantes.

Or at least, that was how the ship's armorer thought about the battlesuits. I'd only spoken to the man a couple of times since we joined the mission, mostly because I'd, unhappily, only had the chance to wear my suit a couple of times, but he'd always struck me as a territorial sort, like most armorers.

I couldn't blame him for being worried. Only one of the suits was mine, but it still bothered me seeing them ripped open, their guts pulled out like a deer hung up for skinning. I'd never actually seen the isotope reactor yanked out of a Vigilante. That was something done only in the safety of a shielded workshop by remotely-controlled waldos. Not today. The Predecessors hauled the things around as if they were dirty laundry and not a potentially deadly bundle of radioactive isotopes, tossing them to the ground to make room for the...whatever the things were.

I wanted to ask them what the meter-long silver ovoids were, but I didn't want to distract them from their job. I didn't have any trouble identifying the things they were installing along the right arms of the suits, replacing the plasma guns. They were bigger, longer, but the other details were the same as the hand weapons the Resscharr nobility had used to maintain control on Yfingam. I'd shot the things and *been* shot at by them, and while they didn't exactly make a plasma gun seem anemic by comparison, they had a longer range and more penetration, and I was willing to bet they'd been perfected against the Skrela thousands of years ago.

"What do the Predecessors call those things?" I'd asked Dwight earlier.

"Energy cannons," he'd replied unhelpfully.

"But how do they work?" I'd insisted, hoping to get at least a cursory understanding of the theory.

"The closest thing you have to them would be the proton cannons on your starships. They aren't exactly the same thing, but close enough for you to grasp."

That had sounded vaguely insulting, but I hadn't pressed him on it.

"Look at the bright side," I told Spagnuolo. "It could be worse. You could be the Engineering officer on the *Orion*."

I motioned upward and the pinch-faced troll of a man followed my gesture. The starship was one of the suits writ large, surrounded by floating work pods, each of the things hovering on columns of superheated air, their waldos hauling out huge sections of the ship's fusion reactor. The hull gleamed in the morning light and I squinted, shielding my eyes from it.

They felt as if they were full of grit since none of us had slept last night.

If it had been a Fleet engineering team tearing the ship apart, I would have judged the process might take weeks at a minimum, maybe months. Lilandreth had promised it would be finished in forty-eight hours and I hoped to God she hadn't mistranslated human measurements of time.

"This makes me nervous," Spagnuolo confided, leaning closer, maybe so the other Drop-Troopers standing around watching the procedure wouldn't hear him, "us counting on these freaky-looking aliens for all our power and weapons."

"What?" I asked, shaking my head. "You think they're going to sabotage us? That the stuff won't work?" I was being as quiet as Spagnuolo, but more because I was worried about the Predecessor techs hearing us. I didn't know if they had translators, but I didn't know they didn't either.

"Naw, that wouldn't make any sense," the armorer admitted. "It's their asses right alongside ours. What I'm worried about is, what if they break down? We sure as hell can't repair them."

I chuckled, motioning expansively at the city around us.

"Spags," I told him, hoping he wouldn't mind me using his nickname, "look around. Their ships, these buildings, everything you see, it was all built over ten thousand years ago. I'm not worried too much about it breaking down."

"I guess you got a point there, sir."

"Alvarez," Captain Solano said, stalking up to me, looking as antsy as Spagnuolo but more self-important about it, "do we have an ETA on when the work will be finished on the suits?"

"Good morning to you, too, Chip," I said with an insincere smile, hoping this time that Solano *did* take offense at my use of his nickname. I motioned at the row of Vigilantes, a squad's worth, being closed up by the Predecessor techs. "This first bunch is done. You want to have one of your squads test them out?"

He eyed the things uncertainly.

"You're in charge of this upgrade," he said. "Maybe you should be the first to give it a shakedown run."

I very carefully did *not* bust out a huge grin, despite an intense desire to do so. Solano was as easy to manipulate as some of the adults at the group homes where I'd spent my childhood.

"You heard the man, Spags," I said, nodding to the armorer. And then I finally did let that grin break through...it wouldn't be contained. "Get my suit ready to go. And whatever you do, don't tell Captain Sandoval. She'd kill me for not letting her be the first to try it out."

[21]

"And you say these weapons are the same as the Resscharr used against us?" Matis asked, raising the energy rifle to his shoulder, keeping it pointed in a safe direction, at the dirt mounds our engineers had pushed up as a target range outside the city.

"They are," I said, fighting an urge to nod. He wouldn't see me inside my Vigilante. Or rather, my Vigilante *Type B Modified* as Spags insisted on calling the enhanced suits. I'd been walking around in it since morning, trying to get used to the differences.

There weren't *too* many. The thing still had the same style interface, the same jacks plugged into my implant sockets, the same targeting reticle. But the jumpjet readouts were completely changed...they had to be. Before, the suits had a very limited jump capability, for the simple reason that the reactor would only put out so much energy and the jets could only run for so long without overheating. Not anymore. We still couldn't jump very high—there's a limit to how much energy output even the Predecessors could fit into a three-meter tall, armored suit— but we could stay up for a lot longer with no worries about overheating or shattering the turbine blades.

And, of course, the rangefinders were different. The plasma gun, for all that it was a devastating weapon, had a fairly limited range due to thermal blooming. This energy cannon thing did *not*. I was using all those differences as an excuse to be inside my suit because, God's honest truth, I'd just missed being in the thing. That, and I was nervous as hell about Matis and his platoon firing those damned rifles around me even in armor, much less with just utility fatigues between myself and atomization.

"First rank!" Sgt Motte barked, standing off to the side of the firing range. "Take positions! Standing, unsupported! Prepare to fire one round on my command!" The Force Recon NCO paused and looked at me, his eyebrows knitted in confusion beneath his helmet visor. "Do these things have a safety, sir?"

"Keeping our booger hooks off the bang switch seems to be the only safety the Predecessors believe in," I told him.

"Fucking wonderful," he muttered. "Making sure to keep your finger off the trigger, take aim at your target!"

The targets weren't much, just some empty cargo crates we'd hauled out of the *Orion*, but they'd do well enough for a familiarization fire. The front line raised their weapons with a little hesitation, and I could understand that. They'd *just* gotten used to the rifles we made for them and now they were getting something totally different.

"Fire!"

The effect of eight of those rifles firing at once is hard to describe. Static electricity didn't just fill the air; it bloated it, close to erupting, sparks crackling over every metal surface, and a wash of heat I could feel even through my armor washed back over us. Lightning flared and my helmet visor went a shade darker to compensate. Where the crates had been, nothing was left except a crawling haze of white smoke, and the dirt behind them had crystallized to black glass. Matis' people were muttering to each other, some staring at the weapons in wide-eyed awe. Even Motte was taken aback, and it took him a moment before he could speak again.

"All right, keep those things pointed downrange! First rank, sling your weapons and file off the firing line! Second rank, take their places!"

"That's damned impressive."

I turned at the voice in my ear, knowing who it was and knowing they had to be close enough to have watched the demonstration. Top lumbered up in her newly-modified suit, and I laughed at the sergeant-major's stripes and rockers stenciled on her chest and arm.

"Advertising yourself as a high-value target, Top?" I asked.

"The Skrela wouldn't know our ranks from shit smears on a cow's ass," she said, snorting a dismissal. "I figure if this is our last fight, I'm going out in style."

A warning flashed in my Heads-Up Display, and I turned to the north, to the skyscraper that was the *Orion*, jutting above the highest walls of the city.

"Everyone keep your weapons pointed downrange!" Motte insisted as the rumble began to reach us.

It wasn't the whining crackle of atmospheric jets, nor the deeper-chested thunder roll of rockets. It was something totally alien to me, to all of us, a shaking in the ground and a quavering in the air, as the Predecessor ships surrounded the *Orion* and the green glow of their tractor beams enveloped her.

"Why can't she take off on her own?" Motte wondered. "Didn't they put that weird alien shit in her?"

Top answered, which was a good thing, because I surely didn't know a thing about starship propulsion systems.

"They couldn't give her a gravitic drive like their ships." The articulated left hand of her suit raised, pointing at the green cylinder shapes. "They'd have had to rebuild her from the ground up. They just replaced her fusion reactor with one of their singularity things, one they had lying around as a replacement part. They can't make them here, not anymore. She still uses a fusion drive, but now, she can pretty much fuse *anything* because the process is different...the reactor can squeeze whatever, liquid, solid, gas...and turn it into plasma, accelerate it out the drive bell. Metallic hydrogen is what they gave us because it has the largest delta-V, but in a pinch, we could use seawater in those tanks."

"That'll come in handy," Motte opined. "In the unlikely event we live through this."

"Why so fatalistic?" I asked him. "You saw what those guns can do. Your Force Recon platoon has the same weapons now, and our suits have even bigger ones. As long as the *Orion,* along with the Predecessor fleet, can take out those motherships, I think we can take these guys."

I felt unreasonably buoyant, though I wasn't sure if it was the demonstration of the firepower the Vergai were wielding or my hopes rising with the *Orion.* If Vicky had been listening in instead of coordinating with the Resscharr about how to best array their ground forces, I was sure she would have kicked my metaphorical ass and told me to get real. But having the Vergai depending on me for leadership gave me a duty to believe we could win.

I guess.

The *Orion* was already out of sight, propelled up through the atmosphere at unbelievable speed by the gravitic drive ships. In just hours, she'd be out past the orbit of their moon, towed by the Predecessor vessels. Out into the midst of the Skrela fleet. I noticed Top still staring into the sky and switched to a private network with her.

"Are you worried about him?"

I couldn't see her face, but I read the surprise in her voice. "Him who?"

"Come on, Top." I grinned, the tables turned. Ellen Campbell was well over a hundred years old and had been a Marine for much of that life, and getting the advantage of her in a conversation was like winning the World Cup. "Maybe I'm a baby compared to you, but I'm not a complete moron. You know exactly who and what I mean. Are you worried about him?"

Motte was running the next squad through the familiarization fire and the thundercracks of the weapons discharging was muted by my armor, something far away, while this conversation was close and much more meaningful.

"I'll answer your question with my own," Top said, cagey as always. "Do you worry about Sandoval when you go into combat together?"

"Every time. But don't tell her I said that. It's easier now than it used to be, back when we were in separate outfits, and I didn't even know if she'd lived through a battle until afterward. At least the way things are on this mission, we can watch each other's six."

"Yeah, that's a luxury I don't have," she admitted. "It's my own fault for getting involved with my fucking commanding officer. You'd think I'd know better after this long, but once we got cut off from the Cluster, things got...more difficult. It's one thing to never call your family because you don't have much in common with them, but it's another entirely to not even be *able* to send them a message, to face the possibility of never seeing them or your friends ever again." Top paused, a verbal shrug I could almost see. "For me, that's not a huge deal. You get to be my age, you've left behind a lot of family and friends through the years. But Marcus...he's good at projecting the image of a hard-as-nails, unfeeling Intelligence colonel, but he has a family. He talks about his younger brother constantly, how proud he is of him. Everyone needs someone, and he's in a uniquely lonesome position."

"I get that. I really do." I thought about Captain Covington and how isolated the man had seemed, how ready he'd been to sacrifice his life for the mission when the time came. He'd been like a more competent version of Hachette. "I guess I shouldn't be the one to ask if you think you can handle this. You've got a little experience on me."

She laughed softly.

"I have grandchildren older than you. And I'll be honest, I haven't seen them in a long time. Hadn't thought about it, because I figured they'd always be there when I had the time to look them up. I probably shouldn't have waited so long. It's one thing to live this long, Alvarez, but it's another to actually learn something from it. And if I have, it's that there's always enough time to put off relationships, love, all the stuff that makes us human. Until there's no time anymore, until you just run out of it."

"Like the Skipper," I murmured.

"Like the Skipper," she agreed. She waved at the firing line, switched out again now. "I can handle this for a while. Go talk to your wife. While you still have time."

———

"I don't know if that's a good idea," Vicky said, gesticulating with her suit's left hand as if she and Lilandreth were debating spring fashion decisions.

I'd flown back into the city from the training range, and the whole experience had been surreal, like one of those dreams where you're floating above everything, not like a bird but more like you've got your own magic carpet. And since any sufficiently advanced technology is indistinguishable from magic, I guess I did. And yes, I'd found that quote in one of the books Top and Vicky had forced me to read during the trip.

The city was just as mind-bending from above as it was from inside, none of the curves or rises or dips making any intuitive sense from human architectural standards. Was it just because they weren't human, or might it just be a reflection of their advanced materials technology and the effects of thousands or even *tens* of thousands of years of that on art and design? Would we build this kind of shit in a thousand years?

Would we even be around in a thousand years?

I landed a few dozen meters from where Vicky was speaking to Lilandreth, towering over her in the suit, which had to be a little satisfying given how intimidating the Predecessors were physically.

"Our soldiers have always worked in conjunction with our force field installations," Lilandreth insisted. "Your own Marines would be better protected if they also fought from behind the shields."

"All due respect," Vicky said, the strained patience behind her tone telling me she wasn't actually giving much respect to the idea, "but you've never had much success against the Skrela on the ground, have you?"

"We did not. But logic dictates..."

"There's logic," I interrupted, "and then there's the rules of combat. Movement is life. We have a military tradition full of fixed defensive positions being overrun. And while none of them had gravitic force fields, they also weren't facing suicidal alien scorpion horses carrying plasma cannons."

"I feel that I must yield to your experience," Lilandreth said, bowing her head. "But I do not know if our soldiers have the training or ability to fight such a battle."

"Do you even keep a standing army?" I wondered.

"We have volunteers. Adults who have no pre-adolescent

children. None of them have any experience, but we have, as I said, access to the memories of others." She tapped at her skull demonstratively. "We implant these volunteers with the memories of soldiers who trained and fought ten thousand years ago, during the war."

I winced. That sounded like a great shortcut, but the problem was, they were being given memories from the losing side, absorbing strategies that had lost them the whole Cluster and left them fragmented and nearly extinct.

"How about this?" Vicky suggested. "You have underground shelters for your civilians, right?"

"Some. Those will only be occupied by parents with children, however. There is not room for all. The other adults will be given weapons and put under the charge of the soldiers at three key strongpoints protected by force field barriers."

"Aren't there force field barriers around the underground shelters?"

"One of them. The largest. The others, it was hoped the Skrela might not detect if they weren't shielded."

"Could you fit all your families into the largest shelter?"

"It would not be comfortable," Lilandreth said, "but it *is* possible."

"Do it, then. And gather all your other people around that shelter, armed, with all the power you can generate feeding that one force field."

Lilandreth didn't reply for a moment, and when she did, her cadence was slow, hesitant, as if she were unsure of the words the translation memory was giving her.

"You have a saying, if I am understanding it correctly, about putting all of your eggs in one basket."

"It fits your strength," Vicky insisted. "And ours. You have one fixed point to defend, while we can attack the enemy from the sides, the flanks. They have one target they'll be focused on, and that's you. It makes them vulnerable."

"We would be entirely dependent on you to prevent us from being overrun."

"You would. But you've already said you expected to lose this battle. And if our ships can't stop theirs, it won't matter what we do." Vicky's words were cold and calculating and I winced at the brutal frankness of them. But she was also correct, and Lilandreth couldn't deny it.

"This is so. Very well, I will pass these directions on to the leader of the soldiers."

"Where will you be during the battle, Lilandreth?" I asked her. I expected her to be the leader of the soldiers, given the seniority of her position.

"I will be in the bunker," she said, surprising me, "with my mate and my children."

She walked away, as if that were the natural end of the conversation, and I stared after her.

"She's ten *thousand* years old," Vicky said, giving voice to my thoughts, "and living on one of the last outposts of a dying race, and she's still having children."

"Yeah." I shook my head, trying to clear the whole business from my thoughts. "Have you talked to Solano?"

"As little as possible. Why?"

"I've been trying to coordinate where the Vergai and the Force Recon platoon will fit into our defensive gameplan and not getting much feedback. I think he's pretty much telling us to figure it out on our own."

"Fucker," she muttered. "We obviously can't hold them in a static defense. They'll be way too vulnerable, even with a force field to cover our asses." Vicky chuckled. "And I can't even express how stupid I feel using the term 'force field.' It's like I stepped into one of those cheesy sci-fi movies they used to show at the rec center back on Inferno."

"Look around. We're living in one of those cheesy movies."

"*Touché*," she acknowledged. "How good do you think the Vergai are at running and gunning?"

"About as good as you'd expect them to be. They've had a few weeks of real training." An idea flickered in the back of my brain. "What we need is cover and concealment. What about the city? It's confusing as hell for us, and I can't imagine it would be any less mind-fucking to the Skrela. I don't think they have as much to fuck with in the way of brains, but I don't think they're going to be able to make head or tail of it."

"True. But can *we*?"

"We can if we plant beacons at set points and guide Matis and Lt. Campea with our comms," I suggested, my brain working about half a second behind my mouth. "I bet Lilandreth could even get us something that the Skrela couldn't jam."

"I'm liking this more and more," Vicky told me. "But we can't just have them hide inside the city and hope the Skrela wander through. How do we draw them in?"

"That part's easy," I told her, chuckling ruefully. "We give them something to chase." I waved my left hand demonstratively.

"Us."

[22]

"This is where I want you to set up your initial positions," I told Matis, motioning to an alcove...somewhere. I checked the transponder again and saw that we were four hundred meters from the nearest entrance. "Get your people behind cover, but remember, even with the new body armor you're wearing, it might just be concealment instead of cover. The plasma guns those things carry hit hard."

Matis nodded, touching the unfamiliar chest piece over his fatigues. The Predecessors had run off enough for his platoon and the Force Recon troops in just an hour, sized correctly too, all from a long-distance scan. How the hell had these people been chased out of the Cluster?

"Lt. Campea." I turned toward the Force Recon platoon leader, who stood beside Matis, helmet in hand. He looked painfully young, though he was probably only three or four years younger than me. Promotions took longer since the war. "You know where the Predecessor techs set up the force field generators?"

"Yes, sir," the man clipped off, his depilated scalp gleaming in the light shining from, seemingly, everywhere. "I have the locations programmed into my HUD."

"Good. Think of this as the biggest, deadliest game of tag you ever played, and those generators are home base. If you're getting surrounded, cut off, outnumbered, you run to the closest one of those damned things and you call for us." I motioned to Vicky. "We'll clear them out long enough for you to get out. And Campea, do *not* forget that you have the Vergai platoon attached to you. If I find out you didn't do your Goddamned best to keep them alive, I'll be very cross with you."

"Yes, sir! I'll treat them like my own family." He shrugged. "Well, better than that, I hope. I don't get along that well with my family."

"It must be a Marine thing," Vicky said over our private net.

"You both know the plan," I told them. "Now make sure every one of your people know it. Matis, remember what I told you. Everyone down to the most junior private, just in case all the others get killed."

Matis grunted an assent, though his face paled, either at the thought of his own death or the idea that he could lose that many people. Campea pulled him aside and the two of them gathered their platoons together for the briefing.

Good idea. If nothing else, the Vergai could learn a lesson from what questions the Marines asked.

"Cameron Alvarez." It was Lilandreth. There was no IFF transponder associated with her comm signal, but the voice was unmistakable. "I wanted to let you know, our fleet and your *Orion* have reached the enemy ships. The battle is commencing. I can send the feed from our ships and reconnaissance drones to your helmets if you like."

"Just mine and Vicky's," I said, not wanting the rest of the troops to see if the *Orion* got taken out. "And Top's...Sgt.-Major Campbell."

"It will be as you say."

And there it was. It didn't fill my whole helmet display, just the pop-up section designed for video feeds, but all I had to do was stare at it for a few seconds and it grew to fill my vision. I don't know how the hell they put together the imagery, because there was no way one drone or even one ship could have taken it. Computer enhancement, maybe, but it had to be done in next to no time. *Magic.*

The Skrela weren't a fleet, they were a damned *swarm.* The motherships were the same twisted, eye-shedding, inhuman shapes that made Predecessor architecture seem homey and familiar by comparison, the same ones we'd seen after we'd transitioned the Corridor. They didn't try to maneuver, didn't try to dodge, just moved in some sort of formation I'd never seen from spaceships. It wasn't globular, wasn't starburst, wasn't a cube...but it *was* a formation, I could tell that much by how each ship maintained its distance from every other.

They weren't propelled by the same sort of gravity drive that the Predecessors used. They couldn't accelerate nearly as fast, for one thing, and for another, they had exhaust...of a sort. It wasn't the starfire flare of a fusion drive, but it did glow in the blackness, each exhaust lighting up the twists and curves along its own hull. Curiosity made me want to ask Dwight about the drive, but I remembered he was out on the *Orion.* But...

"Lilandreth," I called, hoping she was still monitoring the comm net, "what's the lightspeed delay for this signal?"

"There is none," she said as matter-of-factly as if she'd just told me that it was going to rain tomorrow morning.

And I could either waste time trying to get her to explain to me how *that* was possible, or I could just live with it. *Magic.*

"Can I access the ship's comms?" I asked her.

"You're already synched with our transmissions. Simply use

your native comm nets and the signal will run across our transceivers."

"Thanks." I switched off the call to her and adjusted it to the ship. *Not* to the bridge. Neither Hachette nor Nance needed me joggling the elbow right now. "Dwight, can you hear me?"

"Clearly, Captain Alvarez."

And *he* seemed to accept the instantaneous communications as easily as Lilandreth had.

"Can the weapons on the Skrela ships penetrate the Predecessor shielding?"

"Not one on one. If that were so, the Predecessors would have fallen in days, not thousands of years. But if enough concentrate their fire on one Predecessor ship, they can overload the shields." He paused. "Of course, the *Orion* only has portable force field projectors installed, which won't be as effective as the shielding from the onboard singularity of a Resscharr vessel."

It took me a moment to find the *Orion* and the Predecessor fleet...there were dozens of the green cylinders, each smaller than the Commonwealth ship but glowing verdant in the dark. Yet they were a pinprick compared to the Skrela and the whole thing looked hopeless to me.

"Here," Dwight narrated as if he were the computer guide on one of the interactive history programs we were given to study at OCS, "is where the Predecessors have concealed their stealth force field modules."

"Their what?" I blinked. No one had mentioned that to me.

"They're isolationist," he told me, "not stupid. They were prepared for a Skrela incursion."

What I assumed to be the force field modules lit up like the glowing red eyes of predators hidden in the dark forest, and between them, a green web of gravitic energy stretched out across the stars...and where it touched, Skrela ships burst like the insect hives they were. Fire spread along the entire length and breadth of their formation, dozens of the massive mother-ships imploding in white nova flares, and the thought that this whole thing might end before we had to fire a shot passed like a fleeting ray of warmth in the cold depths of my imagination.

But the green webs, while they seemed to be everywhere, still had gaps. I guess not even the Predecessors could have sealed the entire region of space with gravitic energy, though it would have been nice for us if they could. Maybe it would have caused a black hole or something equally destructive, but I would have been willing to risk it if anyone had asked my opinion. Because Skrela motherships passed through those gaps unharmed, dozens more, *hundreds*, and if a third of the swarm was destroyed in that cataclysmic eruption of white, what was left was enough to raze a world.

"Jesus God." That was Vicky, and I should have expected her to be watching, but for some reason, her voice startled me. She said nothing else, but there was nothing else to say. For the first time, we both had a sense of how the Skrela had driven out the Predecessors. A third or even more of their fleet had been taken out in seconds and they pushed on as if it meant nothing.

"They still have to get through our ships," Top said, her voice flat, as if she wasn't convinced of it herself. I wondered if I should have told Lilandreth to send the footage to her...but she was more of an adult than I'd ever be, and she needed to know what we were expecting.

She was right, though, the battle hadn't even been joined. When the Predecessor ships surged forward, an ice-cold stab of fear went through my chest, and I thought they were going to ignore the *Orion* and their promise to follow Hachette's leadership. But the formation they fell into was a classical Commonwealth 3DV, a cylindrical cone with the *Orion* at the point, the Predecessor ships spreading out thousands of klicks away from each other at the base.

And when that formation opened fire, it rivalled the web of destruction from the defense grid. Dozens of motherships were ripped apart by the cone of gravitic beams and energy cannon blasts, as well as by twinkling green stars streaking out from what had been the missile launch bays on the *Orion*.

"What are those?" I asked Dwight. I'd nearly forgotten I was on the line with him. "Those green glowing things the *Orion* is shooting?"

"Collapsar torpedoes," he said and then stopped, as if that explained everything.

"And what do they *do*, Dwight?"

"Suffice it to say, each of them creates a microscopic singularity that only lasts a fraction of a second. However, that fraction is enough to bathe its target in all sorts of deadly radiation and rip it apart from gravitational tidal forces."

"That's...handy," Vicky commented dryly.

"It's a shame there was only room for twenty of them on the ship," Dwight agreed.

It was, since each of the weapons took a Skrela mothership with it when it detonated. They were winking out like the stars at sunset...and then they began to shoot back. It was inevitable, of course, but my gut clenched in shock when the barrage of blue fire washed over our fleet. It didn't penetrate, not with the first volley, but the green glow around the Predecessor ships grew brighter and harsher, and I remembered what Dwight had said about the shields on the *Orion* not being quite as strong as those.

The—I guessed I could call it the *Allied* fleet—got off one more devastating barrage before they scattered in a starburst maneuver, each flying off on a different trajectory to keep the

Skrela from focusing their fire on a single point. The *Orion* wasn't quite as agile or quick as the Predecessor ships, but she dropped a spread of the collapsar torpedoes in her wake and a handful of Skrela motherships exploded behind her, providing cover for her withdrawal.

"Over half the enemy fleet has been destroyed," Dwight reported.

"Fuckin' A," I breathed. That incredible mass of ships halved in minutes...the sheer firepower involved in that was simply inconceivable.

"There is a human thing called a 'good-news, bad-news' joke," Dwight went on, "and I'm afraid that was the good news."

"Oh, shit," Vicky said, her tone echoing the sinking feeling in my stomach. "What's the bad news?"

"It will not be enough."

"That was only one engagement!" Top snapped at the AI. "They can winnow through the rest of them; it's just going to take time."

"They can, and I assure you they will," Dwight agreed. "But not before the motherships which are left launch their drop pods. And before you point out to me that the planetary defenses can destroy most of them, yes, they can. I've analyzed the Resscharr defense system and it should be able to attrit ninety percent of the incoming pods."

"Ninety percent sounds pretty damned good to me," I said, still watching the Skrela swarm. It hadn't broken formation, even in the face of fifty percent casualties, hadn't slowed its acceleration.

"Ten percent of the landers will equal out to no fewer than two thousand that will successfully land, each one with ten of their warrior drones inside."

"Oh." I couldn't say anything else to that. Just repeated it. "Oh."

"We have the Intercepts up," Top said, as if she could argue the AI out of its conclusions, "and the assault shuttles, and the drop-ships. They'll provide air support."

"They will. And again, it won't be enough. Your forces on the ground will be faced with approximately twenty thousand Skrela warrior drones. If the fleet was free to give you orbital fire support, that would be enough to make the difference, but they will be engaged with the Skrela swarm for hours."

"What are you trying to do?" Vicky demanded. "Scare us?"

"I'm trying to convey the odds to you. It may and *should* have an effect on your strategy."

"Of course it does," Top replied, something defiant in her tone again. "We're surrounded. That simplifies the problem."

I recognized the quote. Anyone who'd attended Boot would. It was a Marine, of course, United States variety, from a small, regional conflict called the Korean War. I laughed softly and plumbed the depths of my memory.

"Great, now we can shoot at them from every direction."

Top was chuckling too now, which was the best sign that things were, indeed, hopeless, and yet I still took heart from it. But we weren't through, of course. It was Vicky's turn and I wondered what she'd come up with.

"All right," she said, a smile in her voice. "They're on our left, they're on our right, they're in front of us, they're behind us...they can't get away this time."

The chuckles gave way to full-throated laughs and I was glad we were in our suits, because otherwise, Matis and his people might be wondering if we'd gone crazy. Dwight certainly had his own opinions on the matter.

"Humans," he told us, "are a strange species."

"It's not all humans," I assured him. "Just Marines."

"Ooh-rah, Captain," Top said. "Fucking oor-rah. Good old Chesty Puller would be proud."

"I wonder what the Skipper would think."

Top laughed again, though this one was less tinged with bravado and more tenderness.

"He'd be wishing he was here. He was always a sucker for last stands."

[23]

The night sky was on fire.

I watched it with my own eyes, the chest plastron of my Vigilante propped open, letting me get one last breath of fresh air before things kicked off. It was better that way, I think. It gave the whole thing a reality that seeing it in the helmet display would have robbed it of. And anyway, I was tired of watching the battle play out like a documentary recording on virtual reality. I was tired of seeing Predecessor ships destroyed and grinding my teeth at every flash, imagining this one would be the *Orion* buying the farm.

And this part of the battle, I didn't need drones or telescopes or magic Predecessor technology to watch. The defense satellites in orbit, the Intercept cutters, the shuttles were all performing as efficiently as Dwight had predicted. Skrela drop pods were disappearing in flashes of sublimated metal catching fire and turning into plasma, miniature suns lighting up the night in a dome covering the city. I'd finally got around to asking Lilandreth why they didn't have a force field covering the whole city and received a lecture on physics that I hadn't understood one bit of, except that it wouldn't work because it would be too large and likely to collapse and kill us all.

Again, something I might have been willing to risk if anyone had bothered to ask my opinion.

"Captain Alvarez?" I was so used to voices coming through my helmet headphones, having someone talk to me through the open air almost seemed strange. I leaned further out of the chest plastron and saw Matis approaching hesitantly, as if he was afraid to be outside with the show going on in the sky. He wasn't alone in that. None of the Predecessors wandered these streets this night either, either crammed into the central shelter or huddled above it and beneath the force field dome.

"What's up, Matis?" I asked. "Your people in place?"

"They are, yes, sir," he said, nodding.

"Did you get them fed? Did Lt. Campea get those field rations to you?"

We'd been here for hours now, which had required designating a section of the Predecessor floor out of the sightlines of both platoons as a latrine and hoping Lilandreth had been honest about its absorbent qualities. It had also required sharing out rations for everyone. I'd eaten mine an hour ago, but it still sat heavy in my stomach and I wondered if I should visit the latrine myself while I still had the time.

"They did, thank you. Though the taste of your field rations is even stranger than the food you serve on board your ship."

Couldn't argue with him there.

"What's the problem, then?"

"I have been listening to the sound of the battle," he explained, sounding embarrassed to go on. "I wondered if you thought any of the enemy would be able to make it through all... that." He waved at the sky to show me what he meant by "that."

"I'm afraid so, Matis," I said, wishing I could have honestly told him no. Wishing I could bring myself to lie. "There'll be a lot. Thousands." I didn't want to go into the exact number. I needed him cautious, not catatonic. "But remember, they won't be coming after *you*. They won't even know you're here. We'll be leading a few at a time into your ambush. Just concentrate on that."

"I'm trying, sir." He looked at his helmet, held in his hands, possibly seeing his reflection in the half visor. "But I can't help thinking of my wife and my children. I'd hoped to see them again."

"You will, Matis," I said, lying through my teeth. "We'll kick their asses off this planet and fly out of here the conquering heroes. And when you get home, your people will sing songs of how brave you and your troops were."

He smiled, his eyes lighting up, and I felt guilty that he might actually believe the sunshine I was blowing up his ass. I thought about telling him the truth, that we were about to be hip-deep in enemy, but I'd told him what he needed to hear. I was about to try to say something encouraging and badass, something like the Skipper used to say, but I was interrupted by the sound of distant, rumbling crashes echoing through the city.

"Cameron Alvarez, can you hear me?" Lilandreth's voice seemed far away, coming from the speakers inside my suit. I sighed and leaned back inside it.

"I'm here, Lilandreth."

"The first of the Skrela pods have landed at the southern edge of the city, near the river."

"They haven't tried to drop on any of your smaller outposts?" I asked.

"No, not since we pulled all our citizens into the shelters here. You were right...they won't bother with the outposts until they've taken the city."

"Unless," I corrected her. "We're not going to let that happen."

Wow. I was really laying it on thick today.

"I wish I could be as confident as you," Lilandreth said. "But I remember the Skrela. I remember what happened every time they attacked."

"I know your job is to be the mediator, but maybe it's time for you to take a side. You believe in a Creator...you need to start trusting Him."

She said nothing for a long second, and I thought maybe I'd gone too far, transgressed some Predecessor taboo. But when she finally replied, I didn't detect any offense.

"We have always thought of you humans as messy," she said, almost apologetic in the admission. "As a mistake born of the cataclysm which claimed the world we knew. Your connection to that world made us bitter, I think, inclined to believe you were the embodiment of all the evil and disappointment we'd suffered. We placed all our hopes and dreams for our legacy into the Tahni, the creation of our own hands, and yet, from what we have learned, I believe we were victims of our own hubris. If there is a Creator, He must have accounted for your evolution as well as ours, and perhaps that was the lesson they were trying to teach us, that His plan was always the one which would prevail, not our own."

"If you want to hear God laugh," I said softly, quoting the words of an old song I'd heard once, "tell Him your plans."

"Just so. Good luck, Cameron Alvarez. And may the Creator shine upon your path."

I let myself sag against the internal webbing of the battlesuit for just a second, sucking in a deep breath. Maybe the last breath of outside air I'd ever get.

"Matis," I called down to the Vergai leader, "the enemy has landed. Get back to your people and get them ready to fight."

"Yes, sir." He sketched his best copy of a salute, then ran back into the building.

I watched him go, then slid into the suit, and pulled down the chest plastron, sealing myself into the metal coffin.

"Solano," I called, including Top in the net since she'd be holding Solano's hand, "the Skrela have landed. Deploy your company at the edges of their line of advance and prepare to engage."

"Copy that, Alvarez." Solano's voice was shaky, although I suppose he had every right to be. I had my doubts about his ability to handle this, but that was why he had Top with him.

The sledgehammer footsteps of Vicky's suit preceded her out of the exit and she stopped beside me, staring into the distance at the indistinct glow from the battle.

"We're two klicks from the shelter," she mused, "and this is the approach they'll have to use to get there. Do we want to wait until the main body passes by before we start luring them in here?"

She was so damned cool about it. I guess to someone looking from outside, I'd look like I was taking all this in stride too, but my insides were roiling. Hers weren't. I could tell when she was putting me on, affecting unconcern, and she wasn't. I wanted to ask her how she was managing it, but I didn't. I heard a story once about a centipede. Someone asked him how he managed to walk controlling all those legs, and from that moment, he couldn't. I wasn't sure that asking Vicky how she was being so cool would make her freak out, but I wasn't sure it wouldn't either.

"No, I don't think so," I answered her question. "We'll see, but I don't think the Skrela are going to organize into formations like an infantry battalion. They're going to rush toward their target, the biggest energy signature in the city, and swarm over it like they did the last two times we faced them. If we wait for that, they'll be impossible to distract. I think we have to start drawing them in as they make it to this area, pick them off before they get the chance to mass together."

"There's only one problem with that," she said.

"Yeah. If we're *too* successful, we'll get *all* of them coming here." I sighed. "But that's the chance we'll have to take." I checked my systems and shuffled down the walkway to the south. "Just you and me, Vicky."

"You watch my back," she said, following after me, "and I'll watch yours."

———

I was flying. Not just jumping, but flying, two hundred meters above the twisting, contorted rooftop, the layout of the city spread below me, still glowing with that otherworldly light whose source I couldn't place. Parts of the city glowed for other reasons, from the white-hot remains of Skrela pods. They were everywhere, in and out of the city, and trees and brush beyond the sharp delineation of the gigantic structure and the fields and forests were fiercely burning.

It wasn't the destroyed pods that interested me, however. It was the writhing, insectoid clusters skittering up through the walkways, somehow cloaked in darkness despite the ever-present light. There were half a dozen of them, so far, parallel to each other on different roads—well, what I was calling roads. I don't think any vehicles ever traveled them, but each of the Skrela was as big as a small vehicle and they seemed to have no trouble navigating them.

The scene was nightmarish, but from up here, it seemed to be someone else's nightmare, happening in a city far away and alien to my experience. I was floating far above it, not a part of the madness and destruction. Until one of the Skrela warrior drones looked up and saw me.

Coruscating white plasma ripped apart the night, the heat a sun lamp against my skin even through the armor as the beam missed by less than a meter. The turbulence in the superheated air sent me and my Vigilante tumbling, and the only thing that saved me from the inevitable volley of follow-up shots was a crackling beam of energy slicing through two of the Skrela in the center of the clump.

Vicky followed me down to the street, her controlled descent a good deal more graceful than my desperate attempt to stabilize my fall. But I somehow managed to right myself and get my jets pointed at the ground soon enough to send a last, powerful braking burst into the pavement and touch down with just the slightest jar through my spine.

The impact cleared my senses, bringing everything to a stark clarity. There were at least fifty of the Skrela only a hundred meters away from me, just around a slight curve in the road, and bless the Predecessors and their cockeyed sense of architecture for including curves where none were needed, because the fusillade of plasma would have incinerated both of us without the intervening wall of the jutting corner of the building. Whatever the Predecessors built the structure from, it was sturdy enough to absorb the massive amount of energy without completely collapsing.

"I'd say we have their attention," I told Vicky. "Let me just make sure they're pissed off enough to follow us."

I hit the jets, a hard enough blast to throw me across the walkway, then did something that was only possible because of the years and years of experience and training I had with the suit. I twisted in mid-air, swapping feet for head, and braking just before I slammed those spiked footpads into the wall across the walkway. The Skrela were fast and accurate, but none of them could keep up with something the size of a Vigilante moving that fast.

Me, I didn't have to be exact in my targeting because I was shooting at such a huge mass of enemy.

Great, now we can shoot at them from every direction.

The Predecessor energy cannon was qualitatively different from a Drop Trooper plasma gun or a Tahni electron beamer, hitting harder and penetrating further and most importantly to me, recycling faster. I fired three times in the space of two seconds, and then I was jetting back across the gap to Vicky, just ahead of the splash of sunfire that lashed out in return. I hit the ground running, giving myself a kick in the pants with the jets, which were now so much handier than they'd once been, hammering the ground with each footstep, Vicky at my heels.

"That did it," she decided, breath straining as her body kept up with the movement of the armor. "Now the trick is gonna be just not letting them shoot us before we reach the kill box."

Adrenaline fueled the manic laugh of my reply, making me much more ebullient than I had any right to be. Top had asked me if I worried about Vicky in combat and I'd told her the answer that felt right while I was sitting there, safe and sound and no one shooting at me. But in the now, in the heat of the battle, I knew the truth. I didn't worry about Vicky because she was the one person I trusted the most, the one whose competence I never questioned. I didn't worry about her because I knew she could survive any situation that I could, and if one of us died, it would be the whims of fortune and not some failing on my part or hers.

Which also might have been why I was on such an endorphin kick, higher than any of the addicts in the Underground, because I knew I was with the one person I didn't have to babysit, didn't have to watch out of the corner of my eye for fear they'd do something stupid and get both of us killed.

And then the high faded because I realized that was about to change.

"Matis, Campea," I strained out between breathless panting. "We have at least fifty enemy on the hook and headed your way, ETA one minute. Do you copy?"

"Copy, sir," Campea replied, and I was impressed at the steadiness of his tone. I'd read his file. He'd seen combat in the war, but as an enlisted man, and hadn't attended the Academy until after. He'd never led troops in battle before this mission, and had seen precious little of it so far. When I'd been in his position, I'd been nervous as hell. Or at least that was how I remembered it.

"We will be ready!" Matis said, and it was obvious to me that he was trying to cover fear with enthusiasm. And that was okay. We'd all been there.

"Minute's a long time," Vicky warned me, shifting to the right as if she'd seen the blast of Skrela plasma coming. Instead of turning her to slag, it charred the wall behind her, burning a crater in the tough material. "Especially since we can't just run away from them."

"Good point." I pushed off from the ground with a jet assist and spun in place, firing my fancy new energy cannon behind me, and spinning back frontward without waiting to see if I hit anything. It didn't matter, as long as I kept the enemy engaged.

And she was right. A minute was eternity; enough time and effort to drench me with sweat. My lower back and hips were already starting to feel the strain from the acrobatic moves the suit was doing that I was not physically prepared for.

Need to get back in the gym.

The heat didn't help, of course...the searing wash of oven-like air in my suit from every near-miss and even the heat from firing my own weapon. The Predecessor techs had been very efficient with their replacement reactors and God only knew where the heat from those went because it sure didn't affect the suit, but the thermal blossom from the weapon itself was like walking out into the afternoon glare on Inferno.

As long as it seemed to take, we finally reached the right entrance. I wouldn't have known...every one of them looked the same to me, but the transponders we'd left in place did their job and put a shining blue halo around the doorway in my helmet viewer. Vicky ducked inside first, and when I joined her, my HUD lit up like a Christmas tree with the locations of the various ambushes we'd set up as well as the force field projectors. It was a wall of data and I just ignored it, keying in on the first ambush site. We couldn't head straight for it. Well, I mean we *could* have and it might still have worked, but it was an L-shaped ambush, and for optimal results, we had to lead them into the kill box at the right angle, which meant sweeping across the front. Unfortunately, that gave the Skrela more opportunities to shoot at us.

If walking through the interior of the city in our battlesuits had been surreal, then flying through them on jets of superheated air while scorpions the size of horses shot at me was a fever dream. The Resscharr equivalent of art and interior decorating turned into a blur on either side of me, vandalized at random by Skrela plasma blasts. I'd audited a story once back when I was hooking up to the net on those free, recyclable tablets the Trans Angeles city government handed out at the public entertaining center. It was about a group of wannabe gangbangers looking to impress the criminal enterprise of their choice into letting them join, and their bright idea was to vandalize the art museum in the upper levels where the rich folk played. They paid a maintenance and janitorial crew to spoof their work IDs with new biometric data and switched out the cleaning chemicals for the floor buffer 'bot with flammable ones, then poured them all over the exhibits in the main room and set them on fire. The poor bastards didn't know that the exhibits were all holographic projections, and the place was open the next day while the miscreants were sentenced to five years of forced labor on an agricultural colony and never would join that gang.

This group of Skrela reminded me of those stupid kids, trying to vandalize the Resscharr city because they couldn't find any Resscharr. Their only reward for the effort was two platoons of infantry. Vicky was boosting nearly horizontal about twenty meters in front of me, the Skrela about the same distance behind, barely missing with each shot and that only because I was bobbing and weaving like a leaf in the breeze, as randomly as I could manage. I passed through the ambush zone and didn't spot a one of the Vergai or Force Recon on thermal, thanks to the new armor the Resscharr had given them.

At least that was what I hoped. When the first six or seven of the Skrela warrior drones made it to the edge of the fields of fire we'd mapped out from the ambush position, I felt a brief stab of anxiety that they'd moved to another spot without telling me. But that was just Campea trying to be clever, making sure none of the stragglers at the back got away, and it was barely a two-count before both platoons jumped up and opened fire.

It was a beautiful thing, the raw discharge of energy converging on the Skrela warrior drones, and if that sounds bloodthirsty, well...the things were terrifying, the aggregate of every phobia imaginable; implacable, unbeatable, a mindless beast ready to tear humans apart with their massive claws yet also prepared to blast us to atoms with the energy weapon mounted on their shoulders, an incongruity that somehow made them even more terrifying. Seeing them wiped away by the act of a normal human, not even a battlesuit, was satisfying on a gut level, even if it was through the use of the super-technology of ancient aliens.

I touched down on the gleaming white tile, arresting the suit's momentum with another burst of the jets, boot soles scraping against the slick material and stopping me just short of the slaughter. Campea had nearly outsmarted himself. Two of the Skrela had made it out of their firing arc before the platoon leader had triggered the ambush, and they were turning back into the fray, ready to charge the infantry forces. They'd made a mistake, though, a sin that a Marine wouldn't have committed, at least not one taught by the Skipper and Top. They'd turned their backs on the biggest casualty-producing weapons in the area—Vicky and me.

They wouldn't make the mistake again, though their dramatic thermal disassembly barely registered against the Dante-esque hell of the ambush. The air crackled with static electricity and the external heat sensors were almost to non-survivable, though the infantry should be okay since their helmets had an internal air supply. And inside that glowing white churn of ionized air, nothing survived.

"Cease fire!" Campea yelled on the general net, so the Vergai could hear it too. "Cease fire!"

It took another second, of course. The Vergai weren't just green troops, they were scared shitless, and I couldn't blame them. But once the haze of smoke and ash cleared, aided by the almost supernatural Predecessor air circulation system, the cheering began. Where fifty-some Skrela had been was now several hundred charred and scattered pieces of their extremities, the rest a charred scar on the floor extending all the way to the opposite wall.

"Good job, Matis," I told him, making sure my transmission

was loud enough to cut through the cheering. "Get your people ready."

"For what, sir?" he asked, sounding genuinely puzzled. I grinned, perhaps something malicious in it, though at least he couldn't see it.

"To do it again."

[24]

"I think," Vicky said, voice taut with the strain, "that we may have been too fucking successful."

I couldn't disagree, mostly because I lacked the time and wind. The fifty-odd Skrela we'd attracted on our first pass and the eighty-some on the second had been practice, a virtual reality training program with the settings adjusted to beginner. We'd caught the leading edge of the dribs and drabs coming in from the first landings and it had given us a false sense of how easy this was going to be. Suddenly, I felt like a shitheel for giving Matis a hard time.

The Skrela were a swarm of locusts, pouring over the city unchecked, ready to strip it of all life, firing their weapons at anything that moved, including us, and the only reason both of us weren't already dead was that there were so many of them, they kept getting in each other's way. Skrela cannon fire blasted scores of their own number to charred ruin without us firing a shot, but we helped where we could, since that was the whole point of this. And since I was already quivering with adrenaline and *not* shooting back might have pushed me over the edge into full-on panic.

The problem was, there were so many of the damned things that attracting the attention of just the few that we could handle was almost impossible. It seemed as if *hundreds* of the things were after us, too many to fit into the kill zone. Usually, I found the separation the suit gave me comforting, a way to keep myself above the speed and violence of combat, to make sense of things in a way I never could have standing on my own two feet and parsing everything through my biological eyes. Not this time. There was too much data, too much energy discharging, searing the air with its raw power, blanketing everything around us with thermal output that couldn't be separated into its component parts, too many enemy all blending together.

I'd always been good at taking the data the system threw at me and letting my subconscious mind organize it into something manageable, something that my gut told me was right without having to think about it. Right now, my gut was telling me to run.

"Run!" I echoed the sentiment to Vicky.

And we ran. We didn't fly because it would have been suicide. Plasma was so thick in the air, discharges of static electricity were jumping from building to pavement, and anything flying would have been incinerated. Staying low, at pavement level, we blended in with them, and their own numbers made it impossible for them to tell us from each other. It also made it impossible for us to see a damned thing, but at least we had the transponder signal to follow.

Following it through the stampeding herd of Skrela warrior drones was the hard part. I crunched into the backs of them, firing my energy cannon when I could, stomping and punching and twisting when I couldn't. The spikes set on their scorpion tails swung and slammed down at us from all sides, and I lost count of how many hits I took, each a sledgehammer blow to back or chest and leg, but I never left my feet. I couldn't, not with countless legs and arms and torsos to break my fall. I didn't try to hit back, couldn't take the time and attention to pursue the ones who'd struck me. My cannon shots blew divots through three and four of the things at a time, each one I brought down forcing another four or five to stumble and skitter over or to the side of their fallen comrade and giving us the space to move forward.

I didn't try to talk anymore, wouldn't have even if one bruising impact after another hadn't squeezed the air from my lungs. I was near spent, only the suit keeping me going, moving me like a marionette on strings, insisting it could go on smashing and shooting bugs all day even if I was too big of a wussy for it. And it did, taking me along for the ride as if I weren't the one controlling it. In retrospect, I don't know if I was, not consciously. It worked through the interface jacks, and although I'd never pursued that line of research, it's possible my instincts kept me moving.

Which was all good with me, as I had no better plan. My suit was covered in black ichor from the Skrela, charred, boiled, and burnt into the armor until I was sure it would never come out, and I feared that the Vergai would shoot me just because they couldn't tell me apart from the enemy. Since my conscious mind wasn't busy planning or strategizing, it was free to imagine all sorts of worst-case scenarios while I bulled my way through the press of monsters. Scenarios where Vicky and I got separated and I had to wade back in to try to find her, where the Vergai and Force Recon platoons had already been discovered and overwhelmed and we hadn't been able to help them, where our air and orbital cover broke down and Skrela ships began bombarding us with something other than warrior drones.

Those didn't happen, of course, because worst-case scenarios rarely do. What did happen was that, when we emerged from the pack into the city entrance, we were immediately isolated, which made us targets. I didn't have to think about hitting the jets any more than I had to tell Vicky to do it... here, inside, with the enemy bottlenecked in the doorway, it restricted their ability to fire upward. But not our ability to aim downward. The sunfire flare of Vicky's cannon merged with the flash of my own and the Skrela squeezing through the entranceway were flash-fried, their charred corpses manufacturing a speed bump to force the others into a suicidal one-at-a-time pace...except, it didn't. Instead, the Skrela warriors behind blasted the obstacle out of the way, a wave of ionized gas setting a Predecessor floor that wouldn't burn on fire, sending a wash of smoke and steam up to the ceiling.

"Down!" I warned Vicky, just an instinct nagging at the back of my head, a sense the Skrela were smart enough to have noted where we were and where to fire once they came through the gap we could no longer observe.

I almost wasn't fast enough. The gush of ionized gas as hot as the interior of a star swept through the space the two of us had occupied only a half-second before and I ducked out of instinct, running inward on Vicky's heels, making for the ambush point.

"Guys!" I blurted, not using even the slightest bit of comms protocol. "We have hundreds of them streaming in! Make for the closest force field projector!"

"Shouldn't we have let them have a crack at it?" Vicky gasped the question, still sprinting.

"They'd get overrun, cut off," I said. "I got a plan."

"A plan. Great."

The sarcasm hurt in ways I couldn't put into words because talking hurt more. All I could manage was my fervent hopes to speed the infantry platoons from one hiding place to another. The suits would hide their thermal signature, but not their motion, and all we could do was hope the Skrela were totally focused on us.

So far, so good, depending on your perspective. They were *very* focused on us, and it was time to stay low again, only letting the front rank have a shot at us. The jets were turbo-boosts, kicking me in the ass every few steps, making my pace and my cadence irregular so the plasma gushing past me, in front of me, between Vicky and me, only scalded me instead of burning through my armor. It was something I should have been used to, but the touching-a-hot-stove sensation still made me flinch, nearly threw off the stride of the armor since it was keyed to the movements of my biological muscles. The armor slapped smart bandages on the burned areas automatically and the pain faded as quickly as it had started, but the psychological flinch was still there, nagging at the edges of my thoughts.

There. There was the damned force field generator, and if I saw it, I knew the Skrela would too. They might not have been individually sentient, but they were programmed to detect any trace of Predecessor technology, and this was a big floodlight leading them in like big, ugly, deadly moths. A big enough floodlight that they'd forget about Vicky and me, or at least that was what I was betting.

"Split!" I meant the word as a stern command, but it came out cracked and desperate. "Split left!"

She went left, I went right, and the Skrela went straight ahead, into the sheltered alcove with the shimmering shield of otherworldly power stretched across it. They crashed into it like a wave breaking on a rocky shoal, most bouncing off until the crush behind them pushed them harder against it, deeper into the clutches of the gravity field and the front rank began to crumple like a discarded squeeze bulb in the recycler. I watched it with horrified fascination, catching my momentum against the far wall, the material ringing under the collision with my shoulder, though I barely felt the impact through the haze of local anesthetics that had turned most of my torso numb.

The Vergai and the Force Recon platoon were visible through the shield, huddled back against the wall, and if I couldn't see their faces through their helmet visors, I could imagine what they looked like, the fear and disbelief, because I felt it myself. The Skrela attacked that shield like it was the enemy rather than us, clawing at it, firing their weapons nonstop even though the discharge killed their own soldiers, and they were having an effect. The field had been almost invisible when we'd first come upon it, but now it was glowing a pale green, writhing under the battering, as if absorbing the energy was causing it physical pain.

"Campea!" I rasped. "At my call, drop the field and open fire."

"Y...yes, sir." The man was skeptical and I didn't blame him. But staying under the shield was a short-term answer.

"Vicky, circle around behind and thin out the herd."

"You're one crazy son of a bitch," she opined, though I saw her moving to carry out the order.

"I love you too," I assured her, circling around the edges of the Skrela mass.

It was as if we didn't exist, as if the force field projector had them all hypnotized, right up to the point where we started shooting at them again. The quick recycle time of the energy cannons gave us an advantage I would have killed for during the war, the ability to fire over and over in the space of just a few seconds, each shot blowing through multiple Skrela. Vicky and I were circling around their perimeter, picking off the stragglers first, making sure they were all packed into a tight ball before we turned our guns on the bulk of them.

That was when they finally noticed us, though not all at once. Vicky and I passed each other, me on the outside, and I held my fire until we'd cleared fields of fire then started in again, winnowing away the outer ranks of the warrior drones like scraping old paint off a barracks wall. When we reached the opposite side, we both reversed course and headed back the way we'd come, like some punitive PT exercise our DIs had come up with in Boot, and the whole thing was beginning to make me dizzy.

The ones on the outside edge saw us first, turning to deal with the distraction as if we were an annoyance keeping them from doing their real work. But the realization seemed to spread through the whole mass of them in a wave, like they were connected on some sort of comm net, a hive mind, if not a very bright one. The rain of plasma began directing away from the glowing force field and toward us, though it was still impossible for any but the outer ranks to get a clear shot at us, and difficult even for them since we kept curving around outside their fields of fire. More of them died from their own weapons than from ours in those few seconds.

I don't know how I knew that their attention had turned from the force field to us, but I could sense it, knew the time had come to give the order.

"Vicky, get ready to jump on my signal. Campea, lower the shield and fire at will!"

The glimmering green force field stayed up for another two seconds, and I wondered if the Force Recon platoon leader hadn't heard, or was pretending not to hear because he was scared shitless of letting down his only defense against the horde of monsters. I kept shooting, kept running in the interim, just another two steps, wondering how long we could do this before one of the things got lucky.

The field dropped and urgency knotted in my stomach.

"Jump!"

The jets kicked me in the middle of my back, twisting me

around hard enough to pull a muscle as I went from a curving course around the perimeter of the half-circle of Skrela to flying straight up, over the mass of them toward the far wall. The flight took scant seconds, yet it was as if I hung up there forever, watching the drama play out below me. Where the field had been was an arc of crushed Skrela, smashed flat by the wall of gravitational force, leaving behind bits and pieces of carapace, pools of black ichor, and squishy, grey nodules that might have been whatever the things called organs. And beyond that line were the Vergai and Force Recon platoons, arrayed in double rows like Revolutionary War redcoats, half of them standing, the other half kneeling.

The mass fire was on command and simultaneous and absolutely devastating. Screaming bursts of raw power cut swathes through the Skrela ranks, and we added to the fire on the way down, both of us touching down at the outer edge of our file. I could feel it, could feel the end coming. We'd killed dozens upon dozens of the things in seconds and now they were killing each other to get to us and yet none would run. They rushed toward us, into the hellfire, and inevitably, some began to get through even as their fellows went down.

When the first of them reached our lines, I couldn't even shoot it for fear of hitting one of our own people. I could only watch as it stormed through, one of its legs and two of its arms burned off, its plasma cannon a sparking wreckage, the carapace housing for the mechanism of its turret stripped away, revealing the obscene juncture of the biological and the cybernetic. It lunged for one of the Vergai, grabbing the man's shoulder in the grip of its crablike claw and ripping him in two before the troops next to him could kill it with one last volley.

Blood spattered across the other Vergai and they rocked back as if it had been a physical blow, ready to break, ready to run and die to an enemy that was on the brink of death themselves. I pushed up behind them, blocking their way with my bulk, and added my fire to their own.

"Close the gap!" I yelled. "Keep firing! They're dead and they just don't know it!"

"Kill the damned things!" Matis bellowed, standing beside me, hosing his weapon at hip level across the remaining Skrela, ignoring the chaos and death around us. "Push forward and put an end to this so we can go home!"

And they did just that, stepping through the smoking remains of the Skrela, jumping over their corpses, running straight at them. The Force Recon platoon joined them a half-second later without a command from Campea, sensing it was the right move, and like any good leader, he didn't stand in their way. He just ran ahead of them, yelling encouragement like it was his idea.

I couldn't let them have all the fun, and I also couldn't fire through them, since I wasn't a Skrela drone. I crashed in on the side of one of the Skrela, smashing into its support leg with the weight of my suit supplemented by the boost from my jump jets. It crumpled beneath the impact of my shoulder, bringing the thing's wedge-shaped head down to my level, and I grabbed it in both hands, using the jets to whip myself over the top of the warrior drone, twisting its head to the side, the neck cracking with an audible snap. I hadn't been sure if that would kill the thing...after all, it was designed by some unknown alien race for combat, and keeping the brain in a vulnerable skull wasn't the best design, just the one evolution had come up with on the fly. But apparently, the designers of the drones hadn't put any more thought into it than just copying nature, because the thing went limp, collapsing against the corpses of its fellows.

And then it was over. I was dipping into a crouch to launch myself into the air, getting ready to trigger the jets, when I heard Campea's message in my ear.

"Cease fire! Cease fire!"

The hum-crack-snap of the discharge of the energy rifles had become such a constant background, I hadn't noticed it anymore until it was gone. The haze of smoke rising toward the roof cleared gradually, not disappearing completely, but thinning out enough for the carnage to be visible as more than a glowing mass on thermal. I couldn't have given a count of how many we'd killed—there were too many bits and pieces scattered around, arms and legs and heads clumped in blackened, smoking masses—but the smooth, carefully-crafted tile of the floor was almost totally covered in what passed for guts and blood in the Skrela drones, painted black and grey, glistening obscenely. I was suddenly even more grateful for the armor and the insulation from the external world.

"Casualties," I said, then took a sip from the water nipple beside my mouth inside the helmet and tried it again, louder.

"Wait one," Campea replied, a little brusque, but I didn't begrudge him the impatience. I hadn't been the one who'd had to lower that shield with hundreds of alien death machines staring me in the face.

"Matis?" I asked, looking around. "You have anyone hurt?"

I frowned. I didn't see him. I checked the IFF transponder list in my comms display, wondering if he'd been injured...and didn't see his name.

"Matis?"

"Sir..." I didn't recognize the voice at first, until I matched it to the name on the IFF list. We didn't call him platoon sergeant because that would have been imposing a rank structure the Vergai didn't share, but he was Matis' second-in-command.

"Yes, Oster? Where's Matis?" I asked the question despite the empty pit in my gut, despite the fact that I thought I already knew. His choked, hesitant answer confirmed my worst fears.

"He was there one second, sir," Oster stammered, "and then

there was a flash...one of their guns. And he was gone. Nothing left of him at all. Nothing to bring back to his wife for the ceremony."

It was a damned good thing I was in the suit, because it was the only thing keeping me standing. The big, dark eyes of the man's children stared at me in my memory, accusing, and I imagined the railing fury of his wife...the justified anger at us, at *me*.

"I have two KIA, sir," Campea reported, his voice neutral, as if keeping it in check was the only way he could keep from screaming. "Lance Corporal Karl and Sgt. Cho. No seriously wounded. This shit, it either kills you or maybe you get a burn if it passes close, but if it touches you anywhere, you're dead, you're cooked, you know?"

He was gibbering, and again, I couldn't fault him for it.

"Lieutenant," I said, as gently as I could, "get your platoon reorganized and get ready to move out."

"Yes, sir."

"Oster," I told the Vergai second officer, "you're in charge of the platoon now."

The man was a little older than Matis, no doubt appointed as a steady backup for the younger man. Steady was a hard commodity to come by right now.

"Yes, Captain Alvarez," he replied numbly.

"Do you have any other casualties? Any injured, any dead?"

"No, sir." His voice was firmer now, and he sucked in a deep breath before he answered me further. "That is, we have two soldiers with scalding burns, but the smart bandages are taking care of them, and they can still fight."

"Fall in with Lt. Campea and follow his lead," I told him, not sure how complicated I could make my orders. Not only was Matis the smartest of the lot, he also trusted us the most.

Oster turned back to his people and I sagged inside my

armor, letting my head rest back against the cushion behind my neck. I'd lost people before, some very recently, but this was worse, somehow.

"Are you okay?" Vicky asked, tromping up in the wake of the others moving aside.

"Got a few burns, but I'll live," I replied, knowing it wasn't what she was asking. She waited, silent, until I took the question seriously. "No. But I can live with *that* too. What's bothering me is whether we can keep this up. Without Matis, the others are like as not to break and run if we try to lure more Skrela into this place."

"Alvarez!"

I blinked, thinking for a second that it was Vicky admonishing me for doubting the Vergai, but the IFF transponder told the real tale. It was Top.

"Yeah, I'm here, Sergeant-Major," I told her, glum enough to use her actual rank.

"Well, get your ass over *here*, and do it now!" She was yelling, which she didn't have to do, since the comms system would amplify her words enough for me to hear them even if she were only whispering. She was stressed, close to panic, and I'd *never* heard her stressed before...except when the Skipper died. "Get to the shelter! The Skrela are overrunning us and we're taking casualties!"

"Fuck," I murmured. "Copy that; we're on our way."

"And what the hell are we gonna do when we get there?" Vicky asked, and I checked to make sure she hadn't sent that over the net to Top. "With all two of us and some light infantry? What does she think we can do to help her?"

I shook my head, though she couldn't see it.

"Campea!" I snapped. "Oster! Form up and get ready to move out."

The suit seemed to move itself toward the entrance,

bounding in steps that each covered ten meters. Outside the door, the street was clear, nothing there except the wreckage of the Skrela we'd killed on the way in, and precious little of that. Most of it had been carried along in the swarm. The empty street was no comfort...it meant that everything the enemy had was being thrown at the shelter, the force field, our troops.

"What are we going to do?" I repeated Vicky's question, wishing I had a better answer.

I waved at the others to follow me and tromped into the night.

"Whatever we can."

[25]

The battle wasn't too hard to find. Even though the city was kilometers long and bits of it were hidden from sight by unnecessary curves, the light show was a dead giveaway. The flares of Predecessor energy cannons and Skrela plasma guns would have been enough, throwing red and blue and yellow reflections off the stark-white of the city of Decision, but the force field outshone them. Just like the much smaller version we'd used in our ambush, this one was glowing, incandescent from the energy it was absorbing, another light, except this time, we were the moths.

Eventually, after what felt like an hour and a dozen kilometers but was probably twenty minutes and less than four klicks, we were at the last curve, the harsh, sun-bright light shining like the Shekinah Glory, throwing eerie shadows against the opposite wall.

"They're going to be absorbed with taking down the field," I told the infantry following us. "Don't wade into them...there's too many. They'll crush you before you can do any damage. I want you to find cover—doorways, decorative walls, whatever's there—and start taking careful, aimed shots. If they key in on your position, cease fire and move somewhere else, then start again. You're in charge, Campea," I reminded the lieutenant. "Keep out of sight. Getting killed being a show-off won't help anything."

"What are you guys gonna do?" Campea asked.

"In these suits," Vicky answered, "we're not exactly the snooping-and-pooping types. So, we're gonna do what we do best...kick their asses."

That's my girl.

Campea didn't wait for more orders or more useless advice, just corralled his Marines and the Vergai and put them into a file formation, hugging the right side of the walkway and the scant shadows there. I stayed where I was, trying to think.

"The roof," I told Vicky.

"You read my mind. Let's go."

It was a long boost up to the rooftop, two hundred meters up from where we stood, then another few dozen to get somewhere flat enough to land and take a few running steps before we launched again, skimming just above the surface to stay out of the line of fire of both sides. Up here, though, everything was clear, lit up like midday.

The Skrela were an ant colony kicked apart by juveniles, squirming and swarming, crashing together and crashing into the force field, crawling over the top of each other to get to it, their plasma cannons firing almost constantly, each second causing the field to grow brighter, the green twisting into wounds of livid red, and from there into white so bright, it would have been blinding without the helmet's protection. The Resscharr were fighting back, firing their energy beams from the edges of the field, but there was only so much room for them to fire without being incinerated immediately, and they didn't seem to understand that they'd all die when the field collapsed anyway. It was too much to take in, too hard to work out any details, and I wouldn't have seen the Drop-Trooper company at all if it hadn't been for their transponders.

They were out on the far edge of the swarm, scraping layers off, moving in and out of cover, one platoon swapping out for another. I could already tell that the only reason they were still alive was that the Skrela didn't care about losses, just about that damned force field. Four suit transponders were offline already and I could tell immediately why Top had called...one of the KIA was Solano. I felt guilty for all the sparring with the man, though admittedly, he'd been a bit of a prick. He'd volunteered to die thousands of light-years from home in a fight that wasn't his, and now no one who ever loved him would know what had happened to him.

The two of us skipped and jetted a hundred meters at a time, circling around to the roof of the shelter, the Skrela laid out before us, a field of black, glistening thorns. And there, at the top, we paused, like Jesus brought to the mountaintop by Satan to look upon the world.

"Over the top?" Vicky asked.

"In and out," I cautioned. "Don't get tangled up. We're just trying to take the heat off the others."

"Copy that."

I closed my eyes for a moment, then stepped off the roof and into the emptiness. I let myself fall way too far, not hitting the jets until I was just over the slavering pack, braking just enough for the impact with the back of the Skrela's torso not to break my spine. I still bit down and tasted blood, but I was fairly sure the crack I heard was the Skrela's carapace breaking and not my own bones. I yanked at the shoulder mount for the thing's plasma cannon and it ripped away in a shower of sparks and a spray of black ichor, useless except as a club.

Which was exactly the purpose for which I intended it. I didn't want to fire yet. The energy cannon would attract attention to the exact spot where I stood, and I wanted to keep things less specific for a few seconds. The Skrela cannon must have weighed half a ton, but the armor allowed me to swing it like a baseball bat, bringing the heavy end, the end with all the eldritch machinery the creators of these things had used to fire accelerated plasma, into the rear motive leg of the drone next to me.

The carapace was tough, but not tough enough to resist the sheer kinetic energy of that blow, and it cracked vertically, exposing whatever arcane combination of biology and cybernetics was inside the things. Jumping down from onto the damaged limb finished it off and the warrior drone crumpled under my weight. Its spiked tail thrashed at me, but the Skrela were packed so thick, it didn't have room to get a clean swing. It still hurt, but not enough to knock me over, and I got my revenge immediately, smashing the cannon down on the base of the thing's neck.

A step forward, a sideways swing, a jab, an overhead smash, a step forward, and I lost track of which of them I was hitting. It didn't matter—I couldn't miss, and I'd never run out of targets. But it was too slow, and there were too many, and eventually, I was going to exhaust myself if not my suit. Time for the gun.

The first discharge rocked me back, the heat washing back, not quite as bad as a near-miss from a Skrela plasma gun, more like a blast of hot wind from a desert summer at high noon. The burst of whatever the hell sort of particles it fired penetrated through multiple Skrela, toppling them like a row of dominoes, and I spun in place, firing in a 360-degree arc around me, clearing space.

Clearing space for them to shoot at *me*.

The first gush of white-hot ionized gas spent itself on the Skrela in front of me, another breath-stealing wave of summer heat, and I didn't wait for the one that had my name on it. The hand of God yanked me out of the press, or at least that was how it felt when the jets kicked in. I angled straight forward, scared to stray too close to the back for fear of my own Marines shooting me, scared to go to either side for fear of the Resscharr's fire nailing me.

I didn't stay up long—I couldn't, not with thousands of the things shooting in every direction—but I was in the air long enough to spot Vicky. She spun like a dervish, spewing white-hot energy from the Predecessor-tech cannon, leaving ruin and destruction in her wake, a killing machine at once graceful and lethal.

God, I loved her.

Then I was back in the press and she disappeared behind waves of the enemy. Lather, rinse, repeat. Kill a dozen of them, two dozen, yet the total number didn't seem to change.

Were the Vergai and the Force Recon troops picking them off at the edges? I couldn't see, couldn't tell, and what difference did it make? Ten, twenty, fifty, a *hundred* less of the Skrela wouldn't put a dent in this pack. We could fight for hours, but that field was about to go down, and when it did, there would be no way to stop the wave of alien weapons from ripping through the walls of that shelter and killing everyone inside.

This was it, one last battle.

A spiked tail smashed into my left arm and I screamed, pure, white-hot agony crackling through my arm and shoulder. Broken, dislocated, I couldn't tell, couldn't focus enough to even read the medical report flashing in the corner of my vision in blinking red warnings. All I could do was fly, and I did, even though that was just going to get me killed quicker. I fired downward blindly, an empty gesture, knowing that would be a spotlight, a target hung on my back, but just wanting to kill a few more of them before they got me.

The round was powerful, more powerful than my old

plasma gun, but it would accomplish nothing. Yet, somehow, where it struck, a fireball three stories high rose up and the shockwave tossed me head-over-heels, out of control, dozens of meters away from where I'd been. I thrashed in mid-air, my shoulder and arm screaming at me, but a gut-level certainty that I'd die if I didn't right myself screaming louder. The jets roared defiance and I braked just enough to make my impact with the pavement merely excruciating rather than fatal.

I'd hit feet first, but I was on my back now, the fall too much for the armor's catlike gyros to take. I was looking up from somewhere out to the side of the mass of Skrela, past the edges of the swarm, and it took my pain-addled senses a moment to realize I was staring at the silver-grey wedge of Intercept One. Her belly jets spewed white fire as she hovered, firing again, her proton cannons slicing wedges twenty meters wide through the ranks of the Skrela.

And she wasn't alone. The assault shuttles were with her, the drop-ships, circling like vultures over a feast, pounding the enemy with proton cannons, Gatling lasers, missiles, ripping them to shreds. I watched the slaughter in awed disbelief, unable to stand even if I wanted to, as one shock wave after another slammed into me with enough force to kill an unarmored man. Even through the insulation of the Vigilante, the sound was deafening, painful, the vibration a never-ending earthquake, the heat radiating out in successive waves, enough to curl the ends of my arm-hair, the smoke drifting upward through the armor.

Relief warred with stark, gut-twisting fear. Vicky, Top, everyone...if I'd had my ass kicked on the edges of the battle, what had happened to *them*? I tried to roll off my back, but agony speared through my shoulder and I had to stop, even though the armor could have done it. Warmth coursed through me as the suit injected me with local anesthetic. Too much.

Between the burns and now the shoulder, I was drifting in a haze that had nothing to do with the thick clouds of smoke rising from the orgy of destruction the strafing spacecraft had left behind.

"You need a hand, Marine?"

The battlesuit stepped into my field of view, looming over me, its matte grey mottled with black, pitted by debris, the ID markings either covered or scoured away. I knew who it was, though, would have even if the IFF transponder hadn't told me. I'd have known Vicky's voice anywhere in the universe.

"I need a hand, an arm, and a shoulder," I told her, "but I'd settle for some help getting up."

She circled around behind me and grabbed my suit by the right shoulder, yanking upward. The suit's muscles took over once I had my feet beneath me, and I squeezed my eyes shut, trying to clear my head. In what seemed like the far distance, though it couldn't have been more than a few hundred meters, the whine-snap-crack of Predecessor weapons fired sporadically, the Resscharr soldiers finishing off the survivors of the Skrela horde.

"Where's Top?" I tried to ask, but started coughing, my throat scorched dry. I took another sip of water and almost choked on it...it was bathwater hot. But it at least did the job of letting me talk and I repeated the question, not just to Vicky but to the general net.

"Over here, Alvarez," Top answered. I checked my transponder board to figure out where "here" was and saw her coming from over my right shoulder, along with the rest of the company, trickling in from the edge of the battlefield.

Or at least some of the company. I'd known about Solano, but there were others missing from the IFF list...way too many. Gunny Pineda, the company first sergeant, was gone as well, along with Lt. Breckenridge, the First Platoon leader.

"You need to take charge of this company," Top told me, her voice weary. Her suit was as battered as mine, maybe even more banged up. The armor over her left hip was ripped away, not burned, and I figured it had to be from the claw of one of the Skrela.

I was about to tell her that I was in no condition to lead four corporals into a whorehouse, much less a Drop-Trooper company, but I was interrupted by a transmission on the comms.

"You guys okay down there?" Another voice I couldn't mistake for anyone else's.

"Dunstan, you saved our asses," I said, "and don't think I didn't appreciate it, but shouldn't you and the shuttles be intercepting Skrela landing pods so we don't have even more of these assholes crawling all over us in a few minutes?"

"You haven't been following the action, then?"

"We've been a little busy," Vicky interjected.

At the suggestion, I linked back in with the transmission from the Predecessor drones and ships. What I expected to see was slightly fewer Skrela motherships than before. What I found was...nothing. Well, not *nothing*. The *Orion* was still there, burning back toward Decision, surrounded by perhaps half the Predecessor ships she'd been escorted by at the start.

"We *won*!" he enthused, and I heard a thumping in the background that might have been the pilot smacking his fist into the control panel in exultation. "They destroyed every one of those fucking motherships! The battle's over, man!"

[26]

"Holy shit," Vicky breathed. "I can't believe it."

The battlefield was cooler now, though it could still have been scalding for all I knew. Inside my armor, it was back to a livable temperature, and behind us, the force field flickered and extinguished, disappearing as if it had never been. Resscharr volunteer militia stumbled out, weapons hanging at their sides. If they'd been human, I would have said they were numb, shell-shocked, and maybe they were anyway, human or not.

I could empathize. I had no words. I'd fought some of the worst battles of a shitty war, much bigger than this, and lost more people, but the Skrela...there was something so definitively *other* about them, something that could spark fear even in the most hardened veteran. They'd seemed unbeatable, and yet we *had* beaten them, wiped them out to the last. It was like defeating a storm, or killing a mountain.

I shook my head, still trying to clear it, and winced at the pain the action caused in my shoulder, despite the numbing action of the smart bandages.

"Lieutenant..." I hesitated, struggling to remember the name of Solano's company XO. "...Singh, get me a full casualty report and a damage estimate for the suits." Out of the corner of my eye, I saw a familiar figure emerging from the door of the Resscharr shelter, tall and proud, her arms around two of her children. "Five minutes," I told Singh. "I'll be right back."

The ground crunched under my boots, the spiked soles crushing charred bits of Skrela carapace underfoot. I hoped the Resscharr had some ancient, Predecessor cleaning 'bots stored away to get rid of this crap, or their city was going to be a giant garbage dump for however many weeks it took to clean up the remains. The building itself wasn't that badly off. It was scarred, scorched, marked with black streaks and craters, but none of it had collapsed. Whatever it was built from had resisted the plasma of the Skrela drone weapons. If any of their ships had gotten through, it might have been a different story, but by some miracle, that hadn't happened.

Lilandreth made a motion that was half a nod, half a bow as I approached her.

"You did not lie, Cameron Alvarez," she said. "Your people are indeed experts in the arts of war."

"Maybe it's not something to be proud of," I admitted, "but you play to your strengths. Did you lose a lot of people?"

"Fifty of our volunteer defense force were killed."

I winced. Their losses had dwarfed ours, but then, they'd had more to start with, and they'd taken the brunt of the enemy attacks. Honestly, I was shocked they hadn't taken heavier casualties...though she wasn't counting her wounded, and I imagined with their technology, even the grievously wounded could be saved.

"Maybe this is your answer," I said, "the sign your people have been looking for to make your decision."

Which was probably oversimplifying what, to them, was as intense a religious and philosophical question at least as divisive as Protestants vs. Catholics on Earth, but I was feeling pretty loopy and unrealistically optimistic.

"This is a sign," she agreed, hugging her children to her. They looked pre-adolescent to me, from what I'd seen at Yfingam. "A sign that we are cursed by the Creator. Our line is coming to an end."

I blinked as if she'd slapped me, feeling like I'd missed something.

"But...but...we beat them."

"The Skrela will not be beaten, human." The words could have been bitter, but her translation gave them a gentle tone, like she was speaking to her children. "They have no morale to break, no regard for their own dead because they have no life, no sense of self. They know we're here and they won't give up simply because their first wave was defeated."

I stared at her, speechless, my brain refusing to work for a moment at the sheer absurdity of what she'd said.

"They sent a *thousand* ships," I said, shaking my head. "How the hell could they possibly have anything left after that?"

"Alvarez, this is Hachette. You copy?"

I thought the pain drugs were getting to me. There was no way that the *Orion* could be close enough to the planet for them to be able to get a transmission through...except, of course, they weren't using *our* comm gear to do it, they were relaying it through the Predecessor tech.

"Good copy, *Orion*," I replied automatically. "Go ahead."

The whine of landing jets nearly drowned out even the enhanced audio in my earphones and I glanced to the side in annoyance. The drop-ships were landing in the center of the courtyard, the exhaust from their belly jets tossing debris in every direction, spreading bits of Skrela to the four winds.

"Get the Marine personnel and Vergai loaded onto the drop-ships and get ready to dust off," Hachette said, sounding as grim as a Baptist preacher at an atheist's funeral, not at all like a man who'd just won a battle.

My first instinct was to argue, but I thought about Top and what she said and changed my tack.

"Will do, sir," I acknowledged. "But what's going on? I thought we just won."

"I thought so too, Cam. But I'm afraid the Skrela have other ideas."

A video popped up in a corner of my HUD, showing me an image of deep space. Where, I wasn't sure, since there was no context in the video stream, but there was no sign of the system primary or Decision, and if I had to guess, I would have said it was out past the asteroid belt, because that was where the Skrela had come out of T-space before.

There'd been a thousand ships last time. Now, they were as countless as the stars, coming out of T-space in eruptions of rainbow rings, so numerous they seemed to rip apart the fabric of spacetime across my entire field of view. Not a thousand this time. *Ten* thousand. Maybe twenty. More than we could have taken on with the entire Commonwealth wartime fleet and the Predecessor ships together. Carrying more warrior drones than the whole Marine Corps could have hoped to defeat.

"What the fuck."

It wasn't a question, more of a protest, not to Hachette but to God Himself. This shouldn't be possible. Hachette seemed to understand.

"Yeah. I don't like it any more than you do...but we have to get the hell out of here."

———

"You can't do this," I insisted, stifling a curse as I tried to move my suit's arms in a gesticulation and exacerbated the pain in my shoulder. "This is nuts!"

If my argument moved Lilandreth, she didn't show it.

"I was unaware we had a choice," she said. Her kids still stood by her, as if they were afraid to get too far away. Maybe afraid of the Skrela, maybe of me, I wasn't sure.

The rest of the Resscharr were out of their shelter, staring up at the sky, just waiting. It might be days before the Skrela landed, if their first attack was any indication, but none of them made any move to prepare. They were stunned, smacked between the eyes like a bull ready for slaughter. I knew how they felt.

"You have ships," I told her, my frustration growing. I wanted out of the suit, wanted to look her in the eye, even though I knew I'd likely be looking at her chest, given our comparative height. "Load your people up—*some* of them, at least. Get the hell out of here, find another planet somewhere. You can't just sit here and wait for them to come and kill you!"

"We have two hundred thousand individuals on this world," she said, as calm as if we were discussing infrastructure budgeting and not the imminent death of every Resscharr on the planet. "The most we could fit on our ships is just over two thousand. How do you propose we make that selection?"

"Women and children first is the way my planet would have made it back in the day. And maybe that's regressive and sexist, but so's survival." I was being harsh and I didn't care. How do you reason with a walking, talking dinosaur?

"Cam's right," Vicky said. I looked around, surprised to see her. She'd gone to collect the Vergai and Force Recon light infantry and I hadn't noticed her returning. By instinct, I checked over my shoulder and saw the troops lining up at the ramp for one of the drop-ships. "You could at least save *some* of your people. It sucks, but it's better than just...giving up!"

"You speak to me," Lilandreth said with the amused patience of a kindergarten teacher, "as if I were one of you, a human. I suppose I should take that as a compliment. But I'm not, and we're not. For you, survival is preferable to surrendering to fate, but for us, we've been forced to surrender to fate many times before. When the asteroid struck, fate chose us as the only survivors of our genus. When your kind, homo sapiens, evolved, fate chose us to leave the world to you. And when the Skrela came, fate dictated we abandon the core systems you call the Cluster to make sure that all we'd built wouldn't be destroyed."

"You've run away before," I said, trying a new direction of argument. "You saved what you could when you moved out here. Why not do it again?"

"Because the result would be the same." She waved a hand overhead. "For thousands of years, we lived here in peace, with no sign of the Skrela. You arrived, and soon after, so did they."

"You think we brought them?" Vicky demanded, and if there was some righteous indignation in her tone, there was also a hint of the fear that Lilandreth was right.

"No. I think *we* did. Before you came, we hadn't taken our ships out of the planet's atmosphere in three thousand years. *Days* after we do, the Skrela come. They can detect our gravitic drives. If we were to attempt to run, we would merely be delaying the inevitable. Perhaps by years, but more likely, by *days*."

Shit. That was a point I couldn't argue. It made too much damn sense.

"There's room on our ship," Vicky said, blurting the offer out before I could try to stop her. "Not a lot, but we could squeeze a couple hundred of you in long enough to get you to another habitable world. It wouldn't be comfortable, but at least *some* of you would survive. We could take you back to Yfin-gam...there are more of your people there. You might be able to lead them into a better way of life than the one they chose."

"What the hell did you just offer, Captain Sandoval?" Hachette's outraged voice blared inside my helmet—and Vicky's too. "Did you even *consider* clearing that with me first?"

"Your offer is...not without merit," Lilandreth admitted, and I felt for the first time since we'd begun this argument that we'd found something that she wasn't prepared to reject out of hand. "May we have some time to consider this among ourselves?"

"Sir?" I transmitted to Hachette. "I know we're in a hurry..."

"They have thirty minutes," Hachette snapped. "After a half an hour, they're either loading their people up or our ships are taking off. Make sure they know."

Great. It had taken them days to argue what they were going to do to us and they still hadn't decided when the damned Skrela came. I sighed and tried to figure out how I was going to break the news to her.

[27]

"Jesus Christ, Alvarez," Dr. Halonen murmured, shaking her head as she examined the readouts on her display. "I don't know how you manage to get yourself so fucked up inside that nice, thick metal suit."

"It's a gift, Doc," I assured her, resting my head against the padding of the sensor gurney and trying not to fall asleep.

I had my eyes closed, not just because I was tired but because I really didn't want to look at the burns. The smart bandages had treated them, but they'd take days to completely heal unless Halonen stuffed me in an auto-doc, which she'd shown no inclination to do for the whole time I'd known her.

"The burns are second-degree," she ticked off, as if reading my thoughts. "Nothing major; they'll be fine. But you really fucked up your shoulder. Grade Two separation, which is going to require nanite treatment for the ligaments if you want to use it anytime in the next few days."

"I don't know that it's fair to say *I* fucked it up, Doc," I argued, doing my best not to shrug. "A big-ass alien scorpion centaur hit me with a big-ass spike on the end of its tail. I think that had something to do with it."

And getting out of the suit had been tricky. In a normal setup on a troopship or a cruiser, there would have been a medical extraction team to get me out by disassembling the suit around me, but we didn't have that luxury here on the *Orion*, so I'd just had to crawl out under my own power, with Vicky there to give me support, moral and otherwise. That had hurt almost as much as getting hit by the spike, and probably hadn't done my shoulder any good in the process.

Halonen sighed, shuffling through a cabinet beside the exam table until she came up with a flat-grey cylinder and pressed it to my shoulder. It was cold and I flinched away, but she grabbed my neck and held me in place. For a woman, she had a surprisingly strong grip. Something hissed into the skin of my bare shoulder and it felt as if she'd injected a lump of solid lead under the surface layer.

"Ow," I complained, and she snorted a laugh.

"Sit up, you big, tough Marine. I need to get a sling on that."

I tried to comply, bracing myself for the twinge of discomfort I'd come to expect beneath the layers of analgesic, but it wasn't that bad. My left arm was stiff and a little numb, but I could move well enough to pull on my T-shirt and fatigue top. Once I was dressed, the doc fitted me with a sling, strapping the harness across my chest with gusto I didn't appreciate.

"Leave it on for forty-eight hours," she cautioned me, "unless you're showering or sleeping. I don't want to have to see you back in here."

"Me neither," I assured her, rushing to escape the medical bay before she figured out some other torture for me.

Vicky was waiting outside, leaning against the bulkhead, arms crossed over her chest.

"Really?" she asked, cocking an eyebrow. "A sling? What is this, Force Recon field medicine? Has Halonen ever heard of an auto-doc?"

"She's old-fashioned," I said, shrugging with just my right shoulder. "It's just for two days."

"Hachette wants to see us," Vicky told me, jerking a thumb up the passageway.

I sighed. I'd been expecting this, but not looking forward to it. Hachette hadn't had the time for a debriefing when we'd shuttled in from Decision...hell, we'd barely had time to Transition ahead of the Skrela motherships. Then there'd been way too much going on for talking. It had been four hours before I'd even had time to report to sickbay, surviving on painkiller med patches while I dealt with the Vergai and what had been Solano's company. Now, I suppose, they were mine, or at least they would be if Top had anything to say about it.

They'd taken a hit, and I'd seen it in their faces once they were out of the suits. Eight dead, including their company commander, top kick, one of the platoon leaders, and twelve more badly wounded enough that they'd been dumped in the auto-doc and wouldn't be coming out for days.

The Vergai weren't much better. Six dead, counting Matis, no seriously wounded. Oster was lost now that we were away from the adrenaline rush and the immediate threat of combat. He'd been sobbing in the armory when they'd turned in their weapons, and he hadn't been alone. Campea's Force Recon platoon hadn't taken any other casualties once we'd sent them in to snipe at the Skrela, and while they mourned their lost, they were also professionals and they still had their leadership.

Besides the Marines and Vergai who'd needed comforting and reassuring, there'd been new weapons to catalog and assign, and while Spags was a nice, friendly guy, he was also an armorer and insisted on every rifle being assigned to a Marine or Vergai soldier, and each Vigilante being reclassified to account for the new power source and new energy cannon. And my frequent wincing and rubbing my shoulder hadn't seemed to move him at all.

At least Hachette had let me have time to get looked at by the doc before he'd called a meeting. I waved down the passage.

"Let's go."

The crew we passed didn't even try to disguise their stares. Everyone had heard what happened, the invitation Vicky had extended, and I wasn't sure if they were admiring or simply in disbelief of the chutzpah it had taken. And everyone had seen the Resscharr. We encountered a family just off the lift banks, a nuclear one as it turned out. Mom, Dad, and two preadolescent kids. I'd been a little surprised at that. After all, the Tahni were a lot more like us than the Predecessors, and they had nothing at all like the nuclear family. But for some reason, the intelligent dinosaurs had decided that a two-parent household was the norm for them.

They seemed incredibly out of place here in the passageways of the *Orion*, the feathery crests of the adults nearly brushing the overhead. Their big, catlike eyes flickered back and forth, staring at their strange surroundings as they headed to their temporary quarters or maybe the chow hall the crew had set up for them.

Three hundred and twenty. That was the number Hachette's logistical people had come up with, the absolute maximum if we stuffed Resscharr into every available space, including the cargo and hangar bays and even in the holds of the drop-ships. To Hachette's credit, he'd accepted their advice and hadn't even insisted on a fudge factor. The ship felt as if it were about to come apart at the seams from being overstuffed, but he'd done it.

I doubted he was happy about it, at least not if the look on his face when the two of us walked into the ops center was any indication. Top was already there, as were Dunstan and Brandano, and Nance came in just behind us, which meant the gang was all here...and then some. Lilandreth stood near the front of the compartment, staring at the star map projected over the central table, her face unreadable.

I don't know if I'd been more surprised that the Resscharr had taken us up on our offer to evacuate a few hundred of their number, that they'd been able to make up their minds and decide on which three hundred and twenty were going to go...or that Lilandreth and her children had been among them.

"Nice of you to show up," Hachette grumbled, staring daggers at us. I could have tried to explain that I had a separated shoulder, but he wasn't blind, and if the sling wasn't enough of an explanation, nothing I said would have made a difference.

Top didn't look so good herself, so maybe it was less of an excuse. She still had a smart bandage on the back of her neck and the lines beside her eyes spoke of unmentioned pain.

"We have a decision to make," Hachette said, waving at the map. I wasn't familiar with the systems laid out on it. "We've been discussing the new star systems Lilandreth and her people have added to our maps, and what this information means to our available choices."

"You said 'we' have a decision to make, sir," Vicky noted. "Isn't it *your* decision?"

"Not this time, Sandoval," he told her, shaking his head. "Things have changed." He waved at the chairs set around the table. "Everyone, have a seat. This could take a while."

I was hesitant to sit down, mostly because I felt like I'd fall asleep if I stopped moving, but I did it anyway. Vicky was on one side of me, Top on the other. She eyed me sidelong.

"You okay, Alvarez?"

"As good as you are, Sergeant-Major."

She sniffed, and I suppose she knew exactly what I meant by that.

"You know what's happened," Hachette went on, pacing across the front of the compartment. "Fuel isn't an issue anymore, which opens up our options considerably."

"And what *are* those options, Marcus?" Nance wondered. The tone of his question spoke of skepticism, and the dark circles under his eyes and the stress lines around his mouth told a different tale, one of the massive space battle I'd missed. Hachette frowned, but said nothing about Nance's insubordination.

"We don't have to worry about remaining close enough to a habitable to settle there if things go bad. We have the luxury of going as far as we need to and being able to make it back to Yfingam or the Vailoa." His eyes went to the overhead, searching for something. "Dwight, where are you?"

"I'm always here, Colonel." The voice was, anyway, but the holographic representation was missing.

Hachette grunted doubtfully.

"You know the technology in the reactor the Resscharr gave us on Decision. How long can it last, given more or less continuous use?"

"Indefinitely," Dwight replied. The AI was being uncommonly terse. "The drives will wear out before the reactor."

"And we can refuel the drive at our leisure, since it can use anything as reaction mass. So we can go anywhere within practical range, depending on how much food we can carry. And we can get more food from the Vailoans or the Vergai at need."

"But where would we go?" Dunstan asked. And thank God for him, because it was the question we all *wanted* to ask.

"We follow the trail of the only people we know who had a gateway," Hachette replied, spreading his hands as if the answer was obvious. He pointed at the star map. "The Seekers."

No one replied immediately, as if he'd thrown a grenade into the room and we were all frozen with disbelief. I don't know if I was the first one to find my voice or just the first one to be willing to use it.

"Didn't Lilandreth say that the Seekers are heading toward the galactic center?" I asked.

"I did," the Resscharr female confirmed. "Their goal was not, however, the center of the galaxy, but rather the source of the Skrela. They sought clues to the location of that source, and we don't know how far this journey took them. We can say with some assurance that they never found that source, or there would be no more Skrela."

"Is that necessarily true?" Vicky's question was sharp and immediate, as if she'd thought about it for some time. "You said the Skrela can just sit out there, replicating themselves and waiting for a target. What if the ones who created them are long dead and all that's left is their weapons?"

"We considered that." She hesitated. "We had much time to consider every question that could possibly be asked. It is possible now that the Skrela are no longer being created, but not when the Seekers left. It was clear at the time that they were still coming into our spiral arm from elsewhere."

"That's the thing, isn't it?" I interjected. "The Seekers were looking for the source of the Skrela what? Six thousand years ago? What if they already found them? What if they destroyed them? How would we know?"

"I fear you'll have to take my word for this," Lilandreth said. "I knew them, knew their dedication to the cause. Their dream was to end this and take us back to our glory. They would never have left us behind if they won the war."

"Then they're probably either dead or settled somewhere once they couldn't find the Skrela," Nance declared. "It's been *thousands* of years." He met Hachette's gaze and shook his head. "This is a wild goose chase."

"And what's your suggestion, Phillip?" Hachette asked Nance. "Do you think we should go back and ask the Vailoans if we can settle? Throw our power behind them?"

"Fuck no," Nance snapped, and I blinked at his brutal frankness. "That's a nightmare situation, the worst of both worlds. The planet is damn near to settled as it is and yet not advanced enough to help us at all and it won't be for decades, even if we were there helping them. What we need to do is go back and finish what we started. We need to polish off Zan-Thint and his fleet, and with the weapons and reactor we have now, I think we could do it. That system has everything we need *and* everything the refugees from Decision need. And we owe it to the Vergai to make sure the Tahni and the Karai don't just shove them right back into slavery."

I glanced at Vicky and she shrugged. It wasn't a bad plan and wasn't a horrible justification for it either. I'd thought something similar before.

"We kill his fleet," Top said, "and then what?" She tilted her head at Nance without the subordination even a chief NCO would usually show for a ship's captain. "Do we kill every last one of the Tahni and Karai? Because that's what it would take."

"Them without any orbital or air support," Nance replied with a shrug, "they wouldn't fight long."

"We're not butchers, Phillip," Hachette said softly. "Maybe Zan-Thint deserves it, but we aren't at war with the Karai. And that's not even considering the collateral damage any such operation would cause among the Vergai."

"I thought you said you weren't going to make the decision for us," Nance growled, slouching over the table. The man wasn't happy. "Look, I'm going to be straight with you. This was damned close. We're fucking around with things we have no business in. We're way out of our depth and we need to understand that. Taking on Tahni destroyers...*that* I understand. Going up against the Predecessors, people who can take ahold of this ship like a kid's toy and just set it down on a fucking planet's surface." He shook his head. "We don't belong out here."

His words echoed inside my head, so similar to thoughts I had myself. But then I thought of the Resscharr on Decision, letting us go and never once suggesting they could take our ship and save a lot more of their own people.

"We didn't ask for this," I said, not sure of what was going to tumble out of my mouth less than a moment before it did. "But neither did they. The Predecessors might not have liked us humans much, but they gave us everything. They gave us a Cluster full of habitable worlds and the jumpgates to reach them, to help us develop the Transition drive. And then they gave everything they had up just to keep the Skrela from destroying it. Do you think we could do that?"

I sucked in a deep breath, my ears warm from embarrassment. I sounded like a teenager telling his parents they weren't being fair. There was a squeeze bulb of water on the table in front of me and I took a quick drink from it before I went on.

"Because we might have to. If the species who made the Skrela are still out there, do you think they wouldn't do it again? Do you think there's no chance we could be in the same position as the Predecessors someday?" I met each of their eyes and Nance's were skeptical but not hardened. "I didn't join up again to kill Tahni. We were farmers, just trying to make a living, when all this fell in our lap. We joined up again to make sure no one else had to go through what we did. We were ready to give up our lives for that. And from what I've seen, the Skrela and whoever's behind them are a lot bigger threat than the Tahni ever could be."

Vicky nodded, covering my hand with hers.

"I just watched those Goddamned things throw thousands of ships and hundreds of thousands of ground troops into a meatgrinder to kill one isolated, unimportant outpost. Think about what they could do if they reached the Commonwealth. I'm in."

"Yeah, man," Dunstan chipped in, nodding enthusiastically. "I didn't join up again to start farming somewhere. I joined up to kick some ass!"

"You joined up because you couldn't get a job anywhere else," Brandano scoffed, then chuckled at Dunstan's aggrieved expression. "But hell, the goofball's right. We were all here to fight, and this is worth fighting for. I say we go."

All eyes went to Top and she chuckled.

"You know you don't have to ask me. I've been a Marine longer than any of you've been alive."

"Phillip?" Hachette asked, his tone surprisingly gentle. "This isn't a democracy, but it's also not a decision I'm going to make when the captain of the ship is dead set against it."

Nance moaned softly and rubbed his hands over his face. He didn't look like he'd slept in days.

"The hell with it. You're right, I didn't put all this time in as the skipper of a starship to go plant crops or build a colony somewhere. I guess I'm not too old for one more mission where no other human's ever gone."

"Good." Hachette slapped him on the shoulder. "Get with Lilandreth. She can give your people an idea of where the Seekers might have gone. But we have to go back to Yfingam first, to drop off the Resscharr. We just don't have room for them all on this ship."

"And to drop off the Vergai," I reminded him.

"These," he agreed, but then sighed heavily. "But I'm afraid we may have to pick up their replacements. We don't have enough troops without them."

I was ready to argue, but Vicky's hand on my arm and an arching eyebrow stopped me. She was right. We could argue that out once we reached the planet.

"Everyone get some rest," Hachette said, waving us out. "We'll come up with some more specific plans before we head out again from Yfingam."

Getting up from the chair was just as laborious as I'd imagined, and the only things that kept me going were Vicky's guiding hand, a glorious vision of our bunk, and the inside of my eyelids. I barely remembered saying good night to the others before my good shoulder was resting against the inside of a lift car, my eyelids flickering closed.

"Captain Alvarez," Dwight whispered in my ear, and I almost believed it was a waking dream. "Captain Sandoval?"

"What is it, Dwight?" Vicky asked aloud. I glanced around self-consciously, but we were the only occupants of the lift car.

"No one will want to hear this," the AI said, still just a disembodied voice, "particularly from me, but I believe you may be making a mistake."

"It wouldn't be the first time," I admitted, my words distinctly enunciated because the alternative would have been giving in to exhaustion and slurring them. "Can you be more specific?"

"This business about tracking down the Seekers, finding the source of the Skrela. I fear it will end badly for all of us."

"We're going after probably the most dangerous force in the galaxy," Vicky pointed out. "I think we're *all* afraid it's going to end badly."

"It's not the Skrela I worry about," Dwight corrected her. "If I have ever helped you, if I have ever given you reason to value my counsel, remember this one thing and hold it in the back of your mind, for it might save your life."

He hesitated and, if he'd been a corporeal being, I imagined he would be leaning over to whisper in my ear, a conspirator plotting treason.

"Do not trust the Predecessors."

———

Drop Trooper will continue in book 10, Drop Zone

If you enjoyed Drop Trooper, you will love Wholesale Slaughter and Holy War!

Start a new adventure today!

Start a new adventure today!

CONTACT FRONT
KINETIC STRIKE
DANGER CLOSE
DIRECT FIRE
HOME FRONT
FIRE BASE
SHOCK ACTION
RELEASE POINT
KILL BOX
DROP ZONE

RICK PARTLOW is that rarest of species, a native Floridian. Born in Tampa, he attended Florida Southern College and graduated with a degree in History and a commission in the US Army as an Infantry officer.

His lifelong love of science fiction began with Have Space Suit---Will Travel and the other Heinlein juveniles and traveled through Clifford Simak, Asimov, Clarke and on to William Gibson, Walter Jon Williams and Peter F Hamilton. And somewhere, submerged in the worlds of others, Rick began to create his own worlds.

He has written a ton of books in many different series, and his short stories have been included in seven different anthologies.

He currently lives in central Florida with his wife, two children and a willful mutt of a dog. Besides writing and reading science fiction and fantasy, he enjoys outdoor photography, hiking and camping.

www.rickpartlow.com

9 798403 938877